The Girl
Who Ate
the
Stars

Caroline Busher

POOLBEG

Published 2018
by Poolbeg Press Ltd
123 Grange Hill, Baldoyle
Dublin 13, Ireland
E-mail: poolbeg@poolbeg.com

Typesetting, editing, layout, design, ebook © Poolbeg Press Ltd.

1

A catalogue record for this book is available from the British Library.

ISBN 978-1-78199-8694

Author cover photo by John Busher
Typeset by Poolbeg

Printed and bound by CPI Group (UK) Ltd, Croydon, CR0 4YY

www.poolbeg.com

About the Author

Caroline Busher graduated with a First Class Honours MA in Creative Writing from UCD. She grew up in a Victorian house in the North-west of England. As an only child Caroline spent her days reading books and writing fantastical stories. When she got older she moved to the South-east of Ireland where she now lives with her husband John and her children Fiachra, Caoimhe and Tiernan. Caroline strongly believes that it is the most magical place on earth. Her house is nestled beneath the Blackstairs Mountains. But be warned: if you ever go there you must tread carefully. The mountains resemble sleeping giants and legend has it that the giants might wake up someday.

Caroline is the recipient of two literature awards from Wexford County Council and Artlinks. She was highly commended in the Cross Pens/Writing.ie Short Story Competition, longlisted for the Penguin Ireland Short Story Competition, published as part of the RTÉ *100 Words/100 Books Competition* and shortlisted for Bord Gáis Energy Book Club/TV3 Short Story Award.

Caroline teaches creative writing courses to adults and children and is a curator for Wexford Literary Festival.

The Ghosts of Magnificent Children is Caroline's debut novel.

Also by Caroline Busher
The Ghosts of Magnificent Children (Poolbeg 2016)

Acknowledgements

When I was a little girl, my father took me stargazing and I tried to count all the stars in the sky. I was captivated by the glorious way that they lit up the entire world. It was then that I imagined a girl who had to eat the stars to survive. It was this childhood memory and my love of stargazing that inspired me to write *The Girl Who Ate the Stars*. The sky at night would be nothing if the stars refused to shine. And a book cannot happen without the support and encouragement of many wonderful people. You are the stars who light up my world.

Thank you to my wonderful literary agent, Tracy Brennan. We have reached the stars together. I am so grateful for all your support and encouragement, Tracy. Thanks for believing in me and for getting my books into the hands of a fantastic publisher.

A very special thank-you to the amazing team at Poolbeg Press, who work so hard to bring books into the world. Especially to Paula Campbell who made my dream of being a published author a reality. I feel blessed to be working with you, Paula – the last twelve months have been an absolute joy! Sincere thanks to Gaye Shortland who is a skilled editor. Gaye, your extraordinary attention to detail is exceptional and you are a pleasure to work with.

Thank you to Wexford Public Library Services – to John Carley, Eileen Morrissey and Hazel Percival for appointing me as Reader in Residence, and to all the librarians and staff. It was a privilege working in the five amazing libraries across County Wexford, encouraging children and young people to read for pleasure. Librarians are superheroes and share my belief that a child who reads becomes an adult who thinks. It was an honour for me to be an ambassador for reading across County Wexford last year.

Thanks to Fingal County Council and to Nora Finnegan from Fingal Public Library services, and Dublin Airport Authority, for selecting my book *The Ghosts of Magnificent Children* for the Battle of The Book, and for arranging for it to be read by so many children. It was a wonderful experience that I will never forget.

Sincere thanks to Wexford County Council Arts Department and to Artlinks for awarding me Literature Bursaries in 2014 and 2016. Your continued support of my practice as a writer has enabled me to develop my craft.

Huge thanks to the Tyrone Guthrie Centre at Annaghmakerrig for the space to edit my work. *The Girl Who Ate the Stars* came to life in your beautiful surroundings.

Deepest thanks to the Wexford Literary Festival committee: Carmel Harrington, Jarlath Glynn, Maria Nolan, Richie Cotter, Sheila Forsey, Adele O'Neill, Alison Martin, Imelda Carroll and Tina Callaghan. It is a pleasure working for a literary festival with such an energetic, enthusiastic and hardworking group of people. I am incredibly grateful for all the opportunities that the festival has given to me and thoroughly enjoy working as Vice-chair.

Special thanks to the people of Enniscorthy and to Enniscorthy Town and District Council for your constant support and encouragement.

To the phenomenal writing community in Ireland, thank you. I have met so many wonderful writers over the last few years. Your support, encouragement and friendship has been invaluable. A very special thanks to Elizabeth Murray who is always there for me, regardless of whether she is in Iceland exploring volcanoes or in West Cork fishing. A very special thank-you to the incredible authors who endorsed my work. Thank you, Peadar Ó Guilín and Patricia Murphy.

Huge thanks to Alan McGuire on South East Radio. Alan, you gave me a wonderful opportunity to discuss the Reader in Residence Programme and to promote reading to all your listeners once a month. I really enjoy discussing reading and writing with you.

Thank you to Dr Seán O'Leary, Director of County Wexford Education Centre, and to all the Primary and Secondary Teachers across County Wexford. I have had the opportunity to visit many schools across our beautiful county and have seen for myself just how hard our teachers work. They are truly inspirational people.

To each and every bookseller in Ireland, thank you for encouraging children to read and for placing my book into the hands of readers. Your knowledge and understanding of children's literature is phenomenal. A special thank-you to the booksellers here in County Wexford, especially to Amy Devereux in Wexford Book Centre and to Damian Byrne in Byrnes Bookstores.

And to my family:

Thank you to my parents Séamus and Kathleen Doyle. I am incredibly lucky to have you both in my life. I owe everything to you both and love you with all my heart.

To my husband John. You make everything possible. Thank you for your love, support and encouragement and for understanding what it means to create art.

To my three shooting stars:

Fiachra – I am so proud to be your mother. You have the best taste in music and books and you are a talented writer and artist. You are destined for greatness. Let your star shine!

Caoimhe – thank you for baking me the most delicious cakes ever! Your chocolate brownies are amazing. They were a real treat when I was editing my book. You are thoughtful, caring, intelligent and kind. I never knew how much love my heart could hold until I had you as my daughter.

Tiernan – thank you for all the fun we have together. You are full of energy and joy and I love watching you learn and grow. You have taught me to see magic in the world and the wonder of life. You are a very special boy.

Thanks to my family in Ireland and England. To all my aunts, uncles, cousins and in-laws, thank you for always being there for me. A special thank-you to my dear Aunty May, who is no longer with us. You are a star up in heaven and will always have a special place in my heart. Thank you for introducing me to ghost stories and sharing my love of books. To my father-in-law John for the beautiful photographs and for the fascinating stories about life as a lighthouse keeper.

To my friends old and new: I am very fortunate to

have you in my life. Special thanks to Clare Fletcher who has stood by my side since we first met in infant school. Clare, you will always have a special place in my heart. Thank you, Patricia McNally – your friendship means the world to me and I am blessed to know you. And not to forget Helena Dunbar who brought music into my life. Speaking of music, thank you to my wonderful friends from Enniscorthy Choral Society.

Last but not least, I would like to thank you, the reader, for picking up my book and reading it. A book only comes to life when it is read. I hope you enjoy reading *The Girl Who Ate the Stars* as much as I did writing it!

Praise for *The Ghosts of Magnificent Children*

'*An excellent and original voice, with shades of Neil Gaiman and Lemony Snicket*' Eoin Colfer

'*Beautiful, captivating and evocative. Characters leap from the page and the setting and story stay with you long after you finish. A fresh and exciting new voice in children's fiction*' E.R. Murray

'*An exciting and completely original imagination … Caroline Busher writes with verve, colour and deep compassion for people of all ages … a stunning debut*' Éilís Ní Dhuibhne

'*A startlingly original character in Ginny and a plot loaded in menace*' Abi Elphinstone

'*Vivid, lyrical and completely ingenious, this is a book that will haunt your dreams for a long time to come. A truly magnificent debut!*' Mary Esther Judy
– Fallen Star Stories Blog

'*Dark and original – a dark and atmospheric fairy tale with a Grimm setting and a cast straight out of a Tim Burton movie. I particularly loved Ginny and her special ability. Original magic realism for kids. An impressive debut!*'
Kieran Fanning

The Ghosts of Magnificent Children by Caroline Busher
ISBN 978-178199-8748

Dedication

I would like to dedicate this book to my family – the stars around which my life revolves.

To my parents Séamus and Kathleen, my husband John and my children Fiachra, Caoimhe and Tiernan.

Wolves in Ireland

The last wolf in Ireland was thought to have been killed in 1786 on the foothills of Mount Leinster – three hundred years after they disappeared in England and a century after they were wiped out in Scotland.

However, some had survived in a different form . . . this is their story . . .

The Girl Who Ate the Stars

Fear danced
up her spine
under her ribcage
into her lungs
stars hurtled towards her
comets spun
and twisted
through the air
eyes in a gloomy sky

she flinched
at the bones of
a thousand dead wolves
buried beneath her feet

a golden star
a firebolt fell
from the sky
it fizzled as
it
hit
the
snow

Caroline Busher

Prologue

Lottie's Dream

It is the dead of night and a pack of ravenous wolves howl outside the ancient ruins. Lottie is woken from her sleep. She creeps from her bed and goes outside. Leaves crunch beneath her feet as she enters the Forest of Non-Existence. She sees a wolf with teeth as sharp as needles and fangs as red as blood. A waterfall of children's tears flows over the edge of a glass mountain.

A girl called Cuán, who has two hearts and eats the stars, sleeps in the hollow of a tree made from bone. The sky is black. Cuán wakes from her sleep and moves towards Lottie like a starving beast. She has claws like daggers and amber eyes shaped like half-moons. Her dress is made from the petals of black roses and she wears a necklace made of thorns.

An ill wind blows and a pack of bloodthirsty wolves suddenly appears. They howl and pace back and forth, their amber eyes gleaming like gems in the darkness.

The petals from Cuán's dress fall to the ground to reveal the body of a Wolf Girl. She drops to her knees and growls, the transformation complete. The thorns around her neck dig into her thick fur. She reaches out her claw and the wolves whimper and tremble in fright. They retreat into the forest.

Lottie does not fear her strange companion. She stares into her amber eyes and for a moment she thinks that they are made of stars.

Chapter One

A Ghost in the Sky
1940

"*Run, Albert!*" Lottie Hope screamed. Then she gripped her young brother's hand and ran like a lightning bolt from a storm cloud towards the air-raid shelter. Her flame-red hair flowed about her shoulders and matched the colour of the burning sky.

Houses huddled together like a mouth of overcrowded teeth. One by one their windows blinked at Lottie. They were covered with blackout blinds by terrified families who feared for their lives. Another night of bombing had begun.

The air-raid shelter was at the end of the street in an ancient crypt beneath the cathedral. The children could hear bombs falling somewhere in the distance. Sparks and flames danced like a volcanic eruption in the sky.

A plane emerged like a ghoul from behind the black clouds. It came so close that Lottie thought if she reached out her hand she could touch it. Smoke billowed in the air and the smell of gas coming from a burst pipe caused the children to feel lightheaded. They looked into the cockpit and directly into the eyes of a German fighter pilot. His hazel eyes glistened behind goggles which made him resemble a large fly. He seemed as scared as they were and for a moment it was as though time stood still.

The pilot wasn't much older than Lottie. He was a sixteen-year-old boy from Hamburg. He was the eldest of six boys. His name was Günther which meant 'warrior'. But he didn't feel like a warrior at all. In fact, he was petrified. His pale hands trembled, while his teeth chattered like a sparrow falling from its nest. Günther had a jagged scar above his left eyebrow which was shaped like a shooting star. He had acquired it when he fell from his bike on his eighth birthday. He was being chased by a gang of bullies when the accident happened. It always reminded him that danger was never too far away.

Albert waved at Günther as though he were an old friend and he waved back, while Lottie covered her head with her hands and waited for a bomb to fall on them. A tear fell from her eye and landed on Albert's shoulder.

After a while, Lottie looked towards the sky and realised that the plane and its young pilot had vanished. All that remained was a thin wisp of fog. Lottie rubbed her eyes with the back of her hand. Then she began to wonder if she had imagined it or if she had just witnessed some kind of magic trick.

Her father said that magic was real. He told her stories about magical kingdoms inhabited by witches and wizards . . . but that was before the war. There was no room for fairy tales in Lottie's head any more – she'd had to grow up fast.

Lottie turned to her six-year-old brother. She hated him sometimes – he had a wicked temper and, since he was born, she sometimes had the feeling that her mum and dad hardly noticed her – but deep down she loved him and she felt relieved that he did not understand how close they had come to dying.

"Lottie! Albert! Come quick!" A shrill voice pierced Lottie's thoughts like a needle through a piece of silk.

The children looked up and saw their mother running towards them. She looked like a wild animal. Her arms were outstretched and the moonlight cast a shadow across her face, which made her skin look blue. Flames licked the remains of a house that had been bombed close by. Fuelled by love and fear, she scooped Albert into her arms and called out to Lottie to keep pace with her. They ran towards the cathedral and down the worn steps into the crypt. A cockroach scuttled up the side of the red sandstone wall and disappeared into a small crack in the stone. Seconds later another bomb fell.

Chapter Two

The Underground World

The curved roof of the crypt shook like a bowl of jelly. A plume of dust filled the air.

"That was close!" Lottie exclaimed. She shuddered to think of what might have happened if they hadn't reached the crypt before the bomb fell. She looked down and realised that her left shoe was missing. Her sock was damp and her big toe protruded through a hole. "Darn it. My shoe must have come off in the dash to the shelter." But she was grateful that she still had both her legs.

Bombs rumbled outside like thunder. Inside, people cried as they realised that members of their family were missing.

Lottie's mother Nancy hugged Albert then set him down. He looked about then ran and jumped onto a makeshift bunk bed beside a boy called Billy Bright. Albert smiled at Billy who was a sickly child with a head of red curls and a sprinkling of freckles across his large nose. Billy suffered from terrible allergies and was constantly sneezing. Due to this unfortunate affliction Billy was known as Snot Monster by the boys in school. Albert didn't care about any of that: Billy was his friend and friends stuck together. The bunk bed was covered with a scratchy green blanket which smelt of dirty old socks. However, Albert liked it in the bunker. He imagined that he was in an underground den and that he was on a top-secret mission to outsmart Hitler.

Lottie sighed. She hoped with all her heart that her mother wasn't angry with her.

They should have returned from school hours ago, but Lottie had insisted that they visit the library on the way. It was her favourite place to be. Entering the old Victorian building was like stepping into another world. There were richly carved rosewood bookcases brimming with hundreds of old books. The high ceiling was shaped like a dome and statues of philosophers lined the stone staircase that seemed to go on forever. There was a particular statue that Lottie liked most of all. It was of an angel with its arms outstretched. Lottie imagined the statues in the library coming alive at night-time and walking along the dimly lit corridors. The library contained long mahogany desks which were punctuated with green reading lamps. And the wooden floors were polished until they shone. The library always smelt of beeswax furniture polish and dusty old books. Lottie went there to forget about the war. To read books and to escape to far-off lands where children didn't have to sleep below the ground. Where bombs didn't fall from the sky. And where there were no rations, so that people could eat whatever food they liked.

Today Lottie had lost all track of time. She was reading a book about astronomy when Sylvia, one of the librarians, snatched it from her.

"I was reading that, Sylvia!" Lottie protested.

Then she noticed that Sylvia was wearing her blue woollen overcoat and a red hat on her head that matched the colour of her lips.

"I must close the library, Lottie," Sylvia said urgently. "There are German planes approaching. Don't you hear the siren?"

Now Lottie did hear its warning wail. "I'm sorry, Sylvia – I was so lost in my book!"

Sylvia was very fond of Lottie. She had no children of her own and enjoyed talking to her about books. Lottie wanted to be a librarian just like Sylvia when she grew up. Sometimes, when no-one was looking, Sylvia would allow Lottie to go behind the main desk and check out her own books.

"You must find Albert and get to a bomb shelter right away, Lottie!"

Just then there was a booming sound. The lights flickered overhead and books toppled from the shelves. Lottie sprang to her feet. Crowds of people were heading for the door of the library. There was panic everywhere as people made a dash to get out.

"*Albert, where are you!*" Lottie cried.

She had no time to lose – she needed to find her brother fast. She ran between bookshelves and looked under tables. She thought that she would never find him until at last she noticed him sitting crossed-legged beneath one of the desks reading a book on trains. She was so grateful that she found him. She pulled him out and hugged him tightly.

"Quick, Albert, we must go right away. The Germans have arrived."

Lottie held her brother's hand and they joined the line of people who were scrambling to get out of the library. *"Form an orderly queue, please, ladies and gentlemen!"* Sylvia shouted as she held the main door open and helped people out. *"You will get out quicker that way!"*

Now Lottie looked at her young brother in admiration. He was like sunshine on a rainy day.

"This is so exciting, Mother!" he gasped.

Lottie smiled to herself. She was glad that Albert didn't understand what was going on. To him, the war was just a big adventure. Even though he could see the destruction the bombs caused, somehow he didn't think anything bad would happen to him or his loved ones.

The light flickered overhead which signified that more bombs had dropped close by. They fell each night like coins into a fountain. Lottie imagined the alabaster statues in the library running down the staircase and huddling together beneath the angel's wings while hundreds of ancient books tumbled from the shelves. Then her heart sank as she thought of Sylvia, the

9

librarian. Lottie hoped that she had survived. She knew that Sylvia would stay in the library until everyone had left. Even if it meant risking her own life.

"Do you want to play Snakes and Ladders, Albert?" Billy enquired cheerfully. He took out the board game which had yellow ladders and brightly coloured snakes with forked tongues painted on it.

Albert had a mop of blonde hair which fell into his large blue eyes. Despite the rations and the lack of food, he had a rosy glow in his cheeks. He wore a mint-green shirt beneath a blue sleeveless pullover which his mother had knitted to keep him warm. On his legs, which resembled twigs, were knee-length brown trousers. And on his feet he wore a pair of scuffed brown shoes, which pinched his toes. His pale legs were covered in scrapes and bruises. Albert was quite an adventurer – he was always out exploring the world. He built tree houses, made mud pies and pretended to be a pilot just like his father.

"Here are your gas masks, children." Lottie's mother forced a smile. She knew how much they hated wearing their gas masks and she couldn't blame them.

"Do we have to put them on, Mother?" Albert protested.

The gas masks were made of black rubber and smelt of disinfectant. Albert and Billy often played games wearing them because their big goggles and long snouts made them look like monsters – but they couldn't play Snakes and Ladders properly wearing them.

"You can leave them off for a while, Albert, but you

must put them on when you go to bed."

"All right, Mother," Albert replied as he slid a small yellow counter down a snake's back.

Nancy sat down on a wooden bench opposite the boys and sighed. Lottie thought that she looked very tired. Her eyes were bloodshot, her face pale. Her blonde hair was tied up with a green silk headscarf. She wore a knee-length red polka-dot dress that buttoned up the front. It was nipped in at the waist with a thin brown belt. A red scarf was tied in a bow at the neckline. A forest-green cardigan covered her shoulders. And pearl earrings hung from her earlobes. But, despite trying to look her best, Lottie could see that the war was taking its toll on her.

"Are you all right, Mother?" Lottie enquired. She was a caring child, with a big heart, and she hated it when her mother was sad. Now, her mother hardly ever smiled any more.

"You two gave me an awful fright, Lottie. I thought you were . . ."

Lottie stared into her mother's eyes. She had thought that they had been killed by the bombs. Lottie hated herself for causing her mother to worry so. She should have come straight home from school like she was supposed to.

"Don't worry, Mother – we are safe now."

Lottie placed her head reassuringly on her mother's shoulder and held her hand. Lottie loved her mother's hands. Since the day she was born, her mother had used them to care for her. They cradled her as a baby and held her tight when she had a bad dream. She closed her eyes tight and thought of her father. She could see his eyes, his nose, his smile. Then she felt wretched, as she couldn't remember what his hands looked like.

Her heart fluttered and she hugged her mother. She could smell her rose-scented perfume. "I wonder where Dad is now?"

"I suspect he is flying somewhere over Germany."

"I miss him so much, Mother."

"I know, love – I miss him too."

Albert jumped down from the bunk bed and ran over to them.

"Did Lottie tell you about the plane, Mother? It flew so close. The pilot waved at me." Albert could hardly contain his excitement and his mother smiled despite herself.

"I'm sure he did, Albert."

Lottie knew that her mother didn't believe him. Although she didn't blame her. She was an adult after all and they saw the world in a different way from children. Sometimes Lottie hoped that she would never have to grow up and see the world through adult eyes.

"It's your turn, Albert!" Billy Bright shouted enthusiastically as he wiped the snots from his nose onto the green blanket.

Albert hopped back onto the bed beside his friend.

Lottie looked around the air-raid shelter. It was dark and dreary and reminded her of an overcrowded platform at a train station. There were so many people. Some she recognised and others she didn't. A group of women were huddled together, wearing red-and-green homemade party hats. Nancy explained to her that they were at a party when the air-raid siren sounded, and they must have forgotten to take their hats off in the panic. Lottie knew that it wouldn't have been much of a party – all the food was rationed these days which meant that people had very little to eat. But it was still important to try and carry on with life as best you could.

Mrs Andersen, a plump lady with a wooden leg, owned the corner shop. She walked around the crypt and handed the children small glass bottles of milk. They clinked the bottles together as though they were raising a toast. Then they drank the milk gratefully. That's the thing that Lottie noticed about the war – it made you appreciate everything, even the small things.

A girl about the same age as Lottie sat on a tartan blanket, crocheting a scarf. A pair of round spectacles were perched on the end of her pudgy nose. Two deep lines converged on her forehead and she stuck her tongue out as she concentrated – she didn't notice the sounds of the bombs outside. Lottie decided that the next time the air-raid siren sounded she would bring a notebook and pen with her. Her favourite thing to do in the world was to write stories. She had often considered keeping a secret journal where she could spill her deepest thoughts onto the blank pages, like coins from a jar. Although she knew that it would be impossible to keep anything a secret from Albert.

Lottie loved to tell stories too. Occasionally she would make up stories and tell them to the younger children in school during break-time. She relished tales about two-headed giants who lived in castles in the clouds, fire-breathing dragons who turned entire kingdoms to dust, and enchanted fairies who lived in the shade of the trees at the bottom of the garden. But her favourite stories were the ones that her father used to tell her as he tucked her into bed at night. Those were the stories that travelled with her into her dreams. They accompanied her through the darkest of nights.

An old man, with a long grey beard and a face etched with wrinkles, observed Lottie through beady eyes which were as black as coals. His name was Ezra. Lottie had seen him before. Her mother had told her that he was Jewish and his entire family had been killed by the Germans. He was the only one to survive. Ezra picked up the red piano accordion by his side and played a lively tune. Everyone sang.

Lottie's mother's lips curled into a half-smile which didn't quite reach her eyes. Lottie knew that she was still sad. Instinctively she took her mother's hand and joined in with the singing. It was a desperate attempt to cheer her up.

It wasn't long before the sound of the voices singing drowned out the noise of the bombs falling from the sky. And, for a while, in the tunnels far beneath the city streets, Lottie Hope forgot about the war.

Chapter Three

The House with No Doors

Lottie's mother, Nancy, knew that the children had to be evacuated. And it broke her heart. She placed her hand on the fireplace to steady herself. Then she stared at her reflection in the oval mirror that hung on the chimney breast. The mirror was an antique. It had been in Nancy's family for generations. Its silver edges were tarnished and there was a large crack in the glass. It happened when the mirror fell from the wall unexpectedly. On the day that the war began.

"Seven years bad luck," Fred said from over the top of the newspaper he was reading at the time.

"Nonsense, Fred,' she said. 'There will be no talk of that kind in this house."

She remembered it as though it were only yesterday. She didn't believe in superstitions. However, she could not deny that bad things started to happen the day that the crack appeared in the mirror. It was only a matter of time before their home was bombed. She knew she was being foolish. She couldn't blame a stupid mirror for the war. It was Hitler who was to blame.

She shouldn't keep the children in Manchester. It was too dangerous. She would never forgive herself if they were killed during the nightly bombings. They depended on her to keep them safe. Each night, as she tucked them into bed, she prayed that they would make it through the night.

She looked out of her bedroom window. Storm clouds drifted across the tumultuous sky. They resembled pirate ships sailing the seven seas. In a few hours the clouds would vanish. War planes would appear on the horizon and the sky would be on fire once more. She fiddled with the sleeve on her green cardigan. Her blonde hair was tied up in a bun which was secured with a silver bird-shaped hair clip. She always tried to look her best, for the children's sake. Although it was becoming harder to hide the dark circles beneath her eyes.

The street on which they lived was barely recognisable any more. There used to be thirty-two terrace houses. They were built during the reign of Queen Victoria. They all stood in a row as neat as pins, each one identical to the next. Chimneystacks that resembled the crooked fingers of giants disappeared into charcoal clouds. Wooden front doors opened like hungry mouths onto a cobbled street. Before the war, the clickety-clack of heels could be heard from miles around. Women with curlers in their hair and babies in their arms gossiped about their next-door neighbours. In the backyards lines of washing billowed in the breeze like sails on ships. After school, girls with pigtails played hopscotch and skipping games together, while the boys played football – they dreamed of one day scoring a goal for Manchester United.

But all that was before the war. Things were different now.

Now only four houses remained on the street. The rest of the houses had been reduced to piles of rubble. Homes that had stood for over a hundred years had come tumbling down like dominoes in one night of bombing. It was as though an invisible magician had waved his magic wand and they all disappeared in a puff of smoke. Entire lives were torn apart. Nancy knew that she was one of the lucky ones, but she feared her luck would run out one day too, as that of most of her neighbours had.

One morning Nancy had found her neighbour Mrs Russo sitting in a pile of rubble. She was a black-haired Italian woman with olive skin and brown eyes. She worked in the fish and chip shop and lived at Number 22. The only thing that remained of her three-storey house was her living-room wall. It was the most peculiar sight. The powder-blue flowers on the wallpaper were singed from the force of the blast. Hanging on a rusty nail in the centre of the wall was her wedding photograph, which had been taken twenty years earlier. Mrs Russo had one daughter called Bianca and she had been killed at the start of the war. Bianca was a pretty girl with brown hair and eyes like her mother's. She was twelve years old, just like Lottie. Bianca had a limp and

17

was unable to run fast enough to the air-raid shelter beneath the cathedral when the first of the bombs fell. The force of the blast had killed her.

The morning the house was bombed, Nancy walked across the street and touched Mrs Russo gently on the arm.

"You can't stay out here in the cold, Mrs Russo. Come on. I'll make us a nice pot of tea."

"Thank you, Nancy, you were always such a thoughtful girl. But I will stay here, with this pile of rubble that was once my home."

Tears fell from the woman's eyes. Nancy had a hanky up her sleeve which she handed to her.

"Then I will make a pot of tea and bring it out to you," Nancy insisted, and Mrs Russo simply nodded.

Minutes later Nancy returned, carrying a silver tray. It contained a pot of tea, two china cups and a candle. She had also made corned-beef and cucumber sandwiches.

Nancy placed the tray down on the remains of a wall.

"Is all this for me?" Mrs Russo wrapped her slim arms around Nancy's neck.

"I am sorry that you lost your home. It's so unfair."

"Life's unfair, Nancy. You are one of the lucky ones. But your luck will run out one day too. Get those children of yours as far away from here as possible."

Nancy simply nodded. She knew Mrs Russo was right. It could so easily have been her home that was bombed and her family that were killed. Nancy gathered up some broken-up pieces of furniture. A chair leg and a bookshelf. Then she lit a small bonfire in the rubble and they huddled around it to keep warm. As the amber flames licked the air Mrs Russo lit the small candle and placed it in front of the living-room wall. After a while more people joined them. Each of them brought a candle which they placed beside Mrs Russo's. They burnt old pieces of furniture and talked about the good old days. Before the war began. Then as day turned to night, the distant hum of the air-raid siren sounded and alerted them to danger. One by one they ran for cover. All except Mrs Russo who refused to be beaten. Nancy never saw Mrs Russo again after that night. She presumed that she had been killed by the bombing. Although she tried not to think about it as it made her feel sad.

Nancy would never forget the pain etched on the woman's face. There were no words to describe the loss she felt and no words of sympathy that could ease her pain.

The thought of parting with Lottie and Albert broke Nancy's heart. However, she knew that they wouldn't survive for much longer if they stayed at home with her. It was only a matter of time until a bomb fell on their home.

Nancy sighed as she sat at her oak writing desk. She stared at a photograph of Albert and Lottie. It was in a wooden frame that Fred had carved for their tenth wedding anniversary. The photograph was taken on the beach in Blackpool before the war began. They looked so happy. Blackpool Tower was in the background. Albert had a bucket and spade in his hands. He wore shorts and a string vest. Lottie lay beside him on a blanket. She was reading a book. Always reading a book, that one, Nancy thought. She wondered if her family would ever have such happy times again.

A blank sheet of paper lay in front of Nancy and her pen was poised. Her hand trembled as she fought back the tears that sprang to her eyes. She remembered Mrs Russo's words: *"Your luck will run out one day too. Get those children of yours as far away from here as possible."* This was the hardest thing that Nancy would ever have to do.

Before the war, Nancy enjoyed writing letters. She loved nothing more than the smell of ink on a crisp white sheet of paper. The sense of possibility that she could write anything – a story, a poem or even a letter – made her heart sing with joy. But now letters were used to convey bad news and to arrange for children to be sent away from everything that they knew and loved. Fred wrote letters to her from the war. She kept them all in a bundle. They were tied up with the green-velvet ribbon that she wore in her hair on the night that they first met. In the letters he spoke about how much he missed her and the children. He also talked about how frightened and alone he felt. Nancy always wrote happy letters back to him. She tried to see the silver lining in every cloud. She dreaded the day when the letters from Fred might finally stop coming. Other families had received telegrams to say that their loved ones were MIA which meant 'missing in action'. Or worse still that they were dead.

Nancy thought back to the day two years earlier when she and the children had said goodbye to her loving husband.

Fred was so handsome in his blue-grey uniform. His boots were polished until they shone like new pennies and the brass buttons on his coat glistened in the sunlight. Albert looked so much like his father – he had the same dimple in the centre of his chin and his eyes crinkled in the corners like Fred's when he smiled.

Nancy was devastated on that cold October morning when she stood on the platform with the children. She could see her breath in the air when she spoke. Her fingers were numb with cold. But she would have stood there forever if it meant that she could have prevented Fred from going away.

"Say goodbye to your father, children," she said as she choked back the tears that gathered at the back of her throat.

Lottie ran into her father's arms. She could feel the rough texture of his uniform against her skin. He smelt of lemon soap and shaving cream – it was a smell that she would never forget. She caught sight of her distorted reflection in his golden buttons. Her face looked as though it had been stretched and her eyes were puffy and red. She held back her tears. She didn't want her father's last memory to be of her sobbing – she was a big girl after all.

Fred ruffled Albert's hair. "Be a brave young man, Albert," he said cheerfully.

"Take me with you, Father," Albert begged. "I am ready to fight the Germans too, you know."

Fred smiled, then squatted down in front of his son and placed his hands on his shoulders. Albert trembled like a leaf on a tree. The cold breeze reached under his coat like a thief.

"Listen, son, the War Office has decided to send the older soldiers to war first. We will return soon and then we will send out our bravest and strongest soldiers – and that's where you will come in. The Germans won't know what hit them when you arrive, Albert Hope. You will be our secret weapon."

A great big smile erupted on Albert's face and his eyes shone like stars. "Do you promise, Father? Am I really your secret weapon?"

"I promise, son – and, yes, you are the bravest of all the soldiers. But, for now, I need you to guard your mother and your sister here. Hold the Home Front and make sure that the Germans don't invade while we are away. Do you think that you can do that?"

Albert glanced at his mother and sister. It wasn't a very exciting job. He knew that as soon as his father was gone his mother and sister would start bossing him around again. But he couldn't let his father down. He was counting on him after all.

"Yes, sir!" Albert replied. He saluted his father. Then he ran off along the platform with his arms outstretched, pretending to be a plane.

Nancy smiled. She would never love her husband more than she did at that moment in time. He always knew exactly the right thing to say and do. She wished with all her heart that she could speak to the children the way that Fred did.

As the train chugged away, a puff of smoke trailed through the air like a kite escaping from a child's hand in a storm. It was all Nancy could do to stop herself from running after it. She wondered if she would ever see her darling Fred again.

Chapter Four

The Creature in the Room

Nancy made a fresh pot of tea and then she sat down in the green armchair. It was Fred's favourite chair. The shape of his body was worn into the fabric. Nancy sighed. The amber flames crackled in the fire and devoured the lumps of coal. The cuckoo clock on the wall chimed to announce the passing of another hour. A small wooden bird appeared out of a little red door. Its head was perfectly carved and moved up and down. Tiny wooden wings flapped as the bird cuckooed. Then it scurried back into the heart of the clock through the miniature door. A strand of blonde hair fell from Nancy's green headscarf, which matched the colour of her eyes. Looking down, she noticed that the hem of her blue dress had come down. She had made the dress herself. There were small white doves printed on the fabric. The buttons were shaped like pebbles. Before the war, Nancy had worked as a dressmaker and she had taken great pride in her work. She used to make all of Lottie's dresses, and they looked every bit as good as the expensive dresses in shop windows. The material was cheap but the stitching was exceptional. People had come from far and wide to have a pair of trousers turned up or a dress altered. She had enjoyed conversations with her customers. She loved hearing about other people's lives, apart from the fact that that they admired her work. The money was useful too.

But since the war began she had lost all interest in sewing. The only thing that she cared about now was surviving. She was fearful that she wouldn't hear the air-raid siren over the rattle of her sewing machine and that they would all be killed when a bomb fell.

She rubbed her temples. Her head ached. She had thought long and hard about where to send the children. She had no relatives in the country and she hated the thought of sending them to live with strangers. Stories had begun to emerge about children who were treated horrifically in their new homes. She couldn't take that risk. There was only one place that she could think of sending them and that was the village of Kilbree in Ireland. It was the village where her mother grew up, in a place called County Wexford. It was rooted in a steep valley, with rolling hills. Winding country roads stretched as far as the eye could see. And the River Slaney draped itself over the landscape like a blue-silk scarf around the neck of a princess. Nancy had visited Kilbree with her mother often as a child. But that was such a long time ago now.

Her cousin Hugh Dunlivin and his wife Ida lived there still. Hugh was the village undertaker. He had a daughter called Prudence, who Nancy thought would be excellent company for Lottie. However, for many years the only contact that Nancy had had with Hugh was an exchange of cards at Christmastime. The last time she had seen him was when they were twelve years old. She had never even met Ida and Prudence.

Hugh had been a tall thin boy. His nickname was Teapot as he had large ears that protruded from his long head and a bent nose which resembled a spout. Nancy smiled despite herself. She remembered Hugh fondly – he was a kind boy. They spent hours together playing hide and seek in their grandmother's farmhouse. They ran through the golden fields of wheat and occasionally helped their uncle, Michael, to round up the sheep and milk the cows. Kilbree was a beautiful place. Although Nancy could never bring herself to go back. Not even for her Uncle Michael's funeral.

Guilt rose like a mountain in her chest. She thought of the enormity of what she was asking Hugh to do for her. Would he take in her two children until the war ended? Nancy knew that Hugh and Ida might not like two English children running around their home. This was not Ireland's war after all. But she was desperate and desperate times called for desperate measures. And there was no-one else who she could turn to, in these terrible times when the threat of death lurked around every corner.

Nancy picked up the small china teacup and saucer

from the little table beside her. The cup was hand-painted by her father. It had a chip in it, but it reminded her of happier times. Red roses trailed over the rim as she put it to her lips. Her hand trembled and the teacup rattled as she thought of what she was about to do. The tea had gone cold but she drank it anyway. Nothing went to waste during the war.

Nancy rubbed her head with her hand. There was something on her mind that troubled her greatly – even more than Hitler's bombs that dropped like parcels of death from the sky – and she shuddered to think of it. It was the reason that she had vowed never to return to Wexford. If she had a choice, she would not be sending her children to stay there now. But that was the thing about war – it forced people to do things that they wouldn't dream of doing in times of peace.

A terrifying event had occurred in Kilbree when Nancy was twelve years old. She had blocked it out for all these years. It was as though not thinking about it meant it had never happened. It concerned a girl called Cuán.

Nancy unlocked a small drawer in her writing bureau with a silver key which had tiny hearts engraved on it and hung from a red ribbon. Removing the drawer, she put her fingers into the cavity and pressed a hidden button. Another little drawer sprang open. From it she removed a small antique gold ring and some old photographs. The photographs were taken twenty years earlier, during her last visit to Kilbree. Her mother had given them to her when she passed away. Nancy had locked them away in the drawer until now. She studied each photo until her eyes fell on the one that she was looking for.

It was a photograph of her when she was twelve years old. She was perched on a rock next to Cuán who had pale skin and hair as black as ink. Nancy trembled in fear as she studied the photograph. There was something sinister in the background. It was a dark cloaked figure with glowing red eyes. The eyes were absolutely terrifying since the photograph was in black and white. Nancy had first noticed the figure, with its long spindly hand on Cuán's shoulder, when she was a child. However, she knew that there was no-one else there when the picture was taken. She and Cuán were alone at the time – apart from the photographer, and he hadn't mentioned anything.

She couldn't understand it when her mother insisted that she could see nothing behind Cuán. That had made it even more frightening.

Nancy hadn't looked at the photograph in a long time. However, seeing it again now was petrifying and it sent a chill down her spine. She had told herself over the years that it was her childish imagination playing tricks on her. However, she was no longer a child and there was still no denying it. There was a frightening figure standing behind them in the photograph.

The palms of her hands felt clammy. Her heart thumped like a drum in her chest. She felt sure that the cloaked figure was the cause of what had happened to Cuán all those years ago.

Cuán was special. Nancy knew it the moment she first saw her in the orchard eating a bright red apple. It was on a crisp, unseasonably cold August morning. The wind whistled in the trees and storm clouds drifted overhead. That was such a vivid memory for Nancy.

Nancy remembered it as though it were only yesterday. Cuán was wearing a white cotton nightdress. It struck Nancy as peculiar seeing a girl in her nightdress in the middle of the day. But that wasn't the only thing. Cuán's nightdress was covered in mud. Specks of dirt clung to her pale cheeks. Nancy wondered how Cuán had got herself in such a state. She looked as though she had fallen into a bog. Beneath all the dirt, Nancy could see that Cuán's nightdress was expensive. It had a delicately embroidered lace collar which clung to her neck. If it wasn't for that Nancy would have mistaken Cuán for a homeless girl. Nancy looked the strange girl up and down and she noticed that Cuán wasn't wearing any shoes on her feet, even though there was a harsh wind blowing – her toes squelched in the mud. There were twigs in her hair and Nancy gulped as she watched a large spider crawl across her left shoulder. Cuán looked feral, like a wild animal, out hunting for prey. However, it was her eyes that surprised Nancy the most: they were brilliant amber-yellow.

Nancy had heard rumours about Cuán before. People said that she was strange as she spent so much time alone. None of the children in the village wanted to play with her. They called her names and laughed at her, although deep down they were all terrified of her. She

28

was an outsider, just like Nancy was with her English accent and fancy clothes.

Cuán seemed to sense a presence and she turned to look at Nancy, who quickly hid behind a tree. Cuán cautiously came forward until she rounded the tree and stood there staring at Nancy.

Nancy flushed, ashamed to have been caught spying.

"Hello, my name's Nancy," she said awkwardly.

From that moment she found herself drawn to the mysterious girl, like a moth to a flame.

That was only weeks before it happened.

Cuán vanished in the middle of the night. At the time some people believed that she had heard the wailing of the Banshee, the Fairy Woman, which meant that she had been called to her death. Others said that she was bewitched and that the fairies had taken her. Or she had been taken by werewolves. Nancy's mother said that none of that was true. There had to be a logical explanation. Perhaps Cuán had fallen into a well and drowned. Or maybe she had been abducted.

However, Nancy knew the terrifying truth. It was more frightening than the most bloodcurdling ghost story imaginable, even the kind that make the hairs on the back of your neck stand on end. She had witnessed what had happened – something so unimaginable that she had never told anyone. She knew no-one would believe her, not even her own mother.

Cuán had confided in Nancy. She'd told her things about herself. Frightening things. Nancy had always feared, because she was the last person to see Cuán alive, that she would suffer the same fate as she had. Now she shuddered to think that she was putting her own precious children into such a perilous situation. What if Lottie or Albert were next?

Overcome with anxiety, she wondered if the creature in the photograph could still be there in the sleepy village, waiting to strike again. Or was it just Cuán who had inadvertently conjured something up? Something wicked and terrifying that would have left the village when she had?

Nancy picked up the gold ring and studied the wolf's face engraved in it, with its amber eyes. Cuán had given it to her, saying that it would protect her. In the end, it was Cuán who had needed protection.

She slipped the ring on her little finger – it was too small to go on the others.

Suddenly the old cuckoo clock on the wall stopped ticking and the temperature in the room dropped. Nancy shivered as the fire went out.

There was a presence in the room. Behind her. She instinctively covered her eyes with her hands and peered out through her fingers. Then she opened her mouth to scream but no sound came out. She watched helplessly as a dark shadow crept away from her across the room. Nancy didn't know what it was, but it wasn't human.

Unable to move and paralysed with fear, she watched as the sitting-room door opened. It creaked in resistance as the hand with spindly fingers turned the silver doorknob. Within seconds the creature had gone.

The cuckoo clock started ticking again and the flames

from the fire danced in the grate once more.

She looked down at the photo which lay on the desk. Then she picked it up and held it in her trembling hands. To her amazement the creature was no longer there. She turned on the lamp and studied the photo again . . . but the horrifying figure was truly gone. All she could see was a twelve-year-old version of herself sitting beside a girl who had ceased to exist many years ago.

She threw the photo into the fire. Then she watched as the orange flame turned blue. It licked the photo which curled at the edges in resistance. The last thing to burn was Cuán. Her eyes shone red like rubies as the flames died down. Nancy picked up the poker and prodded the photograph until it turned to cinders. If only it was as easy to erase the memories.

Nancy knew that she would have to put the fate of her friend behind her if she wanted her children to survive the war. And maybe, on being released from the photograph, the creature had returned to wherever dark place he had come from and would never return.

In any case, she must take this risk. She must save her children from almost certain death from the bombs which rained on them night after night.

With a quivering hand and against her better instincts, Nancy picked up her silver pen and, with a start, realised that the gold ring was still on her little finger. Perhaps, as Cuán had said, it had protected her?

Putting pen to paper, she wrote to her cousin and his wife.

Chapter Five

The Red Shoe

July 1940

Dear Hugh and Ida,
*I hope that you are both keeping well. Please forgive me
for not getting in touch more over the years.*

*It is with a sad and heavy heart that I am contacting
you. Manchester is being bombed every night. As I am
sure you can imagine, it is terrifying for all of us. Fred
is a fighter pilot which is the most dangerous job of all.
If Lottie and Albert are to have any chance of survival,
they need to be evacuated immediately. Their school has
been bombed and many of their friends and teachers have
lost their lives. I hope that they are both still safe by the
time that this letter reaches you.*

*Would you be so kind as to allow the children to stay
with you until the war is over? I know it is a lot to ask*

but I have no other option. I am sure that they would be great companions for Prudence.

I hope that you will understand the urgency of my request. I will forever be in your debt.

Yours faithfully,
Nancy Hope

As Nancy sealed and addressed the envelope, a feeling of dread overwhelmed her. She walked over to the window and watched Lottie and Albert playing in the street below. They looked so happy and blissfully unaware of what she planned to do. How could she tell them that she was sending them away? She took her green woollen overcoat from the oak coat-stand and put it on. Then she put on her blue hat and tucked the letter into her pocket.

Nancy ran down the stairs. The brown carpet beneath her feet was threadbare and the walls needed a lick of paint. She ran out the door of her terrace house. The streets were crowded as people hurried about trying to get home before nightfall. It wasn't only the bombs that people feared. Once darkness descended on the city streets, not a light could be seen. Even car headlights had to be covered with paper. This made it difficult for pedestrians to see where they were going.

A girl of about Lottie's age sat on a low wall by the corner of the street. She had wavy black hair and sad brown eyes. Her thin face was grubby. She wore black fingerless gloves and held a small doll in her hands.

She looked so lost that Nancy stopped and knelt down in front of her.

She touched the girl's hand tenderly. "What's your name?"

"My name is Ester."

"Pleased to meet you, Ester. My name is Nancy. It's not safe for you to be out here alone. Where are your family?"

"They are in Poland. My parents sent me here on Kindertransport, because we are Jewish, you know. They said that I would be safer in England. But they were wrong."

Nancy had heard of Kindertransport, which meant 'Children's Transport' in German. It was a service that had evacuated thousands of children, mostly Jewish, from their homes in Europe to save their lives – sending them to Britain and other countries, alone without their parents. Nancy had heard such dreadful stories from Ezra, the old man who played the accordion beneath the city streets each night. He told her that Jewish people were being taken away on trains by the Germans and never seen again.

"But, Ester, didn't Kindertransport arrange for an English family to take you in?"

"Yes, they did – but the family were so cruel to me I had to run away."

Nancy shuddered to think of Lottie and Albert ending up on the streets somewhere.

Nancy studied the small cloth doll. She was perfectly formed. She wore a pink dress and red shoes. Her hair was woven from fine black threads.

"My mother made this doll for me. She told me that I would see her again someday."

Nancy's heart went out to Ester. She examined the

delicate needlework. "Your mother is an excellent seamstress."

"My parents own a clothing factory in Poland. My mother learned to sew from a very young age." Ester's eyes lit up when she spoke of her mother.

"Your mother wouldn't like to think of you out here on the streets alone, Ester."

"Do you think that she is still alive?"

"Of course she is. She's probably sitting at home thinking of you right now." Nancy forced a smile on her lips as her heart ached.

Suddenly Nancy remembered the time. She glanced at her wrist watch. The last post would be collected soon. If she didn't hurry she wouldn't make it. She knew that it could take a week for the letter to reach Ireland.

"I have to go to the post-box, Ester. I'll be as quick as I can. Will you wait here for me? You can come back to my house and stay with me. It's not much, but anything's better than the street."

Ester didn't seem to hear her. She cradled the small doll in her arms and sang a lullaby to her. It was as though she were alive.

Nancy ran as fast as she could. She didn't stop until she reached the post office. She bought a stamp then dropped the letter in the red post-box before she had a chance to change her mind. Then she ran back to the spot where she had found Ester. However, the girl was nowhere to be seen. All that remained was a small red shoe. It must have fallen from her doll. Nancy picked it up. Then she ran around frantically, asking people if they had seen the girl.

"Please, sir, have you seen a young girl carrying a doll?"

"Watch it, lady!"

"Excuse me, madam. I'm looking for a young girl with black hair, carrying a doll. She was here a moment ago."

"Oh dear – no, I haven't seen any little girl."

Nancy ran up and down the busy street for over half an hour, until she realised that it was no use. Ester was gone. Swallowed up by the war like so many people. Tears tumbled from her eyes.

Nancy hadn't been to church in years, but that day before going home she went to the cathedral. She lit a penny candle in front of a statue of Saint Anthony. Then she got down on her knees and prayed. She prayed for the little girl called Ester with black wavy hair and sad brown eyes. Then she prayed for Ester's family back in Poland. Please, God, don't let the Germans take them away on the train. Let them survive the war. She prayed for Fred, that he would make it home safely.

And finally she prayed for Lottie and Albert. "Dear Lord, please let Hugh and Ida agree to take care of my children. Until the war is over." Right now they were her only hope. Nancy knew that if it were the other way around she would have taken in Hugh's daughter Prudence in a heartbeat. The flickering candles in the cathedral reminded her of the stars in the sky, the only lights that remained during the blackout. She opened the palm of her hand and placed the small red doll's shoe on the altar in front of the statue of Anthony – the Patron Saint of Lost Things.

Then she ran home to wait for Hugh and Ida to respond.

Chapter Six

The Dunlivins

Twelve-year-old Prudence Dunlivin picked up the small white envelope from the doormat. Her black cat Tabby purred and rubbed himself against her leg.

Prudence had to squint to read the handwriting. She wasn't wearing her spectacles. This made it difficult for her to follow the neat loops of blue ink penned by Nancy Hope's hand. She squinted at the stamp. It wasn't an Irish stamp. Prudence could see a man's head on it, with a crown at the top – he must be the King of England. Why on earth would anyone in England be writing to her father? Prudence thought. Something told her that it meant trouble.

Prudence was an utterly spoilt child. She had a bright red face which looked as though it had been scrubbed with a wire brush. She also had a foul temper and would start an argument at the drop of a hat. Prudence always looked as though she was dressed for a party, although she was never asked to one.

On this particular morning, when the letter arrived from England, she was wearing a pink dress. A red-velvet ribbon was tied in a large bow around her waist. Beneath it was a lace underskirt. Her large feet were squeezed into satin ballet shoes. And her mousy brown hair was tied up with red ribbons and curled like question marks at the end. Although she hadn't eaten breakfast yet, Prudence was sucking on an orange lollipop, which stained her lips. She had a large gap in between her front teeth which made a whistling sound whenever she spoke.

Prudence stomped off to the dining room. She held the letter in her stumpy hands like a prize possession. Nothing exciting ever happened in Kilbree. Receiving a letter out of the blue was an unexpected treat. Prudence couldn't wait to find out what the contents of the small white envelope were.

Hugh and Ida were seated at either end of a long oval dining table. It was covered in a lace tablecloth and adorned with silver cutlery. The plates and cups were decorated with a weeping-willow pattern. The Dunlivins' house looked more like a hotel than a family home. Ida was house-proud and she acted as though she was better than everyone else. The Dunlivins had breakfast every morning at eight o'clock sharp. Hugh ate a hard-boiled egg. Ida ate a steaming hot bowl of porridge. Prudence ate whatever she felt like – even if that was lollipops.

There was a photograph of Prudence on the wall. It

was taken on the day she made her First Holy Communion. She had her hands joined in prayer and an angelic expression on her face. The photograph made her look as though butter wouldn't melt in her mouth although Prudence was the most cunning and devious child to have ever lived in Kilbree. The Dunlivins' dining-room wall was adorned with many peculiar objects. For example, Ida collected hundreds of tiny figurines of cats – they came from all over the world and hung from silver hooks on the walls. There was one from France. It wore a small blue bow around its neck and had bright green eyes. There was also one from China. It had been hand-painted with gold paint and its eyes moved from left to right all day long.

The Communion photograph and the tiny cats shook as Prudence bounded across the room.

"It's a letter for Dad," she announced, waving the letter triumphantly in the air

Ida snatched the letter from her hand.

Ida was every bit as cantankerous as her daughter. People in the village knew her as a hideous woman. She had head of oily black curls and small beady eyes like a crow. Ida Dunlivin had a wicked streak and was not afraid to show it. Whenever people saw her walking down the street, they would cross the road to avoid her. Some people called her a troublemaker. Others called her a witch. One thing was for sure: she was always gossiping about people in the village. In fact, Ida didn't have a kind word to say about anyone except her darling daughter.

"It's from England – who the devil do we know in

England, Hugh?" Ida scowled at her husband.

"Beats me, Ida," Hugh said wearily as he chewed on a piece of brown soda bread. "Bring it here to me, Prudence. There's a good girl."

Prudence ignored him while Ida glowered and picked up the silver letter-opener.

Being an undertaker was a well-respected job and Hugh took his position seriously. But his wife and daughter did not respect him at all. In fact, they made his life a misery.

Hugh Dunlivin had changed a lot since the days Nancy had known him. He was now a tall thin man. Naturally his ears still protruded from his head, but now his hair was sleek and grey and combed over to hide a bald patch. He had a pale complexion and blue lips. And he always wore a black suit, just in case someone died. His melancholy demeanour was perfect for an undertaker. A bushy grey moustache clung to his top lip, like a caterpillar to a leaf on a tree.

Unlike his wife and daughter, Hugh was a kind and caring person. And he appeared to be years older than he was. He put this down to the constant strain of living with Ida and Prudence, who he sarcastically referred to as his "precious darlings".

Hugh longed for a peaceful life. However, he didn't think there was much chance of that anytime soon. And he had the sneaky suspicion that this letter meant that things were about to go even more sour than before.

In contrast to her husband, Ida Dunlivin was anything but dull. She wore bright pink lipstick and a yellow dress with a red cardigan. Her black curly hair was pinned to the side with a silver hairclip that was shaped like a cat. There was a green wart on the side of her nose, with two black dots at its centre. When they had first got married, Ida was beautiful. However, the more horrible she became the worse she looked. Many people said that she had a bad heart. And there was no cure for that. She was wicked and would do anything to get her own way.

Ida prided herself on making the corpses of Kilbree look better dead than they did when they were alive. Although if anyone annoyed her when they were alive, Ida got her own back on them when they were dead by making them look hideous. On one such occasion a woman called Kitty, whom Ida despised, died suddenly. Kitty was a tall woman with square shoulders and large hands. Her back was bent and she had bow-shaped legs. Kitty owned a cake shop in the village, and much like Ida thought she was better than everyone else. Ida shared her interest in baking but, despite their similarities, Ida and Kitty couldn't stand each other. They competed against each other every year in the village-fete baking competition. Ida spent days baking cakes, in order to be crowned the best baker in Kilbree. People in the village took bets on who would win. The year that she died, Kitty went into the tent on the day of the final of the competition and sprinkled salt over Ida's cakes. All so that she could win and be crowned the winner. Ida was livid and vowed to get her own back on Kitty one day. That day came quicker than either of the women expected. When Kitty died in her sleep, Ida was asked to prepare her body for burial. On the day of the funeral when her family gathered to say their last goodbyes, they could not believe their eyes. Ida had made Kitty look like a clown – complete with a red nose and a bright red curly wig. The priest was furious, and Ida promised never to do such a horrible thing again. Although deep down she felt that it was worth it, to get her own back on her arch enemy. Of course, she had to remove the wig and nose, but there was no time to beautify Kitty's hair and face so she still looked dreadful as they closed the coffin. This pleased Ida greatly.

Hugh tapped his hardboiled egg with the back of a silver spoon as he waited in trepidation for his wife to open the letter.

"*Outrageous, simply disgraceful!*" Ida boomed. Her face turned purple and her eyeballs looked as though they were out on stalks.

"Whatever is the matter, dear?" Hugh asked. He sensed that he was going to receive the sharp end of her tongue.

He hurriedly filled a glass with water and carried it down to Ida at the opposite end of the long table. He sloshed water on the wooden floorboards as he went and narrowly avoided tripping over the cat, which screeched and arched its back in disapproval.

Prudence peered tentatively over her mother's shoulder at the letter. The ink was smudged in places as if by tears. Hugh handed what remained of the glass of water to Ida who dropped the letter to the floor. She was hyperventilating and fanning herself with the envelope.

Hugh crouched down and picked up the letter. The

bones in his knees cracked as he straightened up and returned to his chair. He recognised the handwriting straight away.

"Well, I never! Nancy Hope! There's a blast from the past." A hint of a smile flickered across his lips. It was replaced almost immediately by a frown when his wife glared in his direction. He quickly read the letter.

"*She needn't think that we are going to take her two snivelling brats!*" Ida screeched. Then she wagged her finger in Hugh's direction. "I have heard that those evacuees are riddled with lice! And, besides, this is England's war, not ours!"

"I am sure that Nancy's children are quite clean, dear," said Hugh. "From what I recall, Cousin Nancy was always dressed immaculately."

"*Huh!*" Ida snorted.

Hugh remembered his cousin Nancy fondly. She was a pleasant girl with long blonde hair and bright green eyes. She used to come to stay with him every summer when they were children. They had got on very well and had great adventures together. However, she stopped coming to visit when the strange girl Cuán vanished and he hadn't seen her since. Hugh often wondered if Nancy knew more about Cuán's disappearance than she had said. After all, she was the last one to see her on the night that it happened.

Hugh really wanted to help Nancy. However, he did not know how he could persuade Ida to care for two more children. One child was too much for his wife to manage.

"There's a war on, Ida. Times are hard. I know it's not

Ireland's war, but still . . ."

"If you ask me she just wants to get rid of two brats for a while."

Hugh sighed. The only person Ida Dunlivin cared about was herself.

Suddenly he was overcome with anger. *"For once in your life, Ida Dunlivin, put yourself in someone else's position!"* he shouted, slamming his fist down on the table.

Ida's jaw almost dropped to the floor. She was flabbergasted by her husband's sudden outburst. In all their years of marriage, he had never spoken to her in such a hostile manner. Prudence giggled into her cupped hand.

Hugh didn't know what had come over him. He had never spoken back to his wife before and doubted that he would ever do so again.

"Besides, as she says, the children might be company for Prudence," he said in a much quieter voice.

"I don't want company!" Prudence cried.

"Be nice, Prudence – it wouldn't be forever." Hugh flashed his daughter a look of anger.

Prudence looked at her mother who was still in a state of shock. Then she grunted indignantly, folded her arms across her chest and stormed out of the room.

Ida remained as still as a statue. For a moment Hugh thought that he had gone too far. But then her lips began to quiver and she started to laugh. Hugh stared at his wife incredulously as tears fell from her eyes. She gripped her sides, unable to contain herself.

"Hugh Dunlivin, you astound me! I never thought you had it in you!"

"So they can come to stay then, Ida?" he said, pushing his luck.

"Yes. On one condition." Ida stopped laughing. Her face turned rapidly from purple to pink to white.

"Anything, dearest."

"They must sleep down in the cellar."

"But that's where we store the coffins and corpses, awaiting burial."

"Take it or leave it."

"I'll take it." After all, Hugh thought, it was a safer option than staying in England and waiting to be bombed. He guessed that children living in wartime would be used to seeing dead people and hiding underground.

"That settles it then," said Ida. "I will hear no more about it. Keep them out of my way, or they will be on the first boat back."

"Thank you, Ida, my precious darling. I will write to Nancy. Then I will make the necessary arrangements to have the children collected from the train station in Wexford."

Hugh then finished his egg and read the paper as though it was just a normal day.

However, something told Hugh Dunlivin that things would never be normal again.

Chapter Seven

Leaving Home

"I don't understand why you're sending us away!" Albert protested as his mother stood at the edge of his small metal bed and packed his suitcase.

His bedroom was small and damp. The walls were covered in blue wallpaper. It had started to peel away from the ceiling. The only toys he owned were a few teddy bears, a toy rabbit, a metal drum and some tin soldiers. They sat on a dressing table, over by the window. Opposite Albert's bed was a small fireplace. It was surrounded by green tiles. A threadbare rug covered the wooden floorboards.

"It's for your own safety, Albert," Nancy said as she folded his clothes carefully and placed them inside the tattered brown suitcase.

Albert didn't have many clothes. This made Nancy sad. She wished she had more money to spend on her children. If she did they would have the very best of things. She dreamed of giving them a better life one day. She packed all of Albert's clothes. They consisted of two jumpers, three pairs of trousers, three shirts, socks with holes in and underwear. Nancy sighed as she fastened the buckle of the belt around the old suitcase.

"You don't love us any more!" Albert cried. A large tear fell from the corner of his eye.

He had said the one thing that he knew would hurt his mother the most. Her heart ached and her face crumbled like a sandcastle on a beach when the tide comes in.

Tears sprang to Nancy's eyes and overflowed. "Albert, how could you even think that!" she sobbed.

Albert felt frightened. He had never seen his mother so upset before and he knew that he had gone too far. But his vile temper took over and something told him not to stop. He shook his small fist in front of her face.

"I hate you, Mother, and I hate this stinking war! I am not going anywhere!"

Albert was as shocked as his mother at his sudden outburst. He stormed out of his bedroom as fast as he could, slamming the door behind him. Then he stomped down the stairs. He ran outside to the small garden with a face as red as a tomato. There he sat down beneath an old oak tree and wept.

Lottie heard her mother crying loudly as she placed a photograph of her father into her suitcase. For once she agreed with her irritating young brother. She too would rather stay at home than be sent away to live with strangers. Though she knew that it wasn't their mother's fault – she was only trying to protect them. The countryside was safer than the towns and cities, which were targets for German bombs. Lottie packed her dresses, cardigans, knickers and socks and, just in case there wasn't a library in the place that she was going to, she packed two of her favourite books as well. They were *The Enchanted Wood* by Enid Blyton and *Gulliver's Travels* by Jonathan Swift.

Lottie could hear her mother's footsteps as she walked across the hallway and stopped outside her bedroom door. Then the door handle turned and Nancy stood in the doorframe, with her head slightly bent to one side. Her eyes were red. A fake smile appeared on her lips.

"Are you ready, Lottie? We have to go soon. Miss Bentwhistle told us to be at the school for nine o'clock. We don't want to miss the train."

Her mother spoke as though she would be going with them, although Lottie knew that she was staying behind.

"Do we really have to go, Mother?"

"Not you as well, Lottie! I can't take much more."

"I'm sorry, Mother, but I don't understand. We survived the Christmas Blitz." 'The Blitz' is what the people of Britain called the German bombing campaign. It came from the German word *Blitzkrieg* which meant 'lightning war'.

"We did but lots of people didn't."

Lottie thought about her friends Bessie and Sarah-Jane. Both had been killed on Christmas Eve when a bomb fell on their house.

"I will miss you, Mother!" Lottie cried. She ran into her mother's arms and held her tight. She could feel the beat of her mother's heart beneath the thin fabric of her dress. She smelt like lavender. Lottie breathed in deeply, not ever wanting to forget a single thing about her.

"I will miss you too, Lottie. Just think of it as a holiday – you'll be back before you know it."

Lottie hoped that her mother was right. She held back the tears that had gathered in the corners of her eyes like tiny soldiers about to go into battle.

"I know I can count on you, Lottie. Albert can be hard work at times, but he doesn't mean any harm."

"I know, Mother."

"Help Albert carry his suitcase, Lottie, and take care of him for me, won't you?"

"Of course I will, Mother." Lottie bit her lip and fussed with the hem of her skirt.

A feeling of guilt rose like a wave in her chest as she considered all the times that she lost her temper with her young brother. It was hard being the eldest child in the family. The burden of responsibility landed on her shoulders. And, in a time of war, more was expected of children than ever before.

"There is something I want to give to you, Lottie."

Lottie's mother held a golden ring between her finger and thumb. The image of a wolf's faced was etched into it. Amber shone from the animal's eyes.

"Mother, it's beautiful!" Lottie cried.

"Keep it safe for me, Lottie – it belonged to a dear friend."

Lottie sat on the edge of the bed and placed the ring on her finger. She was surprised to discover that it fit her perfectly.

"Your friend must have been young when she wore this, Mother," she said.

"Yes, she was," said her mother with a sigh.

"But why have I never seen it before?" asked Lottie.

"I had it hidden away. It's precious. You must take the greatest care of it. Keep it on your finger so you don't lose it."

"I will, Mother," Lottie promised fervently.

"I want you to have it in case anything happens," her mother said.

"What do you mean, Mother? You told us that you're sending us to somewhere safe."

Nancy wiped a tear from her eye and smiled. "Of course I am, Lottie. You'll be quite safe with Hugh and Ida, I'm sure of it."

But Lottie knew that there was something about Kilbree that troubled her mother. What did she mean by "in case anything happens"? Then it struck her: her mother must mean if anything should happen to *her*. If their house was bombed and she was killed, she wanted Lottie to have this special ring. The thought was so terrible that Lottie felt her entire world was being torn apart. But she must be brave. Her mother was so upset and Lottie didn't want to spoil their last few hours together.

"The ring is beautiful. I will treasure it always, Mother – thank you."

"Right. Let's get going."

Nancy stood up. Then she brushed the creases out of her skirt with the back of her hand. She picked up Albert's case and Lottie followed her down the narrow staircase and out onto the street.

Chapter Eight

The Great Train Journey

The railway platform was crowded with people. Children stood in line as their mothers kissed them goodbye. Each child was given a brown luggage label with his or her name on it. The labels were threaded on bootlaces. Then they were placed around the children's necks.

"I feel like a piece of luggage!" Albert said.

"Hush, Albert, and stop complaining," said Lottie. "We just have to get on with it."

"That's the spirit, Lottie," Nancy said as she knelt down in front of Albert and placed her two hands firmly on his shoulders.

Lottie realised that her mother was wearing her best dress. The one that Dad had bought for her birthday. It was yellow and had small green flowers on it. It had grown old and the flowers had begun to fade, just like her smile. Lottie realised her mother wanted to look her best in case this was the last memory her children would have of her. Her face was so pale it looked as though it was made of porcelain and could crack at any moment.

"Now, Albert, you do as your sister tells you and be a good boy for Mr and Mrs Dunlivin."

"But I don't know them, Mother," Albert grumbled like thunder.

"Don't worry, Albert, you soon will. And you'll be back home before you know it. Think of it as an adventure."

"It's time for the children to go now, Mrs Hope." Miss Bentwhistle, the schoolteacher, was a tall thin woman. She resembled a blade of grass. Her mousy brown hair was cut into a bob. Dull lifeless eyes stared over the rim of her spectacles. She wore a long grey skirt and a blue blouse with a bow at the neck. On her feet were a pair of sensible black court shoes.

She stood between Lottie and her mother, like a referee in a football match.

"Right," said Nancy. "Of course."

She kissed Albert delicately on the cheek. Then she hugged Lottie who felt like a small child again, not a twelve-year-old girl. The tears that she had been holding back came flooding through and she began to sob.

"Move along, Lottie, there's a good girl." Miss Bentwhistle directed Lottie and Albert away from their mother and on towards the waiting train.

Lottie turned back. However, the crowd had swallowed her mother whole and she could no longer see her.

"Why are you crying, Lottie?" Albert felt frightened, as he was not used to seeing his sister so upset.

Lottie dried her tears. "Because it's just you and me now. But we'll be all right."

"We will see Mother again, won't we?" Albert was beginning to panic.

"Of course we will, Albert."

They walked along the train platform together. Lottie carried the suitcases and Albert their gas masks. A large black steam train was waiting for them. Most of the children appeared happy to be boarding the train. The stationmaster sounded the whistle. Miss Bentwhistle, who was holding a clipboard in her hand, checked off each child's name as they boarded the train.

"Lottie and Albert Hope, you are in carriage Number 1."

"Can I have the window seat, Miss?"

"I don't see why not, Albert. Now don't dawdle, boys and girls. We are behind schedule as it is."

Lottie lifted the two suitcases onto the train. Then she lugged them along the narrow passageway until they arrived at their carriage. Albert sat beside the dusty window and peered down at the train track. He saw a Robin Redbreast picking a berry off the branch of a tree.

After a short time, three more children joined them.

There were two girls who Lottie recognised from school. Their names were Violet and Edith Butler. Their parents owned the butcher's shop. They were dressed in their Sunday clothes. Violet had red ribbons in her hair and wore a green coat. Edith had a royal-blue coat and a pale-blue velvet beret. Lottie studied her own shabby appearance and felt embarrassed. Lottie knew that Violet and Edith would find a new home very quickly. Their mother had made every effort to ensure that they looked their best. Lottie's mother had too – she knew this – however, her clothes were old and worn and no amount of washing and ironing could make them look better. She wished her mother would take up sewing again. In the past, they were always dressed smartly.

A boy entered the carriage. He introduced himself as Douglas Proud. Albert thought that his name suited him. He was dressed in the finest clothes that Albert had ever seen and he seemed to be a very proud boy. His large nose was raised in the air as he surveyed the rest of the children with contempt. He had smuggled his pet mouse Oliver on board the train. He hid the tiny creature in the breast pocket of his overcoat, much to Albert's delight.

As the steam train puffed along the track, Lottie opened Albert's suitcase. She took out his favourite toy, a rabbit called Mr Fuzzy Ears, and some corned-beef sandwiches. Her mother had made the sandwiches for their journey. Albert's eyes lit up when he saw his old friend. He grabbed him and then tucked into his food ravenously. He handed Douglas a small crumb for his pet mouse Oliver. The small fury creature sniffed at it disdainfully and disappeared back into Douglas's pocket. Albert decided that the mouse was as proud as its owner.

Lottie was unable to eat – her stomach felt as though it was full of butterflies. She imagined her mother going back to the house alone and her heart ached for her. Then her thoughts turned to the place where they were going. She hoped that the people would be kind to them. Albert had a wicked temper and could be a very difficult boy at times. Although he didn't mean it – he just couldn't help himself. Lottie knew that it was her duty to take care of her quarrelsome young brother. She had to ensure that he didn't get into trouble while they were away.

As the train trundled down the track, green fields appeared outside the window. They replaced the red-brick houses that they were used to.

"Look, Lottie, a cloud in the field!"

Lottie and the other children looked out of the window. They stared in the direction that Albert was pointing.

"Heavens above, you are a foolish boy!" Douglas remarked. "That is a sheep not a cloud. How could a boy of your age be so stupid?"

Violet and Edith giggled behind cupped hands. And, before Lottie could intervene, Albert jumped down from his seat and kicked Douglas in the shin. Douglas screamed in pain and Miss Bentwhistle flew into the carriage with a face like thunder.

"What on earth is going on in here?" the overwrought teacher demanded.

"That vile and insolent creature kicked me in the leg!" Douglas sobbed.

"Is this true, Albert Hope?" Miss Bentwhistle folded her arms across her chest and tapped her foot on the floor.

"Yes, and I would do it again!"

"Albert!" Lottie gasped. "He didn't mean to do it,

miss – Douglas was teasing him."

"Your brother is quite capable of speaking for himself, Charlotte Hope."

Lottie knew that Albert was in big trouble now. Miss Bentwhistle only used Lottie's full Christian name when she was very cross.

Albert sat down but the teacher walked over and pulled him up by the ear.

"You are sitting with me for the duration of the journey, Albert Hope."

"Please, miss!" Lottie pleaded.

"Sit down this instant, Charlotte!" Miss Bentwhistle roared.

Lottie did as she was told. She watched in dismay as her brother was marched out of the carriage. They hadn't even arrived at their new home and already she had broken her promise to her mother about taking care of Albert.

"This is all your fault!" Lottie spat at Douglas.

Mr Fuzzy Ears had fallen to the ground. Lottie picked him up and dusted him off.

Douglas Proud wiped the tears from his eyes with the back of his hand. Oliver his little mouse peered out of his coat pocket to see what all the commotion was about.

What Lottie did not realise was that Douglas Proud was as scared as she was about going to a new home. As the train trundled forward the four children sat there silently. They each imagined what their new homes would be like. They didn't utter another word until the train came to an abrupt halt at the station.

Chapter Nine

The Missing Boy

Lottie searched the train station for Albert. There were children everywhere. However, her brother was nowhere to be seen. A sense of panic overwhelmed her. She held the suitcases and gas masks in her hands. Then she was ushered into a large waiting room by an overweight man who wore a black suit. He had a whistle tied around his neck with a piece of string. He appeared to be in charge. Lottie wondered where Miss Bentwhistle was. There was a clock on the wall and two long wooden tables had been set for a party. There were jam sandwiches, Victoria sponge cakes and glasses of lemonade. Lottie couldn't believe her eyes! She hadn't tasted cake since the war began.

Two women stood behind the tables. They handed food to the hungry children, who devoured it like starving beasts. The women had unusual accents that

Lottie did not recognise. They both had red faces and black curly hair. The only difference between them was that one of the women was shorter than the other and she had hair growing above her top lip. They wore white aprons with pockets in the front. The aprons covered their knee-length dresses. The shorter woman wore a green dress with daisies on it. She reminded Lottie of a meadow on the spring day. The taller woman looked older. Her dress was navy blue and had a lace collar. She rubbed her face with the back of her hand. She got flour on her cheek and Lottie had to look away to stop herself from laughing.

As Lottie looked around the room she spotted Albert's friend Billy Bright standing in the corner of the room. She ran towards him.

"Have you seen Albert anywhere, Billy?"

Billy was holding two jam sandwiches in his hand. A large dollop of jam oozed from one of them and fell to the floor.

Billy was just about to answer Lottie when she felt someone tug at the sleeve of her coat. She turned around and saw Albert standing there. His large blue eyes looked sad.

"Albert, I thought I had lost you!" Lottie cried. Then she bent down and hugged her young brother. She could feel his heart beating like a drum in his chest.

"I want to go home, Lottie! I miss Mother!" Albert sobbed.

"Please don't cry, Albert – everything is going to be all right. I promise. Just try to be a good boy." She wiped the tears from Albert's eyes with the sleeve of her coat.

"Would you like a sandwich, my love?"

Lottie looked up. It was one of the women from behind the table. The one with the hairy lip. She had kind eyes which crinkled in the corners and a big reassuring smile. In her hand she held a gigantic plate of jam sandwiches, which were cut into triangles.

"Yes, please," Lottie replied, and for the first time that day she felt hungry. She gave Albert two triangles and took two for herself.

"I want some cake too," said Albert to the lady.

"Albert!" said Lottie. "Mind your manners!"

But the lady said, "Certainly, young man! Just go up to the big table and have some Victoria sponge and lemonade."

So that's what they did.

After all the children had eaten, they were told to sit and wait on wooden chairs that had been placed at the back of the room. Then two girls came in and began to clear the table, while the two women who had been serving took off their aprons and put on their coats.

"What are we waiting for, Lottie? Do we have to get another train?" Albert asked.

"I expect we're waiting for someone to take us to the boat for Ireland. We're going to meet our new family."

"I liked our old one!" Albert moaned.

All the children whispered nervously to each other as a group of adults entered the room.

"Here, Albert, you have jam on your face. That won't do." Lottie pulled a handkerchief out from her sleeve.

Then she spat on it and wiped her brother's face. Just as she had seen her mother do.

The man in the black suit who Lottie had seen earlier came in and stood, holding a clipboard in his hand – it looked like Miss Bentwhistle's clipboard. The lady with the kind eyes went and spoke to him. Then she turned and walked towards Lottie and Albert.

Lottie smiled and turned to Albert. "Sit up straight, Albert. I think the nice lady who gave us jam sandwiches is coming to take us to the boat."

The lady smiled and took Albert by the hand. She began to lead him back to the man.

Lottie got to her feet to follow but the lady turned and said, "You wait there, my dear."

Lottie sat down again, puzzled.

Albert walked sluggishly forward, pulling a little on the lady's hand. He hoped that he wasn't in trouble again. Lottie could sense his fear from where she sat.

"He looks like a bonny little lad! How old are you?" the woman with the kind eyes enquired. Her red cheeks were shiny.

"I am six," Albert replied, glancing nervously in Lottie's direction. He hoped that he would say the right things. He didn't intend to be such a naughty boy – it just seemed to happen.

"Would you like to come and stay with me for a bit, Albert?" the woman asked. "I have horses, and chickens too. You can even help me to collect the eggs for breakfast."

A smile erupted on Albert's lips. "Yes, we'd like that!"

he replied. He had never seen horses or chickens before and they sounded much better than Douglas Proud's silly pet mouse. And Lottie could help him to collect the eggs for breakfast each morning.

The woman turned to the man. "I'm sorry but I couldn't take both of them. I have six children of my own. One is all that I could manage."

"I understand," the man replied. Then he took a handkerchief out from his coat pocket and wiped his brow.

Albert looked back at Lottie who had a perplexed look on her face. He knew she was wondering what was being said and why they were talking to him rather than her.

"Albert, say goodbye to your sister, there's a good boy," the woman said. "And don't forget your suitcase and gas mask."

Albert couldn't believe what he was hearing. This wasn't supposed to happen.

"*I won't go without Lottie!*" he spat.

He ran over to Lottie and jumped into her arms.

"Whatever is the matter, Albert?"

"*I won't go with her, Lottie, I won't!*"

"But she's taking us to the boat, Albert, isn't she?"

"*Noooo! She's taking me to her farm! But she doesn't want you, Lottie!*"

"That can't be right, Albert – there must be some mistake."

"*Don't let them take me, Lottie, please!*"

The man with the clipboard and the woman walked stealthily over to where the children stood.

"Come along now, Albert, say goodbye, there's a good boy," said the man, pulling Albert to his feet.

"*Wait!*" Lottie cried. "There's been a mistake! We're going to Ireland to stay with our Uncle Hugh Dunlivin in Wexford. Mother said that you would put us on the boat!"

"Don't make a fuss, children." The man was exasperated.

Lottie threw herself on her knees in front of the woman. "Please don't take my brother! I promised Mother that I would take care of him – please don't separate us!"

"I am so sorry," said the woman with the kind eyes. She twisted her wedding ring as she spoke. "I can't possibly take you both – I only have room for one."

"*But my mother arranged for us both to go to Ireland to the Dunlivins!*" Lottie screamed. "*Miss Bentwhistle knows! Where is she?*"

The man in the black suit took no notice. He dragged Albert kicking and screaming from the room and the woman followed.

"*Be a good boy, Albert, and don't get into trouble!*" Lottie shouted after him through her tears.

She noticed Mr Fuzzy Ears on the floor. She picked him up and ran onto the train platform. There was no sign of Albert or the two adults.

She felt as though her heart was breaking. She had let her mother down and did not know if she would ever see her brother again.

A cold wind whipped at her ankles and sent a shiver down her spine. Rain burst from the clouds above her head and tapped on her shoulders like drumsticks on a drum. She hugged Mr Fuzzy Ears. The small brown rabbit smelt of Albert and of her home. Lottie realised that for the first time in her life she was truly alone. Without her mother, father or Albert. And she began to have dark, scary thoughts, the kind of thoughts that normally rear their ugly heads in the dead of night, when there is no-one else around.

"*Miss Bentwhistle!*" she screamed as she spotted her teacher at the far end of the platform talking to an old lady.

Struggling to breathe, Lottie ran up to her teacher and tugged on her coat.

"They have taken Albert!" she gasped.

"What are you saying, child?"

"The man – with your clipboard – he's taken Albert! They're gone!"

"Oh Lord, there has been a terrible mistake. Lottie, stay here with Mrs Kennedy. I will be right back."

Lottie stood beside the old lady and watched as Miss Bentwhistle ran back along the platform.

The tears that Lottie had been holding back for so long came flooding out, like ink from a pen. She was sick and tired of being brave. She wanted the war to be over so that she could go back home again to her mother.

"*I want my mother!*" she cried. She felt much younger than her twelve years.

Mrs Kennedy placed her arm around Lottie's shoulders. "Things will work out, girl – just you wait and see."

"How can you be sure?"

"You don't live as long as me without learning a thing or two."

Lottie stared at Mrs Kennedy. She realised that she had an Irish accent like her grandma.

"Are you getting the boat to Dublin?" Lottie asked.

"If I don't miss it. I promised your teacher that I would accompany a young girl and boy to Dublin, but they haven't turned up yet. I will have to go soon."

Lottie lurched forward and threw her arms around the old woman's neck.

"That's us! My name is Lottie and my brother is Albert. We're going to stay with the Dunlivins in Wexford – but I won't go without Albert!"

"You won't have to." The old lady pointed. "It looks like Miss Bentwhistle has found him."

Lottie looked down the platform. She jumped for joy when she saw Albert running towards her. His blonde hair was tousled and blowing in the breeze while freckles danced gleefully across his nose.

"*Lottie, it's me! I'm back again!*" Albert ran into his sister's arms as a lone magpie flew overhead.

"*One for sorrow,*" Mrs Kennedy said.

And something told Lottie that the future they faced was far worse than the past they had left behind.

Chapter Ten

Cuán
Twenty Years Earlier – August 1920
Kilbree, County Wexford

Cuán was walking through the forest with her dog Bonnie on an autumn afternoon when she heard a terrifying sound. The shrill cry startled her. It was unlike anything she had heard before.

It had started off as a perfect day. Sunlight streamed through the trees. Leaves rustled and the entire forest was carpeted in golden buttercups. Cuán picked ripe blackberries. They slipped willingly off their stems and onto Cuán palms like gloves onto cold hands on a winter morning. Her fingers were stained purple. Cuán placed the plump berries onto her tongue. Then a branch snapped. And a flock of crows flew overhead. Moments later the blue sky turned grey. It was as though an artist was painting a summer day and changed their mind at the last second.

Then she heard the wailing. Even though Cuán knew the forest like the back of her hand, the sound frightened her. The direction of the wind changed, enough for Cuán to know that danger was in the air. She shoved her hands into the pockets of her green coat and pulled her hood up. Then she quickened her pace. Cuán didn't scare easily. At first she thought that the piercing cries came from an animal caught in a trap. And, for a moment or two, she scanned the dense undergrowth for the hint of a fox's tail. Or the stout black-and-white body of a badger entangled in the vice-like grip of a wire snare. The animals in the forest trusted Cuán. They respected her. She was the only person that they would come to. She had brought home rabbits with broken legs and sparrows who had fallen from their nests. However, as thunder rumbled overhead and rain spilt from the clouds, Cuán quickly realised that she was in danger. No matter which direction she went the sound seemed to be following her. She shivered in fear. Her instincts told her that she was the one being hunted this time. Who would save her, if she fell into a trap?

Cuán was unaware that the deathly cry was supernatural at first. She mistook it for one of the boys from the village playing a foolish trick on her. They often followed her home from school, and called her names. Although they never usually ventured this far into the forest for fear of werewolves.

"Jimmy Doyle, is that you?" she called out into the darkness.

"Cuán . . . Cuán . . . Cuán . . ." Her name was whispered three times on the breeze.

Cuán had tolerated the boys with their cruel taunts and

wickedness for years now.

"People don't like what they don't understand," Maeve had told her when she arrived home from school one day with a black eye and a cut on her knee which had come apart like the seam on a cushion.

"I don't like them either. I just wish that they would leave me alone." Cuán's knee stung. She winced in pain as Ma pulled a small stone out of the cut with a pair of tweezers.

"You poor child! It is because you are the rarest flower that ever bloomed. People can't pass by without noticing how unique you are. The beauty within you is like a mirror. When people look at you, they feel ugly and inferior. They will leave you alone and move on to someone else soon enough. Mark my words." Maeve looked into Cuán's eyes. They were red from crying. Her hands were wound into tight fists like balls of cotton waiting to be spun.

That was six years ago. Cuán was twelve now and still the bullies continued to torment her.

Cuán's black hair was cut to her shoulders and it glistened under the candlelight. Her red lips were shaped like a bow. Her skin was as white as snow. When Cuán was younger Maeve would tuck her up in bed at night-time with her teddy bears. Bonnie was a puppy then, and she would sneak under the covers and nestle under Cuán's arm, her wet nose protruding occasionally to sniff the damp air. Even as a pup, Bonnie could sense danger lurking. Cuán insisted that Maeve left the thick red-velvet curtains open so that she could see the ancient stars shimmering in the black sky. Then Maeve would read Cuán her favourite story. It was the story of Snow White and Red Rose, the two sisters who lived in the forest and promised to stay together for as long as they lived.

"Read it again, Ma!" Cuán would cry.

"Would you not like me to read you something else tonight, Cuán? You must be bored with that one."

"No, Ma, I want that story."

Ma would read the fairy tale to Cuán and her amber eyes would sparkle in delight. Night would fold over them like a scarf and, when Cuán's eyes began to close, Maeve would place the book on the shelf beside her ring with the wolf's face on it. Then she would kiss her goodnight and they would pray together.

"As I lay me down to sleep.
I pray the Lord my soul to keep.
If I should die before I wake,
I pray to God my soul to take.
If I should live for other days,
I pray the Lord to guide my ways."

Maeve's heart would ache. She knew that Cuán needed praying for. She would never have a sister to play with. She doubted that the peculiar child would even find a friend.

Maeve Clancy was not Cuán's real mother – she was the woman who found her in the forest and reared her. No-one knew who Cuán's mother was. Maeve had been out hunting for rabbits when she saw the tiny baby sleeping in the hollow of a tree. A large grey wolf was snuffling at the baby and Maeve feared for the child's life.

Maeve could hardly believe her eyes. A wolf? How could that be? The last wolf in Ireland had been killed in 1786.

Maeve fired her shotgun. Two shots rang out and the wolf ran away. Maeve lowered the gun, smoke rising from its barrels. As she sighed in relief she looked up at the sky and noticed to her amazement a second moon. It was as blue as the ocean and somewhat egg-shaped. Moments later it disappeared. *Once in a blue moon*, she thought …

She gathered up the little bundle and pulled back the fur-lined wrapper that was around it. She saw that the baby was a girl who wore a gold ring round her neck, tied on with a red leather thong. The ring had the face of a wolf etched into it – its eyes were made of amber. Then she noticed that the child's eyelids were fused shut with a layer of mucus. How strange, Maeve thought. It must be some kind of infection.

Maeve turned to leave. The red-faced baby wriggled in her arms and cried. It was as though she wanted to be left in the forest with the wild animals.

"Hush, child. You are safe now," Maeve said and gave the baby her finger to suck.

Then, Maeve felt a presence. She looked around and was surprised to see the grey wolf standing at a distance watching her. But, somehow, now Maeve didn't feel threatened by the beautiful creature.

She took the baby home and bathed her eyes with

warm water. But still the eyelids were fused shut. Perplexed, she applied some healing herbs which contained Irish eyebright, a white flower with purple stipes and bronze-tinged leaves. Then she bandaged the infant's eyes.

Nothing could have prepared Maeve for the day when the bandages came off. The child's eyelids twitched but stayed closed. She bawled and screeched like a cat. Then, as night fell, her eyes opened. Maeve gasped. Cuán's eyes shone like glowing amber in the darkness.

Eyes like a wolf, Maeve thought, and shivered. "You poor, useless creature! What will become of you?" she cried.

Maeve was forty years old and had never married. Now she suddenly felt that it was her destiny to take care of this poor babe.

"My name is Maeve, little one. But you can call me 'Ma'. I will be your ma from now on. And I will call you 'Cuán' – it means 'little wolf'." Then she held the tiny bundle tight and rocked it in her arms until the baby's eyelids shut again.

Maeve wondered where the wolf had come from. Had it escaped from a circus or zoo? She didn't want to report it or even tell anyone about it. She now had the feeling it had actually been protecting the baby. Besides, she didn't want to have to explain to the authorities where she had got Cuán. They might have taken her away. And, she felt love towards the child already. It was as though she had been left there for Maeve to find. Sometimes, looking at her baby's eyes, Maeve couldn't help but remember the many local legends about werewolves with sharp teeth and amber eyes. The sinister tales caused her to tremble with fear.

So she said nothing about the wolf. She hid the gold ring, wondering who had left it around the baby's neck and what it meant. She pretended Cuán was the child of a distant cousin who had died in childbirth. But the other villagers looked at Cuán's yellow eyes and didn't believe her. There was something otherworldly about Cuán. She was the most beautiful girl to have ever set foot in the village. Her jet-black hair and pale skin made her stand out in a crowd. But it was her piercing amber eyes that people feared. The eyes of a wolf. Maeve wondered how she had been so foolish as to call the child Cuán – 'little wolf' – which only fuelled the villagers' suspicions further.

Speculation about where Cuán came from caused people to shun her. Some said she was a werewolf. Others said that she was the Banshee's daughter. They said that the Banshee would come looking for her one day.

"I am warning you, Jimmy Doyle! Come out from behind those trees this instant!" Cuán cried as she stood in the forest, gazing fearfully around her.

But there was no reply.

"Come on, Bonnie!" Cuán turned towards the black Labrador and stroked her soft coat.

The dog whimpered. The hairs stood up on her neck. Her back arched. Her teeth were bared. Bonnie sensed a strange presence.

Cuán felt it too. She knew now it wasn't Jimmy Doyle. It was something fearsome and it was coming for her. She turned and ran, stumbling over rocks and briars. She gasped for breath as she raced towards the ramshackle house, Bonnie at her heels. As they neared the old farmyard Cuán glanced back and saw a dark figure in the distance moving rapidly towards her. Cuán screamed.

She kept on running past a tractor and the old barn. She glanced over her shoulder. The figure was closer. Cuán shuddered as she heard the wail again. Louder and closer than the last time.

"I am coming for you, Cuán!"

It must be the Banshee, Cuán thought, her face crumpling like a piece of paper.

She ran on as fast as she could. Her heart was beating wildly in her chest. Her green coat fell about her body like a cloak. I wish I was a bird who could soar up into the air and away from here, she thought as she reached the red door. She pounded on it with her fists.

"Ma, help me, let me in!"

Then her heart almost stopped when she looked down and realised that Bonnie was gone.

"Bonnie!" she cried.

The eerie cry filled the air. And the figure now appeared in the farmyard.

The moon crept out from behind the clouds. Night-time scrambled in, like a thief in a gold mine. A sliver of moonlight shone down and Cuán could see that it was not a woman after all who was wailing. But a creature with red eyes. It was still calling her name.

Chapter Eleven

The Room of Skulls
1940

Ida opened up the cellar door. A musty smell crawled up Lottie and Albert's nostrils like a snake. She led them down the steep steps into the cold dark room. Then she tugged a cord so that a single light bulb illuminated the darkness.

Lottie's bones ached with tiredness as she dragged the suitcases behind her.

Albert looked around the room. The walls were wet and covered in green mould. Silver cobwebs hung from the ceiling waiting to snare unsuspecting flies. There were mousetraps on the floor. And propped up against the walls were coffins of different shapes and sizes.

"Do you think there are dead bodies in the coffins, Lottie?" Albert whispered.

"Hush, Albert!" Lottie didn't even want to think about the fact that the cellar was the darkest and creepiest and coldest room in the house. The perfect place to keep dead bodies.

They were surrounded by a labyrinth of tall, dusty bookcases. But there wasn't a single book in sight. Not even a book of spells, as one would expect in such a dreary cellar.

Instead of books, there were human skulls. Hundreds of bony, eyeball-less craniums occupied the ancient shelves. They peered down at Lottie and Albert as though they were unwelcome intruders at a supernatural party.

Albert feared that the skulls came to life at night and spoke to each other about their gruesome deaths. Lottie noticed many strange objects in the cellar that looked as though they belonged in the Natural History Museum. A rare collection of butterflies lay inside a grimy glass case. And on the wall above the fireplace hung a white stag's head. Its large antlers pointed towards a crumbling ceiling.

What on earth do the Dunlivins have all these strange objects for? Lottie wondered as she took in her surroundings.

In the corner of the room was the head of a wolf with yellow eyes. Its teeth were visible and it looked as though it were about to attack. She felt sorry for the creature. The air was stifling. Lottie looked around but found that there were no windows – the cellar was illuminated entirely by the one dim light bulb.

In the centre of the room were two small iron beds. They were covered in grey blankets, the kind that would scratch your skin. The yellowish pillows were as flat as pancakes. A *Prayer Book for Disobedient Children* was on top of a bedside locker between the two beds. Lottie noticed that the small wooden door of the locker was hanging off. She could not help but feel that they had been more comfortable in the air-raid shelter beneath the cathedral in Manchester. At least there they could be with their mother.

"You will be staying here for the duration of your stay!" Ida hissed at the children.

"With the coffins and the skulls?" Albert asked. "Do the coffins have dead bodies in them?"

"Do they frighten you, Albert?" Ida asked in such a way that Lottie suspected that she wanted to scare him.

"No!" Albert replied indignantly. He crossed his fingers behind his back, as he always did when he told a lie.

"I thought you were a brave boy – you are nothing but a coward!" Ida hissed at him.

"Don't you ever speak to my brother like that!" Lottie said and placed her hands protectively on Albert's shoulders. She was exhausted from the journey and she'd had enough of Ida's cruel jibes.

"How dare you answer me back! You disobedient, ungrateful child! I have a good mind to wash your mouth out with soap and water!" Ida snarled. "I should send you packing on the first boat back to England. You will both go to bed on an empty stomach tonight. And I want you out from under my feet tomorrow morning. I don't want to see you again until nightfall."

"But where will we go?" Lottie cried.

"I don't care where you go! And you can stop your sniffling, girl!" Ida screeched.

Lottie looked into Ida's cold, unforgiving eyes. She was the cruellest and most heartless woman that she had ever encountered. Lottie began to wonder if she was a witch. That would explain the skulls and strange objects. Mother would never have sent them to the Dunlivins if she had known they would be treated in such an appalling manner.

Albert and Lottie listened to the sound of Ida's heels clicking as she walked back up the stairs. Then she slammed the cellar door shut and a large piece of plaster fell from the ceiling.

"I hate her!" Albert yelled. Then he sat on his bed and cried.

"Don't worry, Albert, we just need a rest. It's been a long day. Things will seem better tomorrow." Although deep down Lottie feared that things might get even worse.

She sighed as she hauled her suitcase onto one of the beds and unpacked her things. They still smelt of home. Lottie closed her eyes and took a deep breath. The familiar scent swam around her lungs. Lottie felt like a mermaid far beneath the ocean waves. When she opened her eyes she almost expected to see her mother standing there with her arms outstretched. Waiting for her. Instead she found herself in the dingy cellar. She looked over at Albert. He looked as miserable as she felt.

Lottie took out her books and placed them on a small

oak dressing table. Hugh had left it there for the children to use during their stay.

She carefully lifted the photograph of her father out of the case last. The silver frame was tarnished. Lottie kissed the photograph and placed it beside her bed. Her father was a handsome man, and he always had a smile for Lottie. Her heart longed see him again. Each night before she went to sleep she looked up at the sky. She thought of her father flying through the clouds. However, there were no windows in the dingy cellar, and there was no way to see the sky. Lottie felt trapped.

When she was home in Manchester she used to go out into her garden. Well, it was more of a yard than a garden really. She would lie on her back on their small patch of grass. Then she would look up – high above the red-bricked houses and chimneystacks, high above the factories and high above the tallest tree in Victoria Park. She would imagine her father in his plane darting in and out of the clouds, like an acrobat somersaulting and back-flipping through the air. She thought of him peering down at all the houses standing back to back like soldiers marching out to battle. He would see all the tiny streets, and the people going about their daily lives hoping and praying that a bomb would not fall and turn them to dust.

Although it wasn't Lottie's town that her father flew over. It was a German town with German streets. It was German people that he dropped his bombs on. Her father was killing German people.

The first time that Lottie had realised this was during

a dream. She dreamt that she was in a German schoolroom and all around her the children spoke a language she didn't understand. Then her father's plane dropped a bomb on them all. Lottie could see her head drifting through the air like a balloon on a string. She woke in a panic and cried like a baby. But she never told her mother about her dream. Mother said that Father was a war hero – he was protecting the people back home. Lottie suspected that German mothers told German children the same thing about their fathers.

With her father gone, after a while Lottie forgot what he looked like. That's why she had asked Mother for a photograph of him. However, when she lay on the grass and looked up to the sky she thought that she could see his face as clear as day.

Lottie missed her mother desperately. She couldn't wait to send a postcard home to her to tell her all that had happened so far. The only problem was where to begin.

Chapter Twelve

Cuán
1920

Cuán woke up in a cold sweat. The cotton sheets stuck to her skin. A glint of moonlight slithered in through the window. It illuminated the ancient hands of the grandfather clock that lurked like a ghost in the corner of the room. The pendulum swung back and forth like a bird returning to its nest, and announced that it was three o'clock in the morning.

Rain pounded relentlessly against her windowpane. A harsh wind whistled down the chimney. Cuán flinched as she thought of her beloved Bonnie. Out there, somewhere. Cold, frightened and alone.

Every time she fell asleep she had the same unnerving dream about the creature with the red eyes. It was hurting Bonnie – she could hear her yelping in pain.

Cuán knew what she must do. She must find Bonnie.

She pulled back the heavy woollen blankets and

stepped from her bed. The floorboards were ice-cold beneath her feet. Her toes tingled and a shiver danced up her spine.

She tiptoed across the room. Goosebumps prickled her skin. She placed both her hands on the rotting sash of her bedroom window and pushed the window up. A gust of wind entered the room. It took her breath away, tossed her hair and blew out the last of the candles.

Cuán crawled onto the windowsill. Then she dropped to the ground with a thud.

The cold air made her shiver. She heard the sound of an owl hooting somewhere in the distance. Thorns and brambles scratched her legs and stones dug into her feet as she tore down the lane. Her white cotton nightdress clung to her legs like a shroud as the rain soaked into her bones. She heard Bonnie barking and followed the sound.

"I'm coming, girl!" Cuán cried breathlessly.

Bonnie's yelps led her to the crumbling remains of the arched double gateway which led to Kilbree Abbey. Legend said that the ancient abbey had been built on a werewolf burial ground and that it was cursed. No-one ever went there alone.

"Cuán! Cuán! Come! Bonnie needs you!"

Cuán suddenly felt ill. Her dream had come true. Her legs trembled as she heard the voice of the creature who was hurting Bonnie.

Cuán didn't stop for a second. She was desperate to save Bonnie who was more than just a dog – she was her best friend.

Then she froze. There, just inside the double arched gateway, was the red-eyed monster. Bonnie was lying at its feet, whimpering. The figure beckoned to Cuán to come inside the gateway.

Without warning, Cuán's body became consumed with pain. It was a sharp, ugly pain. It twisted and turned like a hurricane inside her body.

Her face contorted. Her jaw became long. Her teeth sharp like thorns. She howled into the darkness. She was no longer a girl. The body of a wolf was revealed. Fur and claws replaced her skin and nails.

Cuán dropped to her knees and arched her back, as she cried out in pain beneath the unforgiving moonlight.

Chapter Thirteen

A Strange Dream
1940

Lottie's heart hammered as she sat up in bed. She gazed around her and shrank back with a terrified cry as she saw that she was surrounded by looming coffins and grinning skulls. Where was she? Was she still dreaming?

Then she remembered. She and Albert were in the ghastly cellar of the Dunlivins' house. A single light bulb shed its weak light around without reaching into the dark corners. She had deliberately left it on when they settled down to sleep, knowing Albert would be terrified if she plunged them into total darkness.

She lay back again on her miserably flat pillow and thought about her strange dream.

She had dreamt of ravenous wolves and ancient ruins – a forest and waterfall of children's tears. She had dreamt of a girl with two hearts who ate the stars, with claws like daggers and amber eyes shaped like half-moons. Her dress was made from the petals of black roses and when the petals fell away they revealed the thick fur of a Wolf Girl. She dropped to her knees and growled, and the wolves trembled in fright and ran off into the forest.

Such a strange dream. But the strangest thing of all was that Lottie had felt no fear of the Wolf Girl as she stared into her glowing amber eyes.

Of course! Lottie raised her hand and saw the wolf's amber eyes glowing dimly at her from the ring. That was why she'd had that dream! Uneasy about this horrible cellar, she had dreamt about the ring. The thought calmed her.

Albert stirred and turned over in his bed, but didn't wake.

Lottie realised that she had no idea what time it was. There were no sounds from the house above her so it must not be morning yet. She closed her eyes against the weak light and tried to go back to sleep.

Chapter Fourteen

Beware of the Wolves

"Sit up straight, Charlotte," Ida ordered as they ate breakfast the next morning.

Ida sat at the head of the table. She wore a white blouse with puffed sleeves and a navy woollen skirt. The green wart at the side of her nose oozed. Her voice was shrill, her laugh a cackle. Sunlight shone through the window in rainbow-coloured rays and Albert thought that her long face looked astonishingly like a witch in a fairy tale. He wondered if she had a cauldron hidden in the kitchen.

Prudence sat next to her mother, eating a piece of burnt toast. She had smothered it with what looked like lumpy marmalade. Although Albert thought it could easily have been the brain of a small animal. He gulped down his fear and watched as crumbs tumbled onto Prudence's navy-and-white sailor dress. It had a white collar and a navy bow. She ate with her mouth open. This revealed rotten stubs of teeth ground down from years of eating boiled sweets.

Albert looked on incredulously. He had never seen such disgusting people before.

Hugh Dunlivin squinted and peered at Lottie over the top of his hooked nose. The resemblance to Nancy when she was a girl was striking. She had the same piercing green eyes and a wry smile. The only difference was her hair colour. Lottie's hair was the colour of fire and fell like flames over her shoulders and her blue dress. She was an extraordinarily beautiful girl. Lottie blushed when she noticed Hugh staring at her and she averted her eyes.

Albert kicked her under the table – he was agitated as he was not used to sitting still for so long.

"May we be excused, please?" Lottie asked. She longed to go outside. To dance amongst the fluttering leaves in the forest. And to bathe herself in the heat of the morning sun.

"Not until I say so, Charlotte Hope!" Ida snapped. She dabbed at her seeping wart with a crinkly tissue.

Lottie shifted her gaze towards her brother.

"Where are you off to today?" Hugh enquired. He was unaware of his wife's strict instructions to the children the previous evening.

"The children are going to explore the village today. Aren't you, children?" Ida said, grimacing and sending an expression of disgust in the children's direction.

"Yes, Aunt Ida," Lottie replied.

"Insolent girl! I am not your aunt. You may call me Mrs Dunlivin."

Prudence giggled. She enjoyed it when her mother got annoyed with the two brats from England. Although secretly she envied them. Prudence had always wanted a brother or sister of her own. She had no friends in school. They all thought she was weird because her parents were undertakers. They called her terrible names and hissed at her whenever she walked by. She felt as though there were glass splinters in her heart. And she shed many tears due to their cruel taunts. Prudence wished she could cut their wicked little tongues out. Then they could never taunt her again. She spent most of her days eating hard-boiled sweets and, after school, helping her mother to decorate the corpses in preparation for burial.

"Really, Ida, there is no need to be so harsh with the children." Hugh hated his wife's hostile manner. Ida was such a sweet girl when Hugh first married her. However, the years had turned her sour. And it grieved him to discover that Prudence was turning out to be every bit as bitter and full of rage as her mother.

Hugh turned to Lottie and smiled. He had a feeling that they were going to get along very well, if she was anything like Nancy.

"Prudence, why don't you give Lottie and Albert the grand tour of Kilbree?" he said. "Maybe you could take a boat trip on the river. I'm sure that they would like that. The scenery is lovely at this time of year." Hugh worried about Prudence. She didn't get out much and she had no school friends. Perhaps Lottie and Albert were the friends she needed. "There is just one thing. I heard that wolves are on the prowl again so you will have to be careful."

"Wolves!" Lottie gasped. "I didn't realise that there were wolves in Ireland!"

"They were thought to be extinct. But they reappeared again when I was a lad."

"Mother never mentioned wolves!" Lottie cried. She was petrified.

"Stay clear of the forest, don't talk to strangers and you will be all right, Lottie," Hugh said reassuringly.

But what did strangers have to do with wolves, Lottie wondered. What Hugh had said didn't make sense.

Albert shifted in his seat. "What was Mother thinking of, sending us to a wretched place with wolves?"

"I suspect she wanted to get rid of you once and for all, you fleabags!" Prudence cried.

Albert was unable to sit still a moment longer and he leapt up onto his chair.

"Right, you've had it! Who are you calling a fleabag, Pooey Prudence? You have rotten teeth and you smell of cabbage!"

"Get down from that chair this instance, Albert Hope!" Ida bellowed.

"You little wretch! Just wait till I get my hands on you!" Prudence shrieked.

Hugh Dunlivin watched helplessly as Albert scuttled across the table. He stepped into the marmalade and the butter, then jumped onto the floor, narrowly avoiding the cat. Then he was chased out of the room by Prudence, with Lottie at her heels.

Ida stood up and turned to her husband. She had her hands on her hips and a face like thunder. "I told you they would be trouble, didn't I?" Then she stormed out of the room, leaving Hugh Dunlivin all alone.

He stood up and walked over to the window. It was a beautiful day and a beautiful area. However, Kilbree had a hidden secret, spoken only of in whispers. The wolves Hugh had mentioned to Lottie were actually werewolves. But he hadn't wanted to say that. The thought of treacherous creatures roaming the land would scare the children too much. They lurked in the woods and wandered the land at night. They killed sheep and small farm animals and fowl. Locals believed that it would only be a matter of time before a person was killed. Werewolves had been on the increase since Hugh was a boy but no-one had been killed yet. It was impossible to know how many werewolves there actually were in the area. No-one had seen a pack – they always appeared singly and it was possible that there were only a few. Rumour, of course, said that the land was crawling with them but Hugh doubted that.

There was no way of telling if a person was a werewolf or not. That made the people of Kilbree suspicious of everyone. Especially strangers.

There was one boy in particular whom people suspected of being a werewolf. He lived alone in the forest. A wolf had slept at the door of his caravan until recently, when sheep went missing. Then the wolf was shot by a local farmer in the dead of night. Hugh heard that the boy cried as if the farmer had killed a member of his family, and those who saw him said they could never after forget the look of pain on the boy's face.

However, the werewolves posed a real threat to the people living in Kilbree. They needed to find a way to be rid of them once and for all.

Chapter Fifteen

Cuán
1920

Cuán woke up in her own bed, although she had no recollection of how she got there. She was tangled in the sheets. Her flesh was torn, her muscles and sinews had been stretched, and an incredible pain seared through her entire body. Her yellow eyes were bandaged tightly so that she couldn't see anything apart from the nightmares that crept around inside her mind.

Then, in the darkness, it all came back to her. Thoughts flooded her brain like a river that had burst its banks: Bonnie's cries, the open window, the wind and rain, the foggy atmosphere and running towards the arched gateway that led to Kilbree Abbey as though her life depended on it.

She tried to scream but no sound came out. Panic took hold and she sat bolt upright in the bed. Cuán placed her hands on her face. She felt her nose, mouth and ears. She was relieved to discover her face was her own, not that of a wolf.

"She is awake now, doctor!" came the voice of Maeve.

Cuán screamed.

"Hush, Cuán, there's a good girl!" the doctor soothed as he carefully removed the layers of bandages from her eyes.

The light stung her eyes and Cuán squinted. Everything was a hazy blur. All that she could see were shadows and shapes.

"*My eyes!*" she screeched as the pain got worse. It felt as though her eyes were on fire.

"Close the curtains right away," the doctor ordered.

Cuán could hear the familiar sound of Maeve's slippers shuffling across the floorboards and the gentle tugging sound of the velvet curtains being drawn. Sounds and smells were amplified for her. She could hear a crow cawing in the distance. She could smell stew being cooked somewhere in the village.

She lay back and Maeve bathed her eyes with cooled boiled water – as she had done all those years ago, on the night she had found her as a baby in the forest with the grey wolf.

Everything was fuzzy at first for Cuán. Then the pain eased. And after a moment she saw Maeve standing in front of her. Lines of worry were imprinted on her brow and her eyes were bloodshot from crying. Cuán noticed her linen nightgown on the bedroom floor beside her dressing table. It lay amidst a pile of mud and sticks. It was stained with dirt and torn to shreds.

The doctor was the last to come into view. He was an overweight man and had a top hat on his head. Cuán prayed that he didn't take his hat off as that was a bad sign. It meant that he was staying for a long time and she might not survive. Doctors didn't stay long unless the patient's life was at risk. He had a grey bushy beard. A stethoscope was slung like a python around his neck.

"I need to listen to your heart, Cuán. Do you understand me?"

Cuán nodded. She could not find the words and was terrified that she would growl instead.

The doctor pulled back the bedsheet, revealing the top half of Cuán's body. Maeve looked away. It was an awful sight. Lacerations and scratches covered her skin. Cuán knew it was bad. The thick coat of fur that protected her as a wolf did not protect her human flesh, which meant that the injuries that she sustained as a wolf were evident on her human body.

The doctor stared into her eyes as he listened through his stethoscope. He had never seen such an interesting creature before. Something told him that she wasn't human. Her yellow eyes gazed back at him, and it was as though she was pleading for help.

Thud, thud, came the sound of her beating heart. Then *thud, thud,* again.

The doctor stumbled back. Then he applied the stethoscope again. For a moment he thought that he was hearing things. But as sure as he stood there, he heard it. A second heartbeat, like the beat of a drum, steady and fast, echoing the first. Never had he come across such a case. It was miraculous.

"What is it, doctor?" Maeve asked as she pulled the sheet over Cuán.

"Incredible, that's what it is!"

"I don't understand," Maeve sighed.

"Your daughter has two hearts."

"But that's not possible!"

"Be that as it may. Cuán has a second heart. It beats faster than the first and it is positioned on the right-hand side of her chest. I have to send word to Dublin. This abnormality will need to be documented right away."

A tear fell from Cuán's eye, like a star from the sky. It made perfect sense to her. She had a human heart and the heart of a wolf.

Chapter Sixteen

The Boy Who Lived in the Woods
1940

Lottie and Albert walked swiftly out of the Dunlivins' house. Warm air filled their lungs. It was a far cry from the smoke-filled air from burnt-out buildings that they were used to in Manchester. Lottie drank it in. Each breath she took made her feel stronger. The heat from the sun shone down on them. It was hard to believe that there a war going on in other parts of the world.

They followed the winding country road. As they walked past grey stone walls and a patchwork of green fields Albert noticed a scarecrow with enormous straw arms. It hung from a pole in a wheat field. Its crooked head was fitted with a black hat. A ragged purple overcoat covered its entire body and flapped in the breeze. Black beady eyes followed the children's every move. As they continued along the road, Albert looked back to make sure that the strange-looking scarecrow wasn't following them.

Hand-painted wooden signs punctuated their route. They read *"BEWARE OF WOLVES"* and *"DON'T STRAY FROM THE PATH"*.

Albert stepped closer to Lottie and held her hand. He imagined wolves hiding in the trees. Dancing in the shadows. Waiting to pounce. He recalled the story of Red Riding Hood and how the wolf had tricked her.

"But, Grandmother, what awfully big teeth you have!"

"All the better to eat you up!"

As soon as the words escaped from the wolf's red lips, he pounced from the bed and gobbled up poor Little Red Riding Hood.

Albert swallowed down his fear with a gulp.

"Albert, you look as though you've seen a ghost." Lottie studied Albert's face which was a deathly shade of pale. All the blood had drained from his cheeks.

"I'm frightened, Lottie. All of these warning signs about wolves!"

"Don't worry, Albert. I'm not going to let anything happen to you. Besides, it's beautiful here," Lottie said as sunlight streamed through the clouds.

Everything was so different in Ireland. It was so much brighter and greener than it was back home. In Manchester they had to hide underground every night but in Kilbree there were so many wide-open spaces. The rolling hills and countryside made Lottie feel as though she had stepped into a painting. It was lovely here, she told herself. But the truth was she had a niggling pain deep down in the pit of her stomach. What if Albert was right? What if there were wolves lurking in the shadows?

Besides, she knew that she could never be happy in Kilbree. Not when she was so far from her mother and father. Before she knew it, she was thinking of her beautiful mother. She had no way of knowing if she would ever see her again.

Albert was deep in thought. He felt just like Lottie. Kilbree was beautiful but it would never be home to him. Home was on the cobbled streets of Manchester, where there were factories and cotton mills. Where a great cathedral sat beside rows of shops and the ship canal. Where they were not at risk from wolves who would eat them from breakfast. Albert longed to play football with his friends, and to eat fish and chips wrapped up in newspaper for his tea.

"How long will we have to stay here, Lottie?"

"I don't know, Albert. For as long as the war lasts, I suppose."

Albert hung his head and Lottie could tell that he was sad.

"What's the matter now, Albert?"

"I miss Mother, Lottie. I should never have said those awful things to her on the morning that we left England."

Lottie stopped walking and turned towards Albert. He looked so small and vulnerable as he stood in front of her. His large blue eyes looked at her pleadingly. He depended on her. She could never let him down. And she hated to think of him worrying about the argument he had with their mother. Lottie hugged Albert tightly and whispered into his ear. She needed to let him know that their mother forgave him. In case they never saw her again.

"Mother knows you didn't mean it, Albert. You are just scared, we all are."

Tears fell from Albert's eyes. His blonde hair shone in the sunlight. Lottie didn't know how to console her young brother. She pulled a tissue out of her pocket and handed it to him. He blew his nose and gave it back to her.

"I am a wicked boy, Lottie! What if our house gets bombed? We will never see Mother again and I will never get the chance to tell her how sorry I am!"

Albert had worked himself up into an awful state. He was a bundle of nerves. And had obviously been worrying about this since they left Manchester.

She put her hands on his small shoulders. "Listen to me, Albert Hope. That isn't going to happen. Mother will survive the war. And you will be back home in Manchester playing soccer with Billy Bright before you know it. You'll see, Albert. Everything will work out in the end. The war makes people feel angry. We all say things that we don't mean from time to time. I am sure that Mother has forgotten all about it.

"Do you really think so, Lottie?"

"I know so. Now cheer up, Albert, there's a good boy. There's no need to worry about the past. We need to look forward to the future. To getting home to Mother and Father."

Lottie held Albert's hand and they continued to walk along the winding lane.

All around them were yellow fields of wheat. The

only sound that could be heard came from the sporadic squawking of crows. They stood like haggard old men on wooden telegraph poles. Occasionally a tractor trundled by. Rows of white cottages with thatched roofs lined their path. And two old men who looked like farmers stood at a crossroad.

One of the men wore a flat cap and chewed on a piece of straw, while the other had a furrowed brow and a bald head. He held a black-and-white sheepdog by the collar. It barked aggressively in the direction of the trees and revealed pink gums. It was as though it sensed the presence of another animal hiding in the woods.

Lottie gripped Albert's hand tightly. All the signs had been warning them. Maybe they should have paid them more attention. When the men saw Lottie and Albert approach they narrowed their gaze. They stared hard into Lottie and Albert's eyes. Then they turned away.

"What's their problem?" Albert asked Lottie. He made sure his voice was loud enough so that the men could hear him.

"They don't like strangers around here," said a voice.

Lottie let out a scream and Albert almost jumped out of his skin. They turned around to see who was talking to them and saw a boy of about fourteen years of age. He wore brown trousers and a red-and-black plaid shirt, which was open at the front. His sleeves were rolled up to reveal tanned arms. A black hat sat squarely on his head. Beneath it hung long black hair, which was tied back with a green velvet ribbon. His left ear was adorned with several silver earrings and a red bandana was tied around his neck. His skin was dark and his eyes were as black as berries. Lottie noticed a small scar on his upper lip. It made him look as though he was scowling. He carried an axe in his hand and it gleamed under the sunlight.

Lottie grabbed her brother by the sleeve. "Come along, Albert."

The boy scared and intrigued Lottie at the same time. His unusual accent told her that he wasn't from the village. He was an outsider just like she was, but the way he appeared out of nowhere sent chills down her spine.

Lottie tugged Albert's sleeve. The same thing that frightened her excited her younger brother. And he remained where he was, rooted to the spot, with his mouth open wide and his eyes on the boy.

"Why don't they like strangers here?" he blurted out.

Lottie was curious too but her instincts told her to get away from the boy. Everything about him told her that he was trouble.

As if sensing her fear, the boy placed the axe on the ground and held out a calloused hand.

"Blaise Carey. Nice to meet you."

Lottie stared into his large brown eyes. Reluctantly she shook the boy's hand. She felt the roughness of his skin as their fingers touched and pulled her hand away as an electrical current passed between them.

She blushed, hoping that Blaise hadn't felt it too. But his smile told her that he had.

"I'm Lottie and this here is my brother Albert," she muttered.

"Nice to meet you both." Blaise stood with his hands

on his hips. Then he bent his neck back and howled like a wolf at the old men at the crossroad.

Albert laughed as the farmers pointed at them and shook their fists angrily. The sheepdog by their side whimpered. They turned and left.

"The silly old fools think I'm a werewolf." Blaise laughed as he picked up his axe again.

"Are you?" Albert asked. Fear gathered like a wave in his chest.

Blaise bent down and looked into Albert's eyes. "Of course not."

"So the villagers really do believe in werewolves?" Lottie asked, thinking uneasily of her dream about the Wolf Girl. What a strange coincidence! Or perhaps not? Perhaps her mother's friend who had given her the ring had come from this very village.

"They certainly do. Terrified of them they are!"

"That's silly, isn't it?" said Lottie. She longed for Blaise to ease her fears. What if there were werewolves in Kilbree? Although she knew that was impossible. People couldn't just turn into wolves, could they?

Blaise just grinned.

Lottie had never met anyone like Blaise before. He had been rude to the farmers but she had to admit that she was glad that they were gone.

Blaise sensed her unease. "Let's get out of here. I live in the forest. I don't have any lemonade but would you like to join me for a nice cool glass of water?"

"No," Lottie said. In her mother's absence she was in charge.

Lottie knew that she had to do the right thing. Hugh had warned them not to enter the forest and never to talk to strangers. She had wondered at the time why he mentioned strangers when she had actually asked him about wolves. Now she realised that he was thinking of werewolves but didn't want to scare her too much.

Although she could not deny that it was a hot day and a cool, refreshing drink sounded like a good idea. And there was something that drew her towards Blaise Carey, despite all of her better instincts.

"Please, Lottie, can we?" Albert pleaded. He was enchanted by Blaise. It was as though he had cast a spell on him.

"If you have somewhere else to go, don't let me stop you," Blaise said. The edges of his lips curled into a smile.

Albert gasped as Blaise threw the axe at a tree stump and it split in half. Then Blaise held up both hands as though he was being interrogated.

Lottie thought for a moment. All this talk of werewolves was nonsense. She knew that werewolves didn't really exist. They were simply old wives' tales made up to scare children. Besides, there was nothing better to do in Kilbree. The thought of going back to the cellar in the Dunlivins' house scared her just as much as werewolves. And the day stretched out before them like a blanket.

After a few moments, she turned to Blaise and smiled. "A drink would be lovely, thank you," she said.

Blaise picked up his axe and led the children along an

overgrown dirt track. Dandelions emerged like proud women in yellow hats from cracks in the earth and bees drunk on nectar buzzed around yellow flowers on long green stalks.

"What part of England are you from?" Blaise enquired.

He was intrigued by Lottie because he had recognised her straight away. She looked so much like the photograph of her mother. She was every bit as beautiful. Her flame-red hair made her appear like a warrior from a legend. Blaise wondered how much Lottie knew about Cuán. The Wolf Girl. Her mother Nancy was the last person to see Cuán alive twenty years ago. It was possible that Lottie's mother had told her how to enter Wolf Land. His head was spinning. He had got so close now and he didn't want to scare Lottie and Albert away. He knew that he would have to take things slowly. As he looked into Lottie's eyes he realised that there was something else about her that intrigued him, apart from her possible link to Cuán. She wasn't like all of the other girls he knew. She was different. He had sensed it the moment he saw her. And when he spoke to her he felt as though he had known her forever. In some ways he had.

"We are from Manchester," Albert replied.

"Stretford, Manchester, to be precise," Lottie said. Then she ruffled her young brother's hair – she was so glad that he hadn't been taken from her in the train station. She would do anything within her power to protect him.

"I've never been to England," said Blaise. "However,

my parents travelled to many different countries."

"You're not missing much – the place has been destroyed by bombs," Lottie said matter of factly.

Blaise wondered how she could speak so nonchalantly about the war. He guessed that it had become normal to her. A part of her everyday life. He felt sad for Lottie and Albert. He couldn't even begin to imagine the horrors that they had experienced back home. He had heard such horrific stories about the war. Children being evacuated from their homes. Jewish people in Germany forced to wear yellow stars on their clothes so that they could be identified, then taken away in their thousands. German troops stormed into their houses during the night and took them away on trains. No-one knew what was happening to them. If Lottie had experienced such atrocities back home in England, would that make her more willing to help Cuán and the others who were prisoners in Wolf Land? Blaise didn't know.

They meandered through the trees, lost in their own thoughts as they moved deeper and deeper into the dense forest. The air became cooler and leaves from the trees were like large umbrellas shading them from the harsh glare of the sun.

Lottie regretted her decision to go with Blaise. What if he left them? She feared that they would never be able to find their way back to the village again. And although she knew that there was no such thing as werewolves, she kept thinking that she saw shadows in the trees. Panicking, she looked around, trying to remember which way they had come, but everything looked the same.

A small patch of sunlight shone through the trees. It illuminated the green leaves on the trees as they stepped into a clearing.

"Here we are!" Blaise announced proudly.

Lottie breathed a sigh of relief.

Nestled beneath the trees was a brightly coloured Romany gypsy caravan. It had a curved wooden frame which was intricately carved with beautiful flowers in red, indigo and green, and parts of it were covered in gold. There were four large wooden wheels and a small red door at the front with a ladder leading up to it.

"Can I have my drink now?" Albert asked loudly.

"Albert, remember your manners!" Lottie chided.

Lottie walked around the caravan and noticed that there was a chimney protruding through the roof at the left-hand side of the doorway. A black horse was tied by a frayed rope to the caravan and it was eating yellow tufts of grass, scorched by the heat of the sun. Its ears twitched and Lottie noticed a white patch on the black nose which it raised in her direction.

"I see you've met my girl Snowdrop," Blaise said as he walked towards Lottie.

"Snowdrop? But she's black – oh, it's for the white patch, is it?"

"Yes," he said with a grin.

Lottie laughed. "She's beautiful," she said as she squinted under the glare of the sun. She had never been this close to a horse before. There were donkey rides on the beach in Blackpool during the summertime, but her mother had never let her go on one. She said that she had better things to spend her money on.

"Here, give her this and she'll be your friend forever." Blaise could see that Lottie was a kind girl. He threw a red apple to Lottie. "Put it on the flat palm of your hand for her."

Lottie balanced it on the palm of her right hand and Snowdrop opened her mouth then took the apple and crunched it nonchalantly with her yellow teeth.

Blaise smiled at Lottie, who blushed and looked away.

"Let's go inside!" Albert ordered and started up the ladder.

"Albert Hope, get down here this instant!" Lottie cried.

"It's all right, Lottie, he can go in. Wait, Albert, the door is locked." He smiled at Lottie, producing a beautifully crafted key. "My people don't believe much in locking things up but, as I live alone and have a few precious belongings, I do."

Blaise climbed the ladder, unlocked the door and went inside. Albert darted in after him.

Lottie followed them up the ladder and into the caravan. Inside was every bit as impressive as outside. Everything was carved from oak and had a golden glow. There were built-in seats, wardrobes, and a glass-fronted cabinet inside which were tambourines, decorated with red and pink ribbons. In the centre of the caravan was a chest of drawers which also functioned as a table. It was covered in a green tablecloth and on top of it was an empty teacup and a crystal ball. There was a small cast-iron stove to the left of the doorway, surrounded by a wooden fireplace.

"Blaise, this is amazing!" Lottie exclaimed.

Blaise smiled bashfully. He was happy that Lottie approved of his caravan. "Thank you, Lottie. I suppose it is. But it's just home to me. It's all that I have ever known."

Lottie was very impressed. She had never been into a caravan before. It felt as though she was stepping back in time. Her gaze landed on the crystal ball and she could not help but wonder if Blaise was a fortune teller.

"Please take a seat," Blaise said. His silver earrings jangled in his ear as he removed an old guitar painted with red roses from the wooden seat to reveal blue velvet cushions.

Lottie and Albert sat down. They felt as though they were waiting for a show to begin.

Blaise put three glasses on the table. They were decorated with colourful hand-painted crowing cocks. He poured water into them from a large pottery jug.

Lottie and Albert drank gratefully, amazed at how cool and refreshing the water was.

Then Blaise pulled out a small yellow stool and, sitting down, played a lively folk song on his guitar.

The children clapped enthusiastically when he finished and Blaise grinned in appreciation.

"Where are your parents?" Albert suddenly asked, then he instinctively turned towards Lottie to check that he had not said the wrong thing.

"They are both dead." Blaise blessed himself and hung his head.

Albert felt sorry for Blaise. So many of his friends had lost their parents. At least he still had Lottie. Even though she could be bossy sometimes.

"We're sorry to hear that, Blaise," Lottie said.

"My father died when I was a young boy. My mother died a few months ago." Blaise attempted a smile which melted away like snow on a sunny day.

Lottie's heart went out to Blaise, living all alone in a caravan in the middle of a forest. If the stories about werewolves roaming around at night-time were true, then he was in danger. Lottie noticed that Blaise was looking at a photograph on the small wooden cabinet. The photograph was in a silver frame. It was of a beautiful woman with long black hair which flowed over her shoulders. Her eyes were astonishing – they were large and vibrant. She was wearing a fur-lined cloak and she held the hand of a small boy who was perched on her knee. He couldn't have been more than three years old. He had the same amazing eyes as the woman and he was holding a tambourine. Lottie guessed it was a photograph of Blaise and his mother. She could not believe how much he looked like her. She thought of her own mother back home – she missed her so much.

"Where do you come from originally?" she asked.

"My mother Talia was a Romany gypsy and my father was Irish. We travelled from town to town whenever my mother was summoned."

"Summoned?" Lottie asked.

Blaise put the guitar down and leaned towards the children. Then he whispered to them. It was as though he was worried that someone would hear him although there was no-one there except the three of them.

"My mother was a fortune teller, Lottie."

Lottie gasped. "Is that her crystal ball on the table?"

"Yes. She had a unique gift. She would receive messages in the crystal ball. She would see things – dreadful things – then we would go to the places she saw to help people there."

Lottie suddenly felt scared. "Did your mother see something here in Kilbree?"

Blaise nodded. "Yes, this is the last place she was called to before she died. She had been here before, when she was a child."

Lottie did not like what she was hearing.

"Do you have her gift too?" Albert asked.

Blaise sighed. "No, Albert, I don't see things in the crystal ball. That is why it is taking me so long. I've been trying for a year now. I felt as though I was letting my mother down – I was no closer to finding out the answers until you arrived."

Until you arrived? Whatever did he mean? Lottie didn't know but she was alarmed.

She suddenly stood up. "I think it's time we went, Albert – come along."

"Lottie, please, wait!" Blaise said urgently. "There is something I really must show you."

Lottie reluctantly sat back down. Her heart was pounding.

Blaise walked over to the wooden cabinet. Butterflies were painted around its edges with gold paint. He opened it and took out a newspaper clipping.

He handed it to Lottie.

The headline read: **Tragedy Strikes Kilbree as Girl Vanishes Without a Trace.**

The date was 1920. There was a photograph beneath the headline of two girls sitting together on a rock.

"Lottie, it's you in the photograph!" Albert cried.

"No, Albert, it's your mother with her friend Cuán," said Blaise.

As Lottie stared at the photograph confusion and dread gripped her.

She stood up abruptly again. "Albert, we have to go now."

She was fearful. Blaise had tricked them. He had known who she was all along and had lured them there. But why? As ridiculous as it seemed she found herself hoping that Blaise wasn't a werewolf. If so, they had just walked right into his trap. She could not understand what he was doing with a newspaper clipping with her mother's photograph on it. And such a frightening tragic photograph!

"Come on, Albert."

"I want another drink of water!" he moaned. "I'm still thirsty!"

"We are leaving now, Albert." Lottie's eyes widened which told Albert that she meant business.

"Please don't go, Lottie – I won't hurt you," Blaise said soothingly. "And it's not safe for you to be out in the forest on your own." Then he gently placed his hands on her shoulders and looked into her eyes.

"I don't understand! What do you want from us?" Lottie cried.

Blaise hesitated. "Well . . . when I said Kilbree was the last place my mother was called to, I wasn't being completely accurate . . . after we came here she had another vision in the crystal ball . . . a vision of Cuán calling for help."

Lottie pulled herself out of his grasp, snatched up the newspaper clipping and fled from the caravan.

"I am sorry but I have to go with her," Albert announced politely. Then he darted from the caravan like a mouse escaping from a trap.

"*Hey! Wait!*" Blaise shook his head then followed them outside.

Expecting to see them still in the clearing, he was startled to find that they were already out of sight. The dense forest had swallowed them up, like a child gulping down a sweet.

"*Lottie! Come back, please!*" he yelled as he ran into the trees he had led them through earlier. "*You won't find your way back through the forest! It's not safe!*"

There was no sight of the children and he had the sickening feeling that they had gone the wrong way and would end up lost and wandering around the dangerous forest. He had to find them.

Blaise knew that it had been a mistake to bring Lottie and Albert to his caravan. What on earth was he thinking? It was all too much too soon. He couldn't possibly expect them to understand his mother's gift and his connection to them.

He longed to tell them about Wolf Land. However, he knew that they were not ready to believe him. He would just drive them further away if he told them everything now.

Blaise knew that Lottie was sent to him for a reason. He just needed to find a way to reassure her.

He ran back to get Snowdrop and plunged into the caravan to get her harness. But then he hesitated. The children would hear the thud of Snowdrop's hooves approaching. They could run into the forest to hide and become even more lost. It would be better to go on foot. He replaced the harness.

About to leave, his eye fell on his mother's crystal ball. Suddenly he felt an overwhelming urge to consult it. He knew there was no time to delay but the call of the crystal ball was too strong. He found himself sitting on the small yellow stool in front of it, mesmerised, as if he had no will of his own. He placed his hands over the glass orb then shut his eyes and calmed his mind. He knew that in order for him to see something, he needed to be at peace. The table shuddered violently, and an electrical current pulsated through his fingers. This was the first time that the ball had worked for him. He opened his eyes. An image appeared in the glass orb. It was of a beautiful she-wolf with soft grey fur and glowing amber eyes. Blaise knew that it was Cuán. She was in the middle of a battle, surrounded by fighting wolves – or werewolves? Then the image faded.

"We are coming for you, Cuán!" Blaise promised as he pulled his fingers away from the crystal ball.

110

Full of resolution, he ran again into the trees, praying the children had run in the right direction.

Lottie ran through the dense forest, Albert panting behind her. Her mind was whirling. There were so many questions that needed answers. For example, why hadn't her mother mentioned the missing girl to her before? And what had happened to Cuán? She thrust the newspaper clipping into the pocket of her dress and ran on, shivering as fear ran through her bones. Perhaps there was something terrible hiding in the trees in Kilbree, something dark and unnatural. Maybe even werewolves. And who was Blaise Carey? What did he want with her?

Chapter Seventeen

Cuán
1920

"How are you feeling today, Cuán?" Doctor Ford enquired.

Maeve stood back to let him examine Cuán, her hands clasped together, anxiety etched on her face.

The doctor studied the girl through his watery eyes and listened to her two hearts beating through his stethoscope. Her black hair framed her pale skin. Her amber eyes shone at him. She looked as though she had stepped out of the pages of a fairy tale. Marvellous, he thought. A phenomenon like this would mean that he would never have to work again. It would go down in the history books. He had written a letter to Dublin detailing his discovery and was waiting for the Medical Board to respond. He guessed that they would send for the girl right away to do tests. She would be prodded and poked with needles until they found answers. He gave her a pitying smile: it would be a long road ahead and she would have to be strong.

Cuán wanted to swat him away like he was a fly buzzing around a jampot, but she just told him what he wanted to hear.

"I am fine, thank you, doctor."

She could see the glint of excitement in his eyes. He had never seen a girl like her before. She was a freak of nature. A discovery like this would make the doctor famous. Cuán realised that it would not be long until the whole world found out about the girl with two hearts and amber eyes.

"Your wounds are healing well, Cuán. I think it's time that we discussed who or what gave them to you."

"I told you I can't remember." Cuán turned her head away. Not again, she thought.

"Cuán, I don't think you understand the severity of your attack. If who or whatever attacked you strikes again, you might not be so lucky next time – and what if they hurt someone else? You would never forgive yourself."

"For goodness' sake, Cuán, please just tell us what happened!" Maeve cried.

Cuán understood the severity of what had happened. She understood only too well. But what did they want from her? If she told them that she had changed into a wolf and she had caused the scratches with her own claws they would never believe her. They would probably think that she mentally ill and lock her away in an asylum for the rest of her days.

She needed time to think about what had happened and to deal with it herself.

"I can't remember, Ma. If I do, I will tell you. Please trust me."

Maeve folded her arms across her chest. She was frustrated with Cuán, but when she saw the look of anguish on her face she immediately regretted snapping at her.

"I think that Cuán has had enough for one day, doctor," she said.

"You will think about what I said, won't you, Cuán?" Doctor Ford said as he picked up his black bag.

Maeve handed him his coat and led him towards the door.

"Of course she will, doctor. Now if you wouldn't mind leaving us alone? Cuán needs to sleep."

Cuán hated the way people spoke about her as though she wasn't there – it was as though she was invisible. She pulled the blue woollen blanket over her head, turned on her side and slept – she wasn't sure for how long but when she woke it was night-time.

The flames of the fire had died and she was alone. There was no sound apart from the ticking of her clock. Her body itched from head to toe and her skin felt tight. It had been a week since Bonnie went missing, a week since she had turned into a wolf, a week since this nightmare began.

Cuán staggered out of bed. She picked up her shawl from the rocking chair, placed it around her shoulders and gazed out of the window.

The moon appeared to be closer than usual. Suddenly a star in the sky fell in a bright arc towards the earth. Maeve had told her that if you see a shooting star it means that a big change is about to happen in your life. Cuán hadn't believed her – it was just a superstition. However, as she watched the star plummeting towards the earth on that dark night, she wondered if there was some truth in it after all.

A sudden movement in the trees caught her eye. There was a figure moving outside in the darkness. It darted behind one of the trees. Cuán saw two eyes as red as coal staring at her. She covered her mouth with her hand as she heard her name.

She was being summoned.

"Cuán, Cuán, come to us!" voices begged.

Cuán covered her ears with her hands. But she could still hear the voices. Louder this time and more persistent. It was happening again and there was no escape.

Unable to stop herself and drawn by a powerful invisible force, Cuán climbed through the window and jumped to the ground. The grass was wet with dew and she stood on something sharp – she felt it cut her foot and blood trickled onto the grass. Ignoring it, she began to run. She kept running through the forest until suddenly pain ripped through her body and the bones in her ribcage rattled. She recalled the way that she had torn at her skin the last time and how it had taken weeks for the cuts to heal. So she dug her fingernails into the soil until her claws grew, letting her nails scratch the soil

115

rather than her own flesh. A gnawing pain seared along her spine and into her jaw, her bones stretched until her nose and mouth were those of a wolf. A ferocious hunger moved through her body. She was starving and there was only one thing that would satisfy the hunger. She ran towards Kilbree Abbey and looked towards the sky. After a moment her eyes landed on the star – the glowing orb appeared to be getting closer. The pull of the star was magnetic. She watched as it spun around until it was within reach. Cuán grasped the star with both her claws and devoured it like the starving beast she now was. The relief was immediate and the pain subsided. Her body trembled as she thought of what she had done. *What kind of a girl eats the stars?* she asked herself. *Not a human one. What is happening to me?*

Then Cuán felt a strength that she had never experienced before. She crawled behind a slippery stone, an ancient rock which protruded from the ground like a grey tooth. Then she fell fast asleep and stayed there until the sun rose. When Cuán woke up she was alone and afraid. At first she thought it had all been a terrifying dream. Yet she could still taste the star on her lips. Lying there in her human form, she shivered. Her bruised ribs ached. She was covered in mud and filled with fear.

Looking down, Cuán saw that she had not hurt herself. Digging her claws into the soil had worked – she had not scratched herself this time. And the scars that were there from before had healed.

The sky was dusty pink. Clouds danced like balls of cotton against the blue sky. And the glowing sun smiled down from the spot where only hours before the moon had been. Where the star had tumbled from the sky as easily as a coin into a well. Had she really eaten it?

Cuán thought of Maeve – she would think that she was dead. She hated herself for putting her through all this but it was unavoidable – she couldn't stop her animal instincts from overcoming her.

She ran until she reached the orchard at the back of her house. Then she paused to catch her breath. Her throat was dry and she coughed violently. She needed something to quench her thirst. However, she didn't want to go into the house to face Ma yet. Not like this. She knew it would take a while for her vocal cords to work properly again.

Cuán pulled a red apple off a tree and took a bite. It was delicious and the juice ran down her chin. The apple tasted amazing. The flavour was intensified by the thirst, her taste buds more alive than ever before.

Then a branch snapped. Someone was watching her, hiding amidst the trees. She hoped it wasn't the creature with the red eyes. Cuán threw the apple core onto the ground and cautiously followed the sound. She was startled to discover a girl behind the tree.

Cuán felt ashamed of her shabby appearance. She was covered from head to toe in mud. Her nightdress was torn and there were twigs in her hair.

The girl did not take her eyes off Cuán for one second.

"Hello, my name's Nancy," she said.

Although she was unable to speak, Cuán smiled. Then she gestured towards her throat.

"Can't you talk?" Nancy enquired.

Cuán shook her head and studied the girl. She wore a red cardigan over a plaid pinafore. Her hair was golden although it appeared red in the sunlight. Her skin was flushed and she spoke with a strange accent.

"Is it true that you have two hearts?"

Cuán was furious. Doctor Ford must have told people in the village about her. She would be like a sideshow. It would only be a matter of time before people started asking more questions about her strange behaviour. It was bad enough that some people even blamed her for re-introducing wolves into Ireland, saying that since she was a baby they had begun to make a reappearance.

"No!" she grunted. Then she gripped her throat. It was too painful to talk yet.

"Can I call to see you, when you're feeling better?"

Cuán blushed and nodded.

"Righto, see you later!" Nancy said.

Cuán watched as Nancy skipped away through the trees. Then she turned towards the house and saw Maeve running towards her in the sunlight.

Chapter Eighteen

The Girl Who Never Grew Up
1940

Lottie ran through the forest with Albert at her side. Thoughts pounded through her head. Why had her mother kept this dreadful secret from her past hidden from her? Why had she sent her and Albert to a place where such terrible things had happened? And this Blaise – a stranger who was demanding she help a girl who disappeared in 1920! It was all too much.

She stopped for a moment to catch her breath and to wait for Albert to catch up. She knew that she mustn't leave him behind.

Anger bubbled up inside Albert like a small volcano.

"*I hate you, Lottie!*" he cried.

Lottie sighed. "Albert, you don't understand."

"You think I don't know anything because I'm younger than you. But you're wrong!" Tears fell from his eyes like marbles from a jar.

Lottie knelt down in front of him. "Don't say such things, Albert. I think that you are clever and brave and strong."

"Why did you run away from Blaise? He didn't do anything wrong."

Lottie looked into Albert's eyes and she spoke from her heart. "It's just you and me now, Albert, and it's my job to protect you."

"Protect me from what? From making friends?"

Lottie was frustrated with Albert – she had enough on her mind without him acting up. But she took a deep breath and spoke to him gently.

"But don't you think it's strange that Blaise had this newspaper clipping with our mother's photograph on it?" she said.

"No! He explained that, Lottie! He told us his mother saw the village in the crystal ball and the girl in the photograph. The girl with Mother. That's why he kept the photo!"

"Nonsense, Albert! You can't receive messages from crystal balls. If you ask me, Blaise and his mother are no more than con artists who prey on innocent people. I don't believe a word of it."

"You don't have to," said a voice behind her.

Lottie turned around and saw Blaise standing there. He was leaning against a tree. With his head cocked to one side and his arms folded across his chest. Lottie was mortified. She wondered how much of their conversation he had heard and she immediately felt ashamed. She shouldn't have spoken about his mother in that way – it was disrespectful, especially as Blaise had been so kind to them. He hadn't done anything wrong. He was a victim of the circumstances he found himself in, just like they were.

"Stop creeping up on people and listening in to conversations – it's bad manners!" she said defensively.

"So is running away without saying goodbye, and calling my dead mother a con artist."

Albert coughed into his hand. This was the first time that he had seen Lottie get into trouble for something she said. He was usually the bad one who put his foot in his mouth, and in a strange way he quite enjoyed watching his sister squirm.

Lottie's face had flushed with shame. What Blaise said was true – she shouldn't have run away like that, and what she said about him and his mother was horrible and uncalled for. What she said to Albert earlier was true. The war turned some people sour, and she was obviously one of them. She recalled the photo in the caravan of the woman with the long, black hair. She looked like a kind woman. And Lottie had never met her. It was wrong to make a judgement about a person she had never met before. Especially as that person was dead.

Lottie felt like crying. All that she wanted was a normal life, away from death and war. It didn't seem like too much to ask. She looked down at her hand and studied the antique ring that her mother had given her with its wolf's face. It shone in the sunlight. She wished now that she had asked her mother more about it and the friend who had given it to her. Was it Cuán? She feared it must have been.

Blaise placed a hand on her shoulder and stared into her eyes. "I know this must be a shock to you, Lottie."

Lottie pushed his hand away. "No, Blaise, you don't know anything about me. But I should never have said such awful things about your mother. But all of this happened such a long time ago, long before we were born. I don't see what it has to do with us." A wave of guilt rose in Lottie's stomach. The war really had brought out the worst in her. She was becoming bitter and resentful and she hated herself for it.

Blaise sensed her anguish. He didn't blame her for the way she felt about him. Or for the way that she was reacting. It was natural she should distrust him. Yet, despite his earlier feeling that Lottie and Albert needed more time before he told them the full story, now his instinct was to explain things to them.

"Before Mother died, she had a terrifying vision in the crystal ball. In it she heard Cuán, the girl in the photograph with your mother. She was calling for help. She's trapped in a terrible place – she's been there for almost twenty years now. We have to find her!"

"*We?* Why '*we*'?" Lottie cried. "I don't understand what any of this has to do with me and Albert!"

"My mother's visions in the crystal ball predicted that a girl and her brother would come to help me. Don't you see, Lottie? It's fate that you were sent here. I've been waiting for you." Blaise's eyes shone with urgency.

Lottie would have denied that she was the girl in question – would have said she didn't believe in fate and that the whole thing was a load of nonsense. But there was a connection – she couldn't deny that. Her mother was Cuán's friend. And there was this ring . . .

A thought struck her. "You keep saying 'the girl' – but Cuán must be as old as my mother now if she is still alive."

"That's the strange thing, Lottie. When my mother saw Cuán in the vision she was still a child. It was as though she never grew up."

What kind of a child never grew up? Lottie thought. She walked over to a big tree stump and sat down. Then she pulled up a tuft of yellowing grass and watched an ant crawling over a lime-green leaf.

"That is not possible, Blaise," she said at last. "Everyone grows up!" She watched the ant scurrying back to its nest with the delicate leaf on its back.

"Not everyone grows up, Lottie – not if magic is involved," Blaise replied. He peered at her out of the corner of his eye and hoped that what he had said wouldn't scare her away again.

Lottie pressed her hand into the soil. She couldn't help but feel intrigued by Cuán. The girl who never grew up. Ever since Lottie was a small child she had believed that magic existed. She felt it in her gut. It was a bit like the feeling she had when she woke up in the middle of the night after a nightmare. It all seemed so real and it took a few moments to realise that it was all just a dream. Although Lottie had never admitted to anyone that she believed in magic as they would think she was bonkers. Even now she resisted the urge to get involved. Magic could be dangerous and she had enough danger in her life already.

"Don't you understand, Blaise? Just because my mother knew Cuán doesn't mean that we have to help her," she said.

Blaise sat down on the stump beside Lottie and placed his hand over hers. It felt hot and clammy. Lottie shielded her eyes from the sun and looked at him.

He flicked his hair back to reveal dark brimming eyes.

"You were sent here for a reason, Lottie," he said. "To rescue Cuán . . . the little wolf."

A shiver of dread went through Lottie. "Little wolf? Why do you call her that?"

"Her name." Blaise looked surprised. "Oh, I forgot – you don't know any Irish of course. Cuán means 'little wolf'."

Wolf Girl, thought Lottie, and her heart began to hammer at the memory of her dream.

She pulled her hand away and sat up straight.

"I don't believe in magic, Blaise. All this talk about vanishing children and being summoned doesn't make any sense. And I don't want Albert to be involved – he has been through enough."

She glanced over at Albert. He had his arms outstretched and was playing at being a plane. She folded her arms across her chest and tossed her long red hair over her shoulder. Tears glistened in her eyes as she watched Albert.

Blaise understood Lottie's hesitation. She had a responsibility to care for her younger brother. He was such a happy little boy, so full of joy and laughter, and it was true that he had been through so much. And the war wasn't over yet. Who knew what else they would have to face in the future? By the time they went home to Manchester, many of their friends could have been killed. Perhaps even their parents. Yet Cuán needed their help too. She was depending on them. For her sake and for his mother's sake he had to rescue her. As he looked at Lottie, an idea occurred to him and he wondered why he hadn't thought of it before.

"Lottie, there's someone I would like you to meet." Blaise held his breath and waited for Lottie to respond.

Lottie looked at Blaise. His brown eyes were pleading with her. "Who is this person?" she asked reluctantly.

"You will see, Lottie. All I'm asking you to do is trust me just this once. I will make a deal with you: come to visit this woman with me and if after you meet her you still don't want to help, I will walk out of your life and you will never hear from me again."

Blaise knew he was taking a huge risk, but he had no other option.

"Where is she though?" Lottie asked suspiciously.

"On the edge of the forest. Not far."

That sounded fair enough, Lottie thought. "All right, Blaise," she said. "We will go with you. But I am not promising anything."

Blaise was overcome with emotion. His eyes shone as he hugged Lottie.

"Thank you, Lottie!"

Lottie blushed. She was shocked by Blaise's sudden outburst and she suddenly realised just how much she meant to him.

Chapter Nineteen

The House on the Edge of the Forest

They set out through the trees, Blaise eagerly striding ahead.

The forest surrounded them like a shield. Green leaves fell from the trees which lowered their branches like musicians playing the keys on an invisible piano. A delicate breeze which felt like the breath of a giant caused the wood pigeons to coo. Nettles reached up from the dark soil and threatened to sting their ankles as they came to the edge of the forest.

Lottie fiddled with the button on her dress. She looked through the trees and saw a long lane ahead of her. It led to an old farmhouse. She suddenly felt nervous. She thought of turning around and running back as fast as she could to the Dunlivins.

Blaise sensed her apprehension. "Trust me, Lottie. There's nothing to be afraid of."

Lottie looked at Albert, his blonde hair glistening in the sunlight as he bent down to tie his shoelace.

She frowned as they walked on together. The farmhouse emerged like a bruise at the end of the long lane. Creeping ivy trailed up the walls. It reminded Lottie of the fairy tale, *Hansel and Gretel*, and she hoped that there wasn't a witch with a cauldron waiting for them inside.

Albert ran ahead, full of curiosity.

"Albert! Wait!" Lottie cried out in alarm.

But he took no notice and ran right up to the house and peered in a window.

"Albert!"

Lottie ran after him. She saw the hunched-up figure of a woman through a window. It was to the left of a large front door which looked as though it needed a lick of paint. The rest of the windows in the house had been boarded up with wood. It reminded Lottie of the houses back home after they had been bombed.

Suddenly a black-and-white sheepdog bounded out of the forest and ran around the yard, chasing its tail. Then it ran towards Albert and knocked him off his feet. Albert burst out laughing as the dog licked his face.

Blaise turned to Lottie and smiled, but she wasn't looking at Albert or the dog. Something else had caught her eye.

Lottie placed her right hand into the pocket of her dress and pulled out the crumpled newspaper clipping which contained the faded photograph of her mother with Cuán. They were sitting on a rock in an orchard, with a farmhouse in the background. Lottie gasped. This was the house in the photograph.

Lottie ran around the side of the house and into the orchard. The trees were bursting with red and juicy green apples. Lottie picked one from the tree and sank her teeth into it, just as Cuán had done twenty years earlier.

Albert hurtled around the side of the house with the sheepdog chasing him playfully. "Lottie, where are we?" Albert enquired. Then he threw a stick for the dog and watched gleefully as it wagged its tail and ran to retrieve it.

"Albert, this is Cuán's house. This is where that photo was taken. The one in the newspaper."

"Imagine, Lottie! Mother was here when she was a little girl."

"I know, Albert. It's hard to believe."

Lottie and Albert held hands and walked back to the front of the house where they found Blaise talking to an old woman at the front door. She wore a purple dress and had a green shawl around her shoulders, secured at the front by an unusual brooch. It was embellished with red rubies and under glass at the centre was woven hair as black as midnight. Lottie recognised the brooch straight away as a piece of mourning jewellery. She had learnt all about it in school – how in the Victorian Era people wore such jewellery to remember their dead loved ones. The woman's eyes were small and brown as chestnuts, and she leaned on an oak walking stick with the head of a wolf carved into the top of it.

Albert and the sheepdog were now playing chase and

the dog started barking madly.

"Hush, Bonnie! Come here!" the old woman shouted at the dog, who reluctantly obeyed her orders. She came and sat down obediently on the stone doorstep and wagged her tail.

Lottie and Albert had always wanted a dog, but there wasn't enough room for one back home in Manchester. She was glad in a way. So many of her friend's pet cats and dogs were killed when the bombs fell. Lottie simply couldn't have borne it.

"Bring the children here to me, Blaise," the old woman croaked.

Lottie could not help but wonder if it was a trick after all. What if the woman really was a witch?

She grabbed Albert by the sleeve. "Let's go, Albert!"

"No, Lottie! I'm not going anywhere!" Albert wriggled free of her grasp and ran over to the front door.

"You annoying little wretch!" Lottie mumbled under her breath.

"Lottie, come here!" Blaise said, beckoning Lottie towards them.

As Lottie approached she cast a stern look in Albert's direction but he didn't seem to notice. He was too busy scratching behind the dog's ear.

On closer inspection, Lottie realised that the old woman standing in front of her was no witch at all. If her suspicions were right then the woman was Cuán's mother.

"Come closer, child, and let me see you."

The woman reached out her bony hand towards

Lottie and touched her gently on the arm. Her skin was paper-thin. Lottie saw veins which resembled blue ribbons clutching the narrow bones on the backs of her hands.

"You are Nancy's daughter all right," the old woman said. "Although she didn't have flame-red hair like you do. As pretty as a picture that girl was, and such a kind heart too."

Lottie blushed at this praise.

"Nancy was there for my Cuán when all the other children in the village turned their backs on her."

"You knew our mother?" Albert cried.

"I did indeed. I am Cuán's mother Maeve. She used to call me 'Ma'. It makes me so happy to hear news of Nancy and to see her two beautiful children. Blaise tells me she is well and living in Manchester?"

"But she's missing us now so I think she's sad," said Albert.

"Never you mind, pet – you'll be home to her in no time." Maeve moved into the house. "Come with me, children, and I can show you where the girls were staying on the night that Cuán went walking."

They followed the old woman down a long dark hallway. Cobwebs hung from the ceiling. Albert watched a small spider spinning a silver web. It looked as though it was made from silk. There was a musty smell and the green-and-blue flowered wallpaper had begun to peel from the walls.

"Went walking?" Lottie asked. That was a strange way to describe what had happened to Cuán.

"Yes. You see, my Cuán was no ordinary girl. She was special."

They continued along the hallway until they came to a large oak door. The old lady pushed her arm against it and it creaked in resistance as if it hadn't been opened in a long time. Lottie coughed as dust tickled her throat. The window was boarded up. Two leather armchairs which were covered in what looked like tooth-marks were positioned in front of the open fire. Strange, thought Lottie, that they had allowed a dog to wreck the chairs like that. The room was full of candles. The old woman handed Blaise some matches and gestured towards the candles. He lit them one by one and they flickered in the dark, casting a ghostly light on the proceedings. It was hard to believe that the sun was shining outside.

In the corner of the room was a cabinet full of religious statues. One of the statues was missing its right hand and it had a strange look on its face. Under the candlelight it appeared to be grimacing. Beside the cabinet was a large wardrobe with silver handles. The fireplace was opposite the bed and it was shaped like the open mouth of a lion. It looked as though it hadn't been lit in twenty years. In the corner of the room Lottie noticed a dressing table with a cracked mirror and beneath it was a purple velvet stool that had claws for feet.

Lottie helped the old woman across the room and they both settled into the leather armchairs in front of the fireplace. Blaise stood with his back to the wall and his eyes on the boarded-up window. In all the times that

Blaise had visited Maeve, he had never been invited into Cuán's bedroom. Albert perched himself on the edge of Lottie's chair.

Maeve pressed her back against the leather chair, just as Cuán had done twenty years earlier. And the same feeling of dread that Cuán had felt rose like a wave in her stomach.

"Are you all right, Maeve?" Blaise asked.

"I am, Blaise. You are a good boy. My Cuán would have liked you."

Blaise smiled, his teeth gleaming in his dark face and his silver earrings glistening in the candlelight.

"So tell me, Blaise – what brings you and Nancy's children here to see me?"

"I wanted Lottie and Albert to meet you."

The old woman looked disappointed. She opened her eyes wide and a single tear trickled down her cheek. "For a moment I thought you knew where Cuán was."

"I wish we did, Maeve," Blaise replied.

"She's still alive, Blaise. I can feel it in my creaking old bones. That's why I left everything exactly as it was on the night she vanished, so that she would recognise the place when she returned. You must bring her straight to me when you find her – which I know you will. But she can't stay here, it isn't safe. No – she will have to go somewhere else, far away from here, where no-one will ever find her."

Lottie shifted in her chair as she noticed something on the floor by her feet. She bent down and picked it up. It was a handkerchief with her mother's initials embroidered in the corner with green thread. It was hard to believe that it had lain there for twenty years. Lottie held it and thought of how terrifying it must have been for her mother on the night that Cuán disappeared. It was no wonder she had never mentioned Cuán to her before. Then she looked at Maeve, feeling horribly sorry for the old woman with her sad belief that her long-lost daughter would return.

"So, child, tell me what brings you to Kilbree," said Maeve.

"Mother sent us here to escape from Hitler's bombs!" Albert cried as he tickled Bonnie on the stomach while she lay on her back with her four paws up in the air. "We are staying with the detestable Dunlivins!"

The old woman smiled. "Oh, I have never heard them called that before! Ida is a bit detestable all right and that daughter of theirs could do with learning a few manners. But Hugh Dunlivin is a gentleman. He sings with me in the church choir."

"Huh, he is as bad as his wife and daughter if you ask me!" said Albert boldly. "That's why they make me and Lottie sleep down in the cellar with all the dead bodies! And lots and lots of skulls! Wait until Mother hears about all this – she'll go crazy."

"Nobody did ask you, Albert Hope!" Lottie warned, her face as red as her hair. "Now keep your mouth shut!"

Albert realised that he had overstepped the mark this time. He pulled his hand away from Bonnie and the dog barked loudly.

"Is this true, Lottie?" Maeve asked, shocked.

Lottie couldn't lie. She nodded.

"Oh, Lottie dear, that is awful! Poor Nancy's children – you deserve better than that. I have choir practice tonight in the church. Let me speak to Hugh. He can't keep you in that cellar – it's not right."

"You would really do that for us?" Albert cried.

"Yes, I would, of course I would."

Albert ran over to Maeve and hugged her.

"You are a lovely little boy, aren't you?" said Maeve.

"Yes, I am."

Maeve smiled, her eyes crinkling at the corners and Blaise and Lottie laughed.

Albert lay beside Bonnie on the ground. "Maeve, is Bonnie Cuán's dog?" he asked.

"Oh no," Maeve said with a smile. "Bonnie is much too young to be Cuán's dog. But Cuán did have a dog called Bonnie. She went missing before Cuán disappeared. The strange thing is that she came home again after Cuán had gone. She had injuries – cuts on her body – and she seemed very frightened. I thought maybe she had got trapped somewhere for a few days and hurt herself trying to escape. I healed her injuries with herbs and gave her others to calm her. Soon she was healthy and calm again – but missing Cuán of course."

"So where is Bonnie now?" Albert asked.

"Come with me and I will show you."

They followed Maeve further along the hallway and into an old farmhouse kitchen. It was much brighter in there. Maeve had baked bread for breakfast and a fresh loaf lay on a metal rack beside the cooker. There was a round table in the centre of the room – it was surrounded by four wooden stools. A breakfast bowl and cup were on the table. In the corner of the room, beside the stove, was a grey dog's bed. It was where the younger Bonnie slept every night. There was a brightly decorated cuckoo clock on the wall and an old wooden kitchen dresser was covered in mismatched cups and plates.

Blaise walked over to the back door and unbolted it, and in that moment Lottie realised that Blaise must visit Maeve often as he was so familiar with her home.

As they stepped outside into the orchard a swarm of bees flew by. Bonnie tried to chase them and ran on ahead through the trees. A worm protruded its small brown head from the inside of an apple that had fallen from a tree. They followed the sound of Bonnie's barking and arrived at a small grave. It was marked by a wooden cross and a small bouquet of yellow roses lay on it.

The words *'Bonnie, Cuán's Best Friend'* had been carved into the wooden cross.

"This is where Cuán's dog Bonnie is buried, Albert," Blaise whispered.

Albert tugged at Maeve's purple dress.

"Why are you crying, Maeve?"

"Poor Cuán didn't get a chance to say goodbye to her pet dog, Albert."

"Don't be sad, Maeve. Cuán's dog is in Heaven now."

Lottie handed her mother's handkerchief to Maeve to dry her tears.

"You're right, Albert," said Maeve. "And there's more to the story." She pointed to where the younger Bonnie was barking and chasing crows from the apple trees. "You see, this Bonnie was the first Bonnie's pup – the only one she ever had and she had her late in life. I think she wanted to leave me a gift to remember her by."

"Oh, that's amazing!" Albert said, his eyes round with wonder.

Lottie just wanted to cry. It was all so sad. She knew now that Blaise was right. They had to save Cuán. Visiting Maeve had opened her eyes to the fact that Cuán was a real person, with a mother, a home, a life and a beloved dog. She was not simply a girl in a photograph or a Wolf Girl in a dream.

Lottie knew that she would find her and bring her home even if it meant risking their own lives in the process.

Chapter Twenty

Death from the Sky

"Listen, Lottie!" Albert cried. *"Get up, get up!"*

Lottie and Blaise were resting on the grass in a small clearing on the way back to Blaise's caravan, while Albert swooped around playing being a fighter pilot again.

Lottie hauled herself up and rubbed the grass off her clothes. She noticed a stain on her blue dress. "What now, Albert?" she said as she wondered how she would get the stain out.

Albert suddenly roared: *"The Germans are coming for us! They followed us here!"* His voice trembled as he pointed towards the sky.

Lottie wondered if her young brother had heat stroke. Or whether all this talk of disappearing children was too much for him.

"Oh Albert! Of course not! Please calm down!"

"Just listen, both of you!" Albert pleaded.

Lottie and Blaise listened and suddenly they heard a distant hum that sounded like a thousand bees buzzing.

Lottie recognised the sound immediately. Her mouth felt dry and her legs turned to jelly as fear took hold. It was the sound of a bomber plane approaching fast. They didn't have any time to lose – within moments a bomb would be dropped and they would all be killed.

She yanked Blaise by the hand and pulled him to his feet. "*We need to get underground, Blaise! Help us!*"

Blaise hesitated and a confused look crossed his face. "Underground? I don't understand what you mean."

Within seconds it was as though a blanket covered the sun and daylight disappeared. They looked up at the sky. There was the plane, descending fast. It was spinning and twirling through the sky and the smell of diesel fumes filled the air.

Albert stiffened. "*The plane is going to crash!*" he cried.

"*Follow me!*" Blaise's voice was barely audible above the whirling, whistling sound of the plane.

Lottie and Albert followed him as he ran through the spruce trees. The animals sensed something was wrong too – foxes and squirrels scattered, unsure of which way to go, and birds flew helplessly around and around in circles.

Blaise swung Albert up on his back. They ran towards the river. They were afraid to look up. They were petrified that a bomb or the plane would fall on them.

Then they came to a rocky ledge above the fast-flowing river. Blaise took Lottie's hand and led her down a steep path. At the bottom they found shelter in a narrow cave. It was dark and cold, and moisture dripped relentlessly from its roof. A brown field mouse walked over Lottie's foot. It wasn't the most pleasant place to be. But at least they were safe.

Chapter Twenty-one

Günther the Warrior

Günther's life flashed before his eyes. The German Luftwaffe plane that he was flying plummeted towards the earth like a giant fireball.

He had been on a mission to bomb Wales when his fuel tank ruptured and his propellers failed.

He could see his mother's kind smile and smell her rose perfume as she read a story to him before bedtime. He was no more than four years old. Then he was running through the town with his arms outstretched, pretending to be a bird soaring through the air. All his Christmases came back to him at once. The faces of his brothers and sisters as they decorated the tree and opened their presents. Sixteen years wrapped up in a parcel of memories. Reminding him of everything that he was about to lose and everything he would never see again.

As the plane fell he released a bomb. It hurtled through the clouds and then he heard an enormous explosion.

The ground flew up to meet him as fire engulfed the cabin. He was suffocating. Then the plane hit the ground hard. It was tilted at a precarious angle and he was suspended upside down in his harness. Like an acrobat in a circus.

The air was hot and dense smoke and shards of glass filled the small cockpit. He released his belt and fell through the air. He landed on a jagged shard of metal. It tore his trousers and sliced his leg open like a piece of birthday cake. He shielded his face as the intensity of heat from the fire was overwhelming.

In excruciating pain, he dragged himself away from the plane. A smaller explosion boomed. The door of the plane flew off and hit him on the head. Then seconds before he fell unconscious he saw the image of a girl with yellow eyes. She was standing in front of him holding a star up to the sky.

Chapter Twenty-two

The Cave Drawings

Albert covered his ears with his hands. Seconds later the earth beneath them shook and rocks fell all around them. It was louder than any bomb they had heard back home. They sat huddled together in silence.

"Is everybody all right?" Blaise asked after a few moments. His eyes were wide with fright, but he tried to conceal his fear. Lottie had seen that expression before on her mother's face when she tried to hide the terror she felt from her children.

Albert coughed and spluttered. "Mother told us we would be safe here, Lottie – she lied to us!" Sweat glistened on his brow. Tears sprang from his eyes.

"No, Albert, you mustn't think that – Mother must have thought we would be."

Blaise thought of his own mother and how much he missed her. Sometimes he could feel her presence as though she was right beside him, guiding him through life. "Lottie is right, Albert – your mother was only trying to do what's best for you."

Lottie shot a smile in Blaise's direction and it made him feel happy, despite the terrible situation they were in.

Albert shivered and his teeth chattered. "Bombs aren't supposed to drop in Ireland – the Irish are not in the war."

Lottie got up and moved slowly towards the cave entrance. She peered outside. "That was a much more powerful bomb than usual. The sound and the way the earth shook!"

Albert stroked the field mouse as it stood on its hind legs and sniffed the air. "Do you think the Germans followed us here, Lottie?"

Lottie sat back down and rubbed her head. "Of course not, Albert – it can't be the Germans."

"What will we do now?" Albert enquired. Back home people remained in the bomb shelters until they were told that it was safe to return home. And the bombings they were used to occurred at night – they had never experienced one during the day before.

"We'll wait here a while," said Lottie.

"I can't wait! I'm too scared!" Albert wailed.

"Come with me, Albert. There's something I want to show you." Blaise led Albert and Lottie deeper into the belly of the cave. Their footsteps echoed. Lottie's heart pounded in her chest.

Daylight ceased to reach them. Blaise took a small box

of matches out of his pocket. Then he struck one of the matches against the wall and lit the stub of a candle which lay on the floor of the cave. Clearly Blaise had been there before.

Lottie gasped. The entire cave was covered in ancient drawings of wolves. They were ferocious creatures, with sharp teeth. Above their heads were constellations of stars. Lottie reached out her fingertips and traced the outline of one of the mythical-looking creatures. It was eating a star.

"Cave drawings of wolves!" Albert said. His voice echoed as Blaise held the flickering candle up to illuminate the ancient markings.

Tall shadows fell on the wolves.

"These are no ordinary wolves, Albert." Lottie's thoughts fell from her lips, like rain from a storm cloud.

"Who is that?" Albert asked. His eyes fell on the drawing of a young boy of about eight years of age. His head was nestled against a she-wolf.

"I will tell you a story about the boy in the cave drawing, Albert. It's one that my mother told me when I was a young boy."

Albert was immediately distracted from his fears. Thoughts of bombs and plane crashes left his mind. Instead he was filled with intrigue and excitement as he studied the cave drawing of the boy and the wolf.

Lottie threw a grateful look at Blaise. A story was a great idea to distract Albert.

Then Blaise told a story that disturbed Lottie much more than calming her.

"A long time ago when the world was still covered in snow, there were wolves. They were beautiful creatures who roamed the world in great packs. People say that they swam to Ireland from Scotland and remained here ever since."

As Blaise spoke he moved around the cave. Each drawing he stopped at corresponded to the part of story that he was telling. In one of the drawings there were mountains, in the next there were warriors going into battle with wolves by their sides.

"At first people saw the wolves as their friends. The ancient kings and chieftans would take wolves into battle with them. They made mighty warriors. But over time a different type of wolf evolved. They were not ordinary wolves. These wolves could change themselves into human form. Such a wolf was known as a 'werewolf', which in old English meant 'man-wolf'. In Irish it was called a 'conriocht' which meant 'in the shape of a hound'. They were descendants of a legendary warrior-werewolf named Laighneach Fáelad."

A shiver danced down Lottie's spine and she twisted the wolf ring on her finger.

Blaise picked up a stone and threw it across the cave. "These werewolves possessed the power and predatory instincts of wolves and the intelligence of humans."

"Where are they now?" Albert asked.

"Well, the last real wolf in Ireland was killed in 1786 on Mount Leinster, on the border of Carlow and Wexford. And people say that its body was buried near the Tower of Wolves."

"The Tower of Wolves! That sounds frightening!" Lottie gasped.

"It was. It still stands in the monastic settlement at Kilbree Abbey. It's an ancient round tower. The monks built a round tower to protect themselves and the villagers from the werewolves – in the same way that people built round towers to protect themselves from Viking raids. It is six storeys high and the door can only be reached by a ladder. The monks built a gateway to their settlement with two large granite arches, one behind the other. They still exist today though partly ruined. People say that anyone who enters the gateway will be cursed."

"Scary!" Albert's eyes were like saucers.

"But you asked me about the werewolves, Albert. Well, the real wolves in Ireland were all killed off – which was a tragedy in its way as wolves are intelligent and beautiful animals. But the werewolves survived. It was difficult to identify them as they were human during the day and wolves at night. Some lived peacefully as humans, and even married humans, but occasionally were overcome by their wolfish natures and transformed into wolves that ran wild in the mountains, especially at full moon. But others were evil and bloodthirsty and eventually abandoned their human nature and lived openly in werewolf packs. These eventually drove away the monks at Kilbree Abbey and took over the settlement. The abbey and settlement were built on an ancient werewolf burial ground and the werewolves believed that one day the buried ones would rise from the dead. That is why they claimed it back. The leader of those werewolves was called Deathhound."

As Blaise mentioned the name 'Deathhound' Albert's eyes grew wide as saucers and his mouth dropped open.

Blaise placed the palm of his hand on the drawing of the boy with the she-wolf.

"This boy is Deathhound." Tears glistened and his lips quivered as he uttered the name *Deathhound*. "He was an ordinary boy who grew up to be a wicked man."

"What made him become wicked?" Albert asked, as he peered up at the roof of the cave. Stalactites pointed towards the ground like long spindly fingers.

Blaise closed his eyes and recalled what his mother had shown him in her crystal ball.

The images sprang to life. Blaise recounted it to Lottie and Albert in such a way that they felt as though they were there.

The year was 1348 and the terrible disease called the Black Death had gripped Ireland. Entire villages and towns were wiped out. No-one was safe. On the day the plague arrived at the village, the sky turned purple like a bruise and a rumble of thunder could be heard over the howling of the wolves. Then people began to die.

When the next full moon rode high in the sky, the village chieftain, Donnacha, called his seven-year-old son Ruairí to him.

"It's a full moon, son," he said. "They are restless tonight. Nevertheless, while the moon is full we must go and pray by the Sacred Stone for protection from the plague."

147

The boy knew that his father would never utter the word *wolf*. The mere mention of one could bring wolves to your door.

It's too late to pray, Ruairí thought. He and his father had avoided the Black Death, but most of the villagers had caught it. Ruairí had watched his mother and sister die and he knew that he would probably be next. But Donnacha was a stubborn man. Ruairí knew that there was no point in arguing with him.

Donnacha placed his wolfskin coat over his large shoulders. Then he made his way over to the entrance of the hut, where his spear hung, together with a wolf's tail. He hung the wolf's tail on its leather thong around his neck and took his spear. The villagers believed that hanging a wolf's tail above the door would keep wolves away. Ruairí wished that it worked for the plague too.

Outside the air was sharp and cold. Ruairí gripped his small spear. He turned his face away from the biting wind as he followed his father up the side of Mount Leinster. They reached the clearing where the Sacred Stone stood upright in the ground, over ten feet high, pointing like a huge finger to the sky. Beneath the glare of the full moon they fell to their knees and prayed that they and the remaining villagers would be safe from harm. Ruairí placed his hand in the small pouch hanging from his belt and felt the wolf's tooth. It was smooth to the touch as he stroked it. It had belonged to his mother and it comforted him.

Time passed and Ruairí began to sway with exhaustion. At first Donnacha, lost in prayer, didn't notice. When he did, he gently shook his son who was half asleep.

"Come, son," he said. "I'll take you back."

They made their way back down the mountain, Donnacha striding ahead. Ruairí looked up at the sky, which was barely visible above the trees. He tried to count the stars but there were too many. So he concentrated on the path ahead of him instead. Fires lit the way back to the village – a warning to unsuspecting strangers that the Black Death was present there.

When they neared the village Donnacha halted.

"Go home, son, and sleep. I will go back to the Sacred Stone and pray while the moon is full that the plague will depart from us and the others."

"No, Father, don't go back! The wolves will get you!" Ruairí blurted out.

"Not while I have this!" Donnacha shook his spear with a grim smile. Then he took the wolf's tail from his neck and placed it around Ruairí's. "That will protect you, son. Hang it back in its place over the door of our hut. Go now."

Ruairí dared not disobey. He walked away. When he looked back his father was still standing there, looking after him. Donnacha raised his spear in salute.

Ruairí waited for five days and nights for his father to return, alone in their hut. His stomach ached with hunger. He was weak and tired. He had gone to the other villagers' huts, begging for food, but each and every person had driven him away, sometimes attacking him with sticks, sometimes pelting him with stones. He couldn't understand how people he had known all his life could turn on him like this – even children he had played with. Even if they feared he might spread the plague, why could they not give him a little food? He tried to tell them his father, their chieftain, was missing but they didn't care.

He knew he should go and search for his father, but he was afraid of the wolves who prowled ever closer to the village. On the sixth day he set out. He could hear the cry of wolves in the trees around him. When he reached the foothills of the mountain he saw someone lying face down on the grass.

"Father!" he cried.

He ran and hugged his father's lifeless body. A single tear fell from his eye. The Black Death had claimed his father after all, he thought. But when he examined Donnacha's body he could see that he had not died of the plague. Nor had he been savaged by wolves. No, he had been speared by human hands.

The sky cracked open like an egg. Rain fell from the dark clouds.

Then, as he stared in horror, a grey she-wolf stealthily approached and sank her sharp teeth into his arm. Ruairí cried out in pain and fear.

He staggered to his feet and then found himself going through a terrifying experience. He was transforming into a werewolf.

The she-wolf paced back and forth, looking on. She was, of course, also a werewolf and she had bitten him so that he could join the pack.

That night Ruairí's human life ended. He was raised in the forest by the werewolf pack. At night he slept in a cave and found comfort in making cave drawings on the rock. He knew he could not go back to his village nor did he want to. The she-wolf who became his mother had told him that his father Donnacha had been murdered by humans that night of the full moon because they suspected him of being a werewolf and blamed him for bringing bad luck to the village in the form of the plague.

Fuelled by grief and anger, Ruairí grew up to be the most terrifying werewolf to have ever lived and his wolf-pack renamed him Deathhound.

Albert and Lottie had listened to Blaise's story with bated breath.

"Poor Ruairí!" said Albert. "It wasn't his fault that he became a werewolf!"

"No, it wasn't," said Blaise, "but he didn't have to choose the path of evil. Yet he did. Deathhound learnt magic and, using it, found a portal into another world, a world called Wolf Land. He and his followers passed through it and quickly took control. And Wolf Land became a very evil place. As it is to this day."

"Except it doesn't exist, right?" said Lottie sharply.

Albert looked at her uncertainly and then at Blaise.

Blaise didn't meet his eyes and just continued his story. "The portal is at the gateway the monks built. Legend says that it is guarded by the souls of dead werewolves. Deathhound put a curse on Wolf Land when he took control. Night became eternal. There was no sun in the sky but there were two moons – one a blue one which had appeared for the first time when Deathhound had entered Wolf Land. It was always winter. The birds in the sky and fish in the rivers died. Then the animals. Only werewolves can survive there now."

"That sounds horrible!" said Albert. "But why did he do that to his own place?"

"He did it out of hatred. Hatred of humans. With no birds or animals to hunt and no food growing in the frozen ground, the werewolves had nothing to eat. Then Deathhound cast a spell which meant that the werewolves could only survive by eating the stars."

"Why?" Albert asked. "And what has that to do with hating humans?"

"Humans know they need the sun and the moon to survive – but they don't realise that they need the stars too. And every time a werewolf eats a star, there is one less star in the sky."

"In their sky! Not ours!"

"Well, that's the thing – you see, Deathhound had discovered from ancient books that if a star dies in Wolf Land it dies in the human world too."

"What will happen when the werewolves eat all the stars?" Albert asked.

"Our world will end."

"*Oh no! What can we do?*" Albert cried.

"It's all right, Albert – it's just a story," Lottie said, although her skin crawled as she imagined Wolf Land and Deathhound. "There's no such place as Wolf Land, or a werewolf called Deathhound – is there, Blaise?"

Blaise stared at her but remained silent.

Lottie glanced at Albert, who looked as terrified as she felt.

"Blaise, answer me! You're scaring us!" Lottie cried.

Blaise turned to Lottie. "I swear, Lottie. I know that Wolf Land exists. Because my mother . . ." he hesitated, "my mother showed it to me in her crystal ball. Wolf Land is where Cuán went on the night she vanished. And now she too eats the stars to survive. And Deathhound exists. And is still alive after all these centuries. Through evil magic he has become immortal."

Lottie was swamped with doubts again. She could tell by the look in Blaise's eyes that he believed what he was saying but it was all incredible.

"I believe you, Blaise!" said Albert.

"*Albert!*" Lottie cried. "Another world ruled by an immortal monster called Deathhound! It's too much!"

"Well, if Hitler wins the war then our world will be ruled by an evil man too, Lottie!"

Blaise put an arm around Albert and pulled him close.

Lottie stared at her brother, wide-eyed. "But this is a whole different situation, Albert. You're too young to understand. When I agreed to help Cuán I knew nothing about evil werewolves and portals to other worlds!"

"I am going with Blaise to help Cuán with or without you, Lottie!" Albert cried.

His two hands were wound into small fists and a determined look was in his eyes. Lottie would have laughed had the situation not been so serious.

153

Blaise smiled at Albert. "Brave boy!" He turned to Lottie. "It is dangerous, Lottie. If we enter Wolf Land we will be risking our lives. Deathhound is evil. And he will kill us if he finds us there. He has also conjured up demons called Thought Monsters, wicked creatures with red eyes who feed off negative thoughts. Fear attracts them and they hunt down their prey by sensing it. They serve as his spies. And they also lure children like Cuán into Wolf Land."

Lottie shuddered.

"So, I won't deceive you, Lottie. Wolf Land is dangerous and terrifying. But it is not just Cuán who needs our help – there are other children too." He paused to allow her to take this in and then continued even more earnestly. "You must believe me – I wouldn't dream of taking you and Albert there if there was any other way. However, it seems I can't rescue Cuán without you. My mother's visions clearly predicted that a girl and her brother would come to help me. That has to be you and Albert."

Lottie turned away from him. "How could your mother learn all that detail about Wolf Land just from looking at visions in her crystal ball?" she muttered.

Blaise was silent for a few moments. Then he said, "The truth is, there are people now in Ireland who have escaped from Wolf Land. My mother met them on her travels around the country over the years. Some of them had left Wolf Land not as babies but when they were older, so they remembered it. She questioned all of them and wrote down everything they said in a journal. She never let me listen to those conversations – she felt I was too young during those years – and she planned to give me her journal when I was older. She also drew a map of Wolf Land in it. I can show you the journal and you can see for yourself."

Lottie glanced at him. He sounded both convinced and convincing.

"Please, can we help, Lottie?" Albert begged, darting in front of her and fixing his big blue eyes on her face.

Lottie bit her lip. "I don't know, Albert. I promised Mother I would protect you."

"But Mother would want us to help her friend! This could be our one chance to save people. We couldn't do anything back home to help people survive the war. So many of our school friends have died, Lottie. Maybe we could help these children. And Father would be proud of us!"

Lottie hugged Albert tightly. He was skin and bone. "I love you so much, Albert Hope!" she cried.

All this time Lottie had stupidly thought that the war meant nothing to Albert. That he was too young to understand what was happening. But he was taking everything in. Every one of her friends and neighbours that had lost their lives were Albert's friends and neighbours too. Of course Albert understood. He was just being brave and putting his best foot forward all this time. At that moment Lottie felt so proud of her little brother. She understood his desire to help other people. He was right: if they couldn't help back home maybe they could help here.

Blaise watched her silently as she pondered.

At last she spoke. "So we need to pass through the gateway into the settlement, through this portal into Wolf Land?"

Blaise sighed in relief. She believed him.

Albert laughed as he clapped his hands.

"Oh Lottie, thank you!" said Blaise. "But you need to know it's not easy to get into Wolf Land – I have gone to the abbey many times but the portal was always closed."

"And there isn't another way in?"

"Not that I know of, Lottie. That's why I thought you could help me."

"What made you think that?"

"Your mother was the last person to see Cuán alive," said Blaise, "so I thought maybe she told you something about the portal."

Lottie shook her head. "I am sorry, Blaise. Truly I am. But Mother never mentioned anything to me about Wolf Land – or even Cuán."

"I know. I realised that soon after meeting you." Eyes downcast, Blaise sat with his mouth pressed against his fist.

"Did your mother not write about it in her journal?" asked Lottie.

"Yes, and she told me all about it. But she didn't know if there was a way to open it when it is closed."

"If there is a way we will find it!" Albert announced.

Blaise smiled at him, amused but heartened by the little boy's courage.

Lottie moved to where Blaise was sitting. "I promise

that we will help you," she said. Then she hugged him. He smelt of pine trees and oranges.

Blaise hugged her back. "That gives me heart," he said.

Albert suddenly looked downcast. He fiddled with a thread that had come loose on his jumper. "What if more bombs come?" he said glumly. "If we're all killed we can't help anyone."

Lottie faced her brother. "We have survived worse than this before, Albert. We were in England during the Blitz. And now we have Blaise. The three of us can survive anything together."

"Even werewolves?" A frown appeared on Albert's face as he spoke.

"Yes, even werewolves," Lottie reassured her brother. Then she cast a warm smile at Blaise.

But she knew that her words were meaningless. From what Blaise was telling her their future was terrifyingly uncertain.

Chapter Twenty-three

Cuán
1920

"That was quite a fright you gave your mother, young lady. You can't keep sneaking off like that." The rasping voice whispered the warning into Cuán's left ear.

Cuán blinked her eyes open as the dull morning light scattered around the room. It reflected off the metal rail on her bed and a rainbow of colours erupted on the wall. Cuán's head was fuzzy and she didn't recognise the voice.

"Who are you?" she asked.

The words scratched her throat as her eyes opened fully, like the petals of a flower in full bloom, and she looked at the person standing in front of her.

The figure of an old woman in a black shawl emerged. She had watery blue eyes and her wrinkled skin was as thin as paper – Cuán could see the bone underneath.

"Alice Fortune's my name. I am a nurse. Your mother

asked me to come and keep an eye on you."

Cuán glared at the woman. She had a set of wooden rosary beads wrapped around her hand. And she had a long, shrivelled neck which jiggled from side to side when she spoke. Cuán hauled herself up onto her pillow.

"How long have I been asleep?" Her head throbbed and her lips were dry.

Alice hunched over to get a closer look at Cuán's yellow eyes. "You've slept for three days now – we're transferring you to Dublin at the weekend."

"You can't!" Cuán cried.

Alice placed her hand on Cuán's arm. "Calm down, there's the girl. There is a pot of rabbit stew in the kitchen. I'll get some for you."

"I don't want your rabbit stew!" Cuán said defiantly.

Alice's eyes grew wide. "Listen, miss, you will do as you are told while you are in my care. I know about girls like you. You think that you know everything, but you don't."

Cuán threw her a look of panic. Then her eyes darted across the room to the bedroom door. "Where's Ma?"

Alice sighed and mumbled something under her breath. Then she said, "Your poor mother has gone away for a few days, to rest. You broke her strength. But you won't break mine. You are a wicked girl!"

Cuán felt anger surge through her body. She dug her fingernails into her bed as an insatiable itch covered her entire body. It was happening again. She was about to change. It couldn't happen now. Not in front of this evil nurse. They would lock her up – or worse still they would kill her.

"Rabbit stew!" Cuán blurted out.

"I beg your pardon?" the old woman said with a frown on her face.

"I would like some rabbit stew, please," Cuán managed to say.

"That's more like it. Now, don't you move a muscle. I'll be right back."

Cuán forced a smile although the skin around her jaw felt taut. The familiar pain travelled beneath her skin, through her ribcage and into her hearts.

Unable to breathe, she fell from her bed and landed on the floor with a thud. Then she scratched at the furniture and tore the mattress open. Feathers flew through the air like a whisper. She scratched her arms and legs until they bled.

Within minutes she was a wolf again. A wild creature. She ran around the room, consumed with panic. She tried to get out of the window but it wasn't open. She was trapped.

Cuán scanned the room. She could hear footsteps in the hallway and the sound of voices outside the room. She recognised them as those of Doctor Ford and Nurse Fortune. Doctor Ford entered first. He was wearing his black overcoat and carried a black bag in his hand, which he dropped to the floor.

Never in all his years had he seen such a horrific sight.

"Good heavens above!" he cried.

Nurse Fortune reluctantly followed him into the room. Steam rose from a piping hot bowl of rabbit stew, which she carried on a tray. She dropped the tray to the floor and the rabbit stew splattered up the wall. Then she screamed at the top of her lungs. The furniture was destroyed with teeth and claw marks. The mattress had been torn to shreds and Cuán lay on the floor, in human form, barely able to move and covered in cuts and bruises.

Doctor Ford's eyes narrowed. "Don't just stand there, woman! Help me," he ordered.

Nurse Fortune fumbled with her apron for a moment, unsure of what to do. Then she helped the doctor to haul Cuán's lifeless body back onto her torn mattress. Only to discover that her yellow eyes were fused shut.

Doctor Ford was furious. Sweat lined his brow. He took a handkerchief out of the pocket of his overcoat and dabbed his forehead. "How long did you leave her alone? You were supposed to stay with her at all times!"

Alice Fortune paced up and down the room. She wiped her hands on her dress. She couldn't understand what had happened any more than Doctor Ford could. "Five minutes was all that I was gone. I went to fetch her some stew. Then I heard you knock at the front door. I answered it and came straight back."

Doctor Ford discarded his woollen overcoat on a chair. Then he opened his bag and pulled out a small brown medicine bottle. He was determined not let anything more happen to Cuán. It was a miracle that she was alive at all. And a miracle that he had discovered her.

"Fetch me some hot water in a bowl and a towel and hurry! We need to clean and bandage these wounds before they become infected." He pulled the cork from the bottle.

"Of course, doctor," the nurse said as she scurried towards the bedroom door. She was relieved to be leaving the evil girl behind her.

Just before Nurse Fortune reached the bedroom door, the doctor swivelled around to face her.

"There is one more thing: don't tell a living, breathing soul about what you witnessed in this house today – *do you understand me?*"

Nurse Fortune nodded her head and silently left the room. She would never mention a word of this to anyone – in fact, she would never speak again as long as she lived, such the shock of what she had witnessed. She vowed that she would never return here as soon as the day was over. There was some kind of spell on this girl. There was no mistake about that and she didn't want anything to do with it.

Chapter Twenty-four

Cuán

"Please don't let them take me away, Ma!" Cuán pleaded with her mother as a storm raged outside the thatched cottage. A flash of lightning illuminated the small kitchen. It sent a kaleidoscope of colours cascading like a waterfall across the floor.

It had been three weeks since Cuán changed into a wolf and her cuts were beginning to heal at last.

"It's for your own good, Cuán," Maeve sighed. She was unable to look Cuán in the eyes as she lit two candles and placed them on the table.

Cuán gulped back the tears. "Why are you letting them do this to me, Ma? You always knew that I was different from the other children. You said that it made me special, and now you are punishing me for it."

Maeve picked up a cup and gripped the handle tightly. Tears streamed from her eyes as she turned to face Cuán. She understood how difficult life was for her.

People said that she was bewitched by the fairies and not of this world. But taking her from the forest was a decision that Maeve didn't regret. Not for one second. Even after everything that they had been through over the past few weeks. It had been a mistake to accept help from that nurse – she blamed herself for leaving Cuán alone with her.

Maeve shifted her gaze and looked into Cuán's yellow eyes. "Sit down, child," she instructed.

A clap of thunder boomed overhead. The kitchen was small and contained a table with two chairs which were positioned in front of the open fire. Cuán pulled one of the chairs closer to the fire. It scraped across the floor and made a screeching noise. Then she sat down and joined her hands together. It looked as if she were about to say her prayers.

Maeve pulled up a chair beside her and held her hands. "You are special, Cuán. You came into my life when I thought I would always be childless and alone. Then you turned up in the woods and gave me something to live for."

Cuán never doubted Ma's love, not even for a second. That's why she felt so confused by her actions now.

"Then why are you sending me away? Are you ashamed of me?"

Maeve sighed. "How could I ever be ashamed of you, my darling girl?"

Cuán buried her face in her hands and cried. She could not understand how Ma of all people could do this to her. Maybe that awful nurse was right – maybe she had broken Ma's resolve.

Cuán sobbed until her jaw ached. "I promise I won't go wandering at night again and I will play with the English girl Nancy every day. I can be normal like everyone else if you give me a chance!"

Maeve stood up and walked across the room with her hands on her ample hips. She stood and pondered. She needed to be honest with Cuán.

She walked back over and sat down again. Her face appeared ghostly in the waning light. Then she sighed.

"You can never be normal, Cuán. You have to accept that, we both do. I am sending you away not because I am ashamed of you but to keep you safe. People around here don't understand you – they never have. We need to discover what is causing you to go running off in the middle of the night. Maybe when the doctors test your two hearts we can find a clue that will lead us to your real family. Then we can finally get some answers."

Cuán gasped in amazement. Her mother's words cut to the bone.

"You are my real family, Ma – you always have been."

Cuán was devastated, although part of her was curious to find out who her original family were. She needed to know why they had abandoned her in the woods as a baby. Perhaps they would be able to explain why she had yellow eyes and changed into a wolf who ate the stars.

A sudden knock on the cottage door caused them both to jump.

165

Maeve ran over to the rain-streaked window and peered outside, although she could only see her own reflection staring back at her.

"Who on earth could that be at this time of night?"

Cuán rolled her eyes. "It's Nancy, Ma – you asked her to stay with me tonight."

"Oh, dear Lord, of course it is – the poor girl will get her death of cold out on a night like this."

Nancy had become a regular visitor to Cuán's home lately. Doctor Ford had suggested that Maeve should ask one of Cuán's friends to stay some of the nights. Since the nurse left unexpectedly, Maeve had been staying up to "keep watch" herself and it was taking its toll on her. She was utterly exhausted and Doctor Ford feared she would fall ill. Then she wouldn't be able to take care of Cuán at all. So tonight was Nancy's first turn to watch.

Cuán hated to think that she was a burden although she genuinely liked it when Nancy came to visit. On the first day that she called over, Doctor Ford had arranged for a photographer who worked for the *Echo* newspaper to come and take a photograph of the girls outside in the orchard. He thought that it might do Cuán good to have something to take to Dublin with her that would remind her of home.

Maeve opened the door and was relieved to see it was indeed Nancy standing there. But she was soaked to the bone.

Nancy was an odd girl. She didn't make friends easily. The village children didn't like her very much because she was English. She was an outsider much like Cuán.

This meant that they both understood what it felt like to be on the outside looking in.

Maeve grabbed Nancy by the arm. "Come in, girleen – it's a bad night out there." Then she held the front door partly open just long enough for the girl to step inside.

"The perfect night for a ghost story," Cuán muttered beneath her breath.

Maeve smiled at Cuán as she helped Nancy out of her blue overcoat. "Cuán, why don't you take Nancy to your bedroom. She can change into her nightdress and dry herself off in front of the fire. I'll bring you in a hot drink and a plate of my scones."

Despite Maeve's smile and cheerful words, Nancy could sense the tension between Cuán and her mother. Her friend's hands were trembling. Her eyes were bloodshot from crying. Common sense told her to make her excuses and leave but she was drawn towards Cuán like a child to a cream cake. She longed to be near her. Besides, her mother had told her that she would be doing an act of Christian duty by staying with Cuán that night and looking after her. In any case, in Nancy's eyes life was always one big adventure.

She followed Cuán along the cold, dark hallway and into the bedroom. There was a window which looked out on the orchard. Two leather armchairs, covered in scratch-marks, were positioned in front of the open fire. Nancy's mother had explained to her that sometimes Cuán was unwell and had seizures. She wondered if Cuán had scratched the furniture. Her mother had warned her that if anything happened to Cuán when she

167

was alone with her, she should run and fetch Maeve straight away.

The room was full of candles. They flickered in the dark, casting a ghostly light on everything. In the corner of the room was a cabinet full of religious statues. One of the statues was missing its right hand and had a strange look on its face. Under the candlelight it appeared to be grimacing. Beside the cabinet was a large wardrobe with silver handles. In the corner of the room was a dressing table with a cracked mirror. Beneath it was a purple velvet stool that had claws for feet.

The fireplace was opposite the bed. It was shaped like the open mouth of a lion. Large flames crackled and hissed as they devoured a log that had turned black, and gave off an occasional puff of smoke.

Nancy shivered as she stood in front of the fire and dried her hair with a towel Cuán had given her. Gradually the heat from the flames warmed her skin. She took her nightdress out of her overnight bag and changed into it. Putting on her blue dressing gown, she tied the cord and stepped into her green slippers.

They both settled into the leather armchairs in front of the roaring fire.

Cuán pressed her back against the leather chair, a feeling of dread rising like a wave in her stomach.

"Are you all right, Cuán?" Nancy asked. She was worried about her friend as there was a look of fear in her yellow eyes.

Cuán shifted in the chair and shook her head. "Ma is sending me away."

Nancy couldn't believe what she was hearing. "Why would she do such a thing?"

"Because I am broken!" Cuán cried, then she rubbed her nose with the back of her hand.

"Broken?" Nancy said, giggling nervously.

Cuán's eyes narrowed. "Can I tell you a secret?" she whispered.

"You can tell me anything, Cuán," Nancy replied.

Cuán needed Nancy to know that what she was about to say was serious and she needed to know that she could depend on her. "If you ever repeat what I tell you, I will be killed. Do you understand me?"

Nancy shuddered and her smile melted away. "Yes, I mean no, I don't understand, but you can trust me, Cuán."

A knock at the door interrupted them and Maeve walked in with a tray containing a plate of scones and two steaming cups of cocoa.

"Why the long faces?" she enquired as she put the tray down on the dressing table. She dragged the purple stool across the floor and placed it in front of the girls. Then she put the tray on it.

The tired woman sensed that she had interrupted something. She could not help but wonder if Cuán confided in Nancy and told her things that she wouldn't tell her. A pang of jealousy twisted in the pit of her stomach.

Nancy glanced at Cuán who looked away.

"We were just talking about school," Nancy lied. "I was telling Cuán that I hated mathematics."

Maeve yawned. She desperately needed sleep. And she knew that she had to take advantage of Nancy being there with Cuán.

"I am going to bed now, girls. I will be down the hallway if you need me, Nancy. Be sure to call me *at once* if Cuán shows any signs of . . . being unwell."

"I will," Nancy promised. "Don't worry."

The girls stared at Maeve, both of them willing her to go.

"All right then, I will leave you girls to it. Goodnight."

She went out and shut the door. They listened to the sound of her slippers receding along the hallway. Then they waited until her bedroom door shut with a bang.

Nancy stood up and walked over to Cuán. Then she sat down on the floor in front of her and held her hand.

"My dear Cuán, I promise that I will not tell your secret to anyone as long as I live."

Cuán looked into Nancy's large eyes and she knew that she could trust her. Right now she had to speak to someone about what she was going through or no-one would ever truly know what had happened to her.

Cuán's eyes were blinded by tears and her voice trembled as she spoke: "What I am about to tell you will be hard to understand – it will scare you more than you can imagine and once you have heard it you may never want to see me ever again."

Nancy swallowed hard, willing her fear to go away. "Whatever it is, I won't leave you, Cuán. We are friends."

"Don't say I didn't warn you and don't worry if you need to leave – it may become too much for you. But bear one thing in mind – if my story is frightening to listen to, just imagine what it is like for me to experience it."

"I am here for you, Cuán!" Nancy exclaimed. Although under the flickering candlelight, as she stared into Cuán's eyes, there was a part of her that wanted to run away and never see her strange friend again.

Chapter Twenty-five

The Monster in the Fog
1940

Günther didn't know how long he had been unconscious but he had to move fast. There would be swarms of people looking for him soon. They would want to punish him for bombing their homes and factories. The ringing in his ears made it impossible to hear anything. Even the sound of the birds singing in the trees was lost to him. Lying there, he looked down at his leg. A shard of metal protruded through his trousers and blood dripped onto the ground. He knew that his leg needed medical attention before infection set in. His head hurt – he raised his hand to it and when he took the hand away it was drenched in blood. It was bad but it could have been a lot worse. At least he was alive.

He looked around for clues as to where he was but could find nothing. He appeared to have landed in a field on the edge of a forest, but he realised that he could be anywhere. His military training told him that he needed to find cover away from the crash site.

Günther flinched when he noticed three figures moving towards him. He tried to move his leg and pain shot through his aching body like a bullet. He held his breath and shuddered violently. Then he screamed out in pain as the figures loomed over him. There were two boys and a girl. He seemed to recognise the girl and the younger boy somehow, but this did not seem possible. He took a deep breath and tried to speak but the smoke from the plane had filled his lungs. It inflated them like balloons while he coughed and spluttered.

The young girl knelt beside him. Then she placed her ear against his chest to hear his heartbeat. As she spoke, he realised that he could hear again.

"Blaise, we need something to bandage his leg and he has a wound on his head too that's bleeding badly."

Seeing the pilot injured pulled at Lottie's heartstrings. He made her think of her father and she knew that she had to help him, although her legs had turned to jelly and the only first aid she had ever administered was on dummies in the Brownies.

Albert didn't feel as brave as his sister. His lip quivered and he faltered.

"Lottie, I'm scared."

Lottie threw him an angry look. "Not now, Albert. Be brave!" she ordered, then she turned her attention back to the pilot. She had no time for Albert's babyish ways in such a crisis.

She peered into the pilot's hazel eyes and ran her

finger along the jagged scar above his eyebrow. Then she realised that she had seen him before. She inclined her head to get a closer look at him then she clasped her hands together in disbelief.

"It is *you*, isn't it? You're the pilot we saw in Manchester!"

Günther stared into her eyes. It was hard to believe that she was the same girl.

A plume of black smoke rose from the cockpit of the plane. Then a giant fireball hurtled through the air and almost hit a nearby pine tree.

"We need to get away from here and fast!" Blaise yelled. *"The plane is going to explode!"*

Blaise grabbed Günther by the arms and dragged him along the grass. The pilot was heavier than he looked and he screamed out in pain.

A safe distance away from the wreckage of the plane Blaise let Günther down on the grass. They all gazed back at the burning plane.

Blaise turned to Lottie. "I'll run back to my caravan – I'll bring Snowdrop to carry him away from here."

"Hurry, Blaise!" Lottie cried.

Adrenalin surged through Blaise's veins and propelled him forward. He knew every twist and turn of the forest and darted through the trees as swift as a fox.

He ran up the small rickety steps of the caravan. Snowdrop raised her head to see what the commotion was about. When he disappeared into the caravan she swished her tail and turned away.

Inside the caravan Blaise took his mother's journal from a secret drawer and shoved it into a pocket inside his waistcoat. He then took a white sheet to use as bandages and pushed it into a big cloth shoulder-bag, together with two big bottles of water.

He grabbed Snowdrop's harness and left, locking the door behind him.

"We are going to need your help, girl," he said to the docile creature as he put her harness on.

He leapt on her bare back and dug his heels into her sides. They galloped back through the forest, darting in and out of the trees like eagles through a cloudless sky until the smoke reached out to them. Blaise covered his mouth with his sleeve as the plane emerged like a monster in the smoke.

He couldn't see Lottie and the others as he plunged into the blanket of smoke.

The explosion was louder than anything Blaise had heard before. He watched helplessly as the green wing of the German bomber plane flew over his head. A tornado of soot swirled around him and the air was grey with ash.

"*Lottie!*" he screamed out, fearing that his friend was gone.

Chapter Twenty-six

Cuán
1920

The storm raged outside like a ferocious giant with a toothache. It rattled the doors and tapped on the windows. Cuán could feel herself being pulled away by an invisible force. Her name was whispered like a secret on the wind. There was a sour taste in her mouth. Her breath was shallow. Her skin prickled and her eyelids flickered. However, she refused to surrender. Nothing would stop her now. She waited patiently until midnight. She needed to make sure that Maeve was asleep. She didn't want anyone or anything to prevent her from what she was about to do.

As soon as the old grandfather clock in the room had chimed twelve times, Cuán reached over and gripped Nancy by the wrist.

"It's time now, Nancy. I need you to check that the window is locked. Take the key to the door now and put it in your pocket before we begin. If I become – ill – don't hesitate. Run out the door and lock it behind you. Do *not* open the door again no matter how much I beg you to. Do you understand me?"

Cuán looked beautiful, her black hair shining like silk under the flickering candlelight, but Nancy was frightened by her sudden movements and strange words. There was a hunger in her eyes and she was like a feral animal caught in a trap. Nancy felt as though danger lurked inside her. Fear swam through Nancy's veins. Her stomach curdled and her heart ached.

Nancy wrenched her hand from Cuán's grip. Instinct screamed at her to run away, Instead, she said, "No, Cuán, I won't lock you in. What if you have a seizure again and you need help? No – your ma told me that I must get her straight away if anything like that happens. I don't understand why you would want me to lock you in."

Nancy felt foolish for allowing herself to end up in such a predicament – with a girl she hardly knew anything about.

Cuán's pupils dilated as she stared hard at Nancy.

"Don't you see, Nancy? It's so that I don't escape."

"Escape? I have no idea what you mean. You're not making sense." Nancy's face drained of colour. Her fingers were splayed as she held onto the armchair.

Then, as Cuán blinked, Nancy saw something in her friend's eyes. It was not anger or fear but sadness. The kind of sadness you feel when your heart has been broken into a million pieces.

"Trust me, Nancy," Cuán pleaded.

She recognised the fear in Nancy's eyes. She had seen it before in the eyes of children from the village who said that she was evil. She imagined how much more terrified Nancy would be if she turned into a wolf right before her eyes. Although she would never willingly do that. But she felt powerless. No matter how hard she tried she could not prevent herself from changing into a wolf. It frightened her as much as it did everyone else. She had the scars on her body to prove it. What scared her most was the lack of control that she had over her mind and body – her biggest fear was that she would attack Maeve and others around her. Nancy was in great danger, staying with her all night long. But she had to tell someone her story before it was too late, someone she could trust.

Most of all she needed Nancy to guard her ring. Her instincts told her that the ring was powerful. She would tell Maeve that she had lost it. No-one would ever suspect Nancy of having it. Within a few days, Nancy would be home in England and not a soul would go looking for the ring there.

"What you are saying frightens me, Cuán," Nancy gasped. Her bones trembled beneath her skin.

"I need you to lock me in. I want you to be safe."

Nancy had heard enough. Her fear turned to anger, like a caterpillar turns into a butterfly within a cocoon. Blood rose in her body. Her pale cheeks flushed red. She slapped her hands against the chair, then stood up and marched towards the door in a determined manner.

"Safe from what?" she demanded, turning around. "I am going home to my mother. You are not making any sense, Cuán. Are you deliberately trying to terrify me? People were right about you. I should never have trusted you."

How had she allowed herself to become friends with Cuán? The room they were in felt smaller then. The candlelight didn't reach into the corners and she felt trapped.

She turned again and gripped the doorknob.

Cuán rushed to Nancy and reached out. She dug her fingernails into her shoulder blades and pulled her back.

Nancy swung around and faced her.

"Wait, Nancy! I will explain everything to you. But I need you to trust me. You are all that I have." Cuán covered her eyes with her hands as she began to cry. Her shoulders heaved up and down as she sobbed.

Nancy bit her lip hard, piercing the surface. Her lip bled. It tasted of iron. She licked it away with her tongue. She had gone too far. She couldn't understand what was happening but she couldn't leave Cuán on her own. Not when she needed her most.

She moved back towards the bedroom door. Then she took the key from the lock and placed it in the pocket of her dressing gown. Her legs trembled as she approached the window. Branches scratched at the glass, like spirits waiting to get in. Nancy didn't know whether she should be more afraid of what was outside of the room or of what was inside.

She tugged at the heavy window and it wouldn't

budge one bit. When she was satisfied that the catch was secure, she returned to where Cuán was again sitting at the fireside.

"There," she said. "I have done as you asked. And I will listen to what you have to say." She placed her hand on Cuán's shoulder and felt her quiver like a leaf about to fall from a tree. Then she went and sat in the armchair opposite.

Fear danced up Cuán's spine. The familiar tingle beneath her skin curled around her ribcage. Beneath her heart and into her lungs. She resisted the urge to scratch her eye sockets. Not tonight, she told herself. But she knew she had no say in the matter. Once her wolf heart gained control she was powerless. Yet she needed to push the feelings away. At least until she had explained everything to Nancy, the girl with flushed cheeks and soft yellow hair the colour of buttercups. The girl she called her friend. She blinked away her tears and told her story while there was still time.

"I don't know where I was born or where I came from, Nancy. But I suspect that I am not of this world."

Cuán stared into Nancy's eyes. They were wide open with fear and trepidation.

The room was quiet apart from the crackling logs on the fire and the howling wind outside that was trying to get in. Cuán sat on the edge of the armchair and peered into the fire. Shadows shifted across the walls.

"Sometimes I have dreams, Nancy – dreams that I am trapped in another world."

"They are just dreams, Cuán! We all have them. Father

told me that dreams don't mean anything."

Cuán smiled. "I thought that at first, but the dreams are as real to me as you are now. In my dreams I am a prisoner. I wake up in a box made of glass – it is suspended in the air – above my head is a sky full of stars. I eat the stars to survive."

Nancy shifted uneasily in her seat. "When did you start having these dreams, Cuán?"

"I have always had them. But they've become more vivid since I went wandering at night-time. They are trying to tell me something, Nancy. It is like a puzzle and I am the missing piece. You see, Ma found me in the woods when I was a baby. My eyes were fused shut and I was accompanied by a beautiful wolf."

So the rumours were true, thought Nancy in astonishment. Cuán wasn't the child of Maeve's cousin. And she had been found in the forest with a wolf.

"So you don't know where you came from then?"

Cuán shook her head.

Nancy couldn't imagine what that would be like. She thought of her own mother and how much she looked like her and she felt sorry for Cuán who didn't know who her family were or where she came from.

"When Ma found me I had this tied around my neck – it is the only clue that I have, Nancy."

Cuán reached within her nightgown. Tied to a string was a shiny gold ring. She pulled the piece of string over her head and handed the ring to her friend.

Nancy had never seen anything like it before. "Cuán, it's beautiful!" she said as she studied it. It was elaborately decorated with golden leaves and in the centre was the head of a wolf with amber eyes.

"I need you to have it, Nancy." Cuán turned away to hide her tears.

"No, Cuán, I couldn't possibly!"

Cuán needed to be brave – it was important to her that Nancy did this one thing for her – if she faltered now the ring could be taken from her and it would be lost forever.

"Guard it for me, Nancy. It is precious to me and I feel it has special powers that have always protected me. Ma is sending me away tomorrow to Dublin. I will be locked in a hospital while they experiment on me and try to find out why I am the way I am. The ring will be taken from me. I know that I can trust you to take care of it."

Nancy understood. She nodded and put the string around her own neck.

"You see, Nancy, the doctor has discovered that I have two heartbeats – two hearts."

"But that's impossible!" Nancy gasped.

"Nancy, if you don't believe me, go straight to Ma now and ask her. She will tell you it is true. That is why they want to experiment on me."

Nancy gazed at her, her thoughts whirling.

"I know that one of those hearts is the heart of a wolf," said Cuán.

Nancy was again wondering if her friend had gone insane. Yet Cuán was speaking calmly and convincingly.

"I know that I am a wolf, Nancy. I change into a wolf sometimes."

Nancy always suspected that there was something

different about Cuán – it was the reason that she was drawn to her. Was what she was saying possible?

"What does it feel like to change into a wolf, Cuán?" she asked, needing to hear more.

Cuán sat up straight in the chair and closed her eyes. "Intense pain fills my entire body, my skin itches and feels tight, my stomach twists and I feel as though I need to get sick. At some stage, I go unconscious. My human heart stops beating and my wolf heart takes over. Afterwards, I am left like this."

Cuán lifted up her top and showed Nancy her scars.

Nancy covered her mouth to stifle a scream "Cuán, they are awful! Who did that to you?"

"I did it to myself, Nancy, when I was a wolf. My claws are so sharp and I feel an urge to scratch myself." Cuán was ashamed to admit such a thing and she hoped that Nancy didn't judge her – it was out of her control.

Whether or not Cuán could truly turn into a wolf, thought Nancy, it was clear that she had the power to hurt her at any time. She had to ask one final question. It was the one that she feared the answer to most.

"Would you hurt me, Cuán?"

Cuán's black hair framed her pale face. Her amber eyes glistened with tears as she spoke truthfully to her friend. "I honestly don't know, Nancy." She bit down on her bottom lip and buried her head in her hands. She was overcome with shame.

"But we are friends. You asked me to stay here tonight. And now you are telling me that you could change into a wolf and kill me!"

183

"Yes, that is exactly what I am saying, Nancy. That is why I told you to lock me in. You must understand I have no control over my actions, I am powerless."

Cuán knew that what she was saying sounded terrible.

Tears sprang from Nancy's green eyes. "So you want me to risk my life to hear your story?"

"Yes, I suppose I do."

Nancy sat down on the old armchair. Every bit of common sense she had told her to open the door right away and run home, but she found she couldn't move. There was honesty in Cuán's voice and Nancy felt compelled to listen to her.

"There is something else I need you to know. Sometimes I see people."

"People?"

"They are more like creatures, I suppose. Deathly creatures with red eyes. They follow me everywhere I go. They whisper my name. I heard them calling me tonight before you first arrived."

Nancy was staring at her in horror. "Cuán, don't say such things – you're scaring me." Then she strained to listen but all she could hear was the tick of the grandfather clock and the scratching of the branches against the window.

Cuán sighed. "I'm sorry to have to frighten you, Nancy. But please believe me, it's important that I tell you everything."

"Why?"

"In case they come here again tonight."

Nancy shuddered. It seemed as though she had got herself into something far more dangerous than she could have ever imagined.

"I need to sleep now, Nancy. Will you stay awake and guard me?"

Nancy nodded. In any case, there was no way that she could have slept after what Cuán had just told her. Her rational mind was still rejecting what Cuán had told her, but her instincts told her it was all true. She felt terrified as Cuán blew out the candles and they both crawled into bed but at opposite ends.

The storm had died down now but it was still raining hard. Nancy could hear Cuán's laboured breathing and guessed that she was asleep. She lay there in the darkness, afraid to move in case she triggered something in Cuán, something that might turn her into a wolf.

At some point during the night, Nancy's eyelids grew heavy and she fell asleep. She was woken moments later by the sound of breaking glass.

"*Cuán!*" Nancy cried.

She jumped out of bed and, as her eyes adjusted to the murky darkness, she looked out the window and beneath the stars she saw a beautiful grey wolf running as if for its life.

Chapter Twenty-seven

The Veil Between Two Worlds
1940

"*Lottie!*" Blaise yelled again.

He was blinded by the dense smoke that surrounded him. The heat from the flames burnt his skin. He couldn't see Lottie and Albert anywhere. What if they are dead? I should have stayed with them, he thought. I should never have left them alone. It shocked him just how much he cared for two children who he had only just met.

A shrill sound reached out to him like a hand through the darkness.

"*We are here, Blaise, hurry!*" Lottie's voice was like a light at the end of a dark tunnel.

Blaise was overcome with relief.

"*I'm on my way, Lottie!*"

Blaise covered his mouth with his hands to prevent the smoke from entering his lungs. He followed the sound of Lottie's calls, running as fast as he could. There wasn't a moment to spare. When he got there he saw the German fighter pilot lying on his side, gasping for air. He was still bleeding from the wound on his forehead as well as the shard of metal entrenched in his leg. Lottie was sitting on a rock with her legs crossed. Albert sat beside her, tears streaming from his eyes. His blonde hair was covered in soot. Lottie looked as though she was in a trance. Blaise knew that she was shell-shocked. It happened to soldiers at war. The bombing, the plane crash and seeing the pilot injured had brought the horrors of the war she had experienced in Manchester back to her.

Blaise jumped off Snowdrop and knelt in front of Lottie. Glancing at Albert, he began to wonder if it was the wrong decision to take the boy along with them. He was only a young child after all.

He pulled Albert into his arms and patted his back. "It's all right, Albert. I am here now and I am going to take care of you both."

Albert smiled through his tears and nodded. He knew that everything would be all right as long as Blaise was taking care of them.

Then Blaise turned his attention back to Lottie. Her long red hair was the colour of the flames that engulfed the plane. Her eyes were bloodshot. Blaise did what his mother always did to him whenever he had a nightmare. He held Lottie's face in his hands, gazed into her eyes and smiled. A smile trembled on her lips.

"You are a brave girl, Lottie Hope, a very brave girl!" he whispered into her ear.

The need to protect Lottie and Albert was overwhelming and primitive. He cared for them as though they were his family. There was something about Lottie that reminded Blaise of his own mother. She was strong. Stronger than she realised.

It was as though Blaise had activated a switch inside of Lottie. She blinked her eyes and looked around. And within moments she was back to herself again. She pushed Blaise away as though he were a bumblebee buzzing around a jam sandwich. Then she leapt to her feet.

"We need to move the pilot this instant, Blaise – he can't breathe with this smoke! And the plane could explode again at any moment!"

"That's the girl, Lottie!" Blaise said.

Blaise knew that Lottie was right. They had no time to lose. He unslung the bag from his shoulder and handed it to Lottie. Then he moved towards the pilot, placed his hands under his shoulders and began to pull him further away from the wreckage of the plane. He was heavier than he looked and it took all of Blaise's strength to move him. When they reached a place where the air was less stifling, Blaise laid him down gently on the grass. Then he turned to Lottie.

"Pass me the water and the sheet in that bag, Lottie. We need to get the metal out of his leg and clean his wounds."

Lottie did as she was told. She handed Blaise the sheet and watched as he tore it into strips for bandages. It reminded her of the way her mother would tear up old rags to curl her hair. Every Saturday night before the war, Lottie and Albert would have a sausage with bread and butter for their tea. Then Mother would prepare a bath for them in front of the open fire. Albert would play with his wooden train set, positioning it on the worn old rug. The wireless would be on in the parlour, playing her mother's favourite song "We'll Meet Again" sung by Vera Lynn. Father would be smoking a pipe and reading the newspaper at the kitchen table. And her mother would spend ages singing songs and doing Lottie's hair. She'd wind old rags around the flame-red strands and, as if by magic, the following morning she would have a head full of curls. As Lottie closed her eyes she could almost reach out and touch her mother's face. She could hear her mother laughing and singing merrily. And she could smell the smoke from her father's tobacco and hear the rustle of the newspaper as he turned the pages. Thinking of happy times before the war made her feel sad.

Lottie bit her lip. She shook her head and turned her attention back to the pilot. She wasn't so sure that Blaise was doing the right thing. She guessed that the injured boy needed more than a bandage made from rags.

"Shouldn't we get a doctor, Blaise?" she said.

Blaise knew that they should. Without medical treatment the pilot might not survive.

"*No doctor!*" the young pilot screamed. His entire body trembled and his face turned a deathly shade of grey.

Lottie knelt down beside him and held his hand. He

was like a young child who was afraid of monsters hiding beneath his bed.

"What's your name?" she asked gently.

"Günter," he gasped.

"My name is Lottie," she said, trying to lessen his fears. "This is Blaise – and that is my young brother Albert."

Günther nodded. He was unable to speak with pain.

"How old are you?" asked Blaise.

"Sixteen."

Blaise shook his head in amazement. He himself was almost as old as this young pilot who had been sent out alone to bomb cities and probably die.

"Now, Günther," he said, "you have lost a lot of blood. Perhaps too much. And you need to have your leg treated properly. We need to go to the hospital."

Günther grabbed Blaise by the arm and pleaded with him. "Please, no hospitals! They will punish me for bombing your cities! I would have rather died with my plane than be a prisoner of war."

"But, Günther," said Lottie, "this isn't England. Don't you realise? This is Ireland – the south of Ireland – and Ireland is neutral in the war. Germany hasn't been bombing here."

Günther's eyes widened in disbelief.

"It's true," said Blaise. "This is County Wexford on the south-east corner of Ireland."

"Oh," said Günther faintly, "I thought I was over Wales . . . I must have flown too far west . . ." He stopped, grimacing in pain.

"So, you see, we can take you to a hospital," said Lottie.

"*No!*" Günther exclaimed, as strongly as before. "They will hand me over to the English!"

Lottie looked at Blaise. Perhaps the pilot had the right to choose his fate?

Blaise shrugged. "Very well. We will do the best we can," he said and bent again over Günther's leg. "You speak very good English," he said, to distract Günther as he pulled the piece of metal from his leg.

Günther screamed out in agonising pain.

Lottie looked away. She had a delicate stomach and seeing all the blood was too much for her.

"What part of Germany are you from?" Blaise enquired as he washed the wound.

A small smile curled like a comma at the edge of the pilot's lips. "I am from Hamburg."

Blaise nodded in recognition. "My parents visited Hamburg once before I was born." He used one of the strips of sheet to bandage Günther's wound.

He glanced back at Lottie – she looked unwell. The last thing he needed was for her to faint. Then he would have two patients to care for.

"Are you all right, Lottie?"

"I'm sorry … I feel a bit sick … it's the blood …"

"I'm so sorry, Lottie," said Blaise. "You're an evacuee – you came here fleeing from war and bombings. And now this!"

"Yes, I feel I might as well have stayed at home!" Lottie blurted out. "I miss home despite the Blitz. I miss my mother."

Blaise knew what it was like to lose those you love. He missed his parents dreadfully. There wasn't a day went by that he didn't long to see them again. All he had now were memories of them.

"Home is where your friends are, Lottie, and we are friends." He poured water on the gash on Günther's head to clean it and wound a bandage around his head.

Lottie smiled at Blaise despite herself. He was always so optimistic. She envied him. She wished with all her heart that she could find a way to carve the good out of the bad and to remain hopeful like Blaise did. However, some situations were just too awful.

She knew that she needed to pull herself together. She turned her attention back to Günther. He looked slightly better now that his leg was bandaged.

"If you won't go to the hospital then we will need to hide you some place where you will never be found," she said.

"But where, Lottie?" Albert asked.

Blaise stood up. "I know the perfect place. Somewhere no-one will ever find you, Günther. It's called Kilbree Abbey."

"Kilbree Abbey with the Tower of Wolves!" Albert blurted out incredulously. "But that place is cursed, Blaise! You said so yourself."

"Yes. But don't you see, Albert? That's what makes it the perfect place to hide Günther. No-one ever goes there. They're terrified of the ancient curse."

Albert darted over to Lottie, threw his arms around her waist and hung on tight.

"Don't be afraid, Albert!" she said. "I'll take care of you."

She gently removed his arms and, grabbing Blaise's hand, pulled him out of the earshot of the wounded pilot.

"Albert is right, Blaise!" she hissed. "From what you told us, Kilbree Abbey is the entrance to Wolf Land. Which means it is full of werewolves. They would smell Günther's blood a mile off."

"The portal to Wolf Land is closed, Lottie. The werewolves can't get to us."

"But the portal could open at any time!"

"Look, we don't have a choice, Lottie. This entire place will be crawling with people in no time because of the crash!"

"I think that I would rather face an angry mob of people than ravenous werewolves."

"Me too!" said Albert.

"*Lottie!*" came a weak voice.

They all went back to the Günther.

"Please, Lottie, let Blaise hide me in that abbey. It is my only chance. I do not want to be captured – or even killed by the people."

Lottie stared into Günther's eyes. She thought back to the first time that she saw him back home in Manchester. How his plane flew so close above her head. He could have dropped a bomb on her and Albert. They would have been killed instantly. However, he chose not to. He did the right thing. She owed it to him to at least try to save him from being captured. Although Ireland was neutral in the war he would be sent back to England and end up in a British prison camp. And he was right – if the people of Kilbree found him, they might well kill him, thinking he had tried to bomb them.

Lottie held Albert's hand tightly. "What are we waiting for? Let's go."

"Thank you, Lottie," said Günther. "I will never forget what you have done for me."

"Save your thanks until we get there, Günther," said Lottie with a sigh.

Blaise recalled his mother describing the portal leading into Wolf Land to him. It was soon after they had arrived in Kilbree and they were walking back from the village at the time. She called it the Portal of Starlight.

"What exactly is a portal, Mother?" Blaise asked.

"Well, the word 'portal' means a doorway or entrance. But this portal is more complicated than a simple entrance. It generally remains closed and is then invisible and unreachable, but then it opens for a while, at times which seem random. It may be to do with some complicated alignments of the stars. Because of this, few have crossed between the two worlds over the centuries . . . until the entry into Wolf Land of the evil werewolf Deathhound."

"Deathhound! A terrible name!" said Blaise, shocked.

"And well deserved," said Talia. "You see, once upon a time Wolf Land was a good place to live in. It was much like Ireland but, of course, it was populated by werewolves. They lived much as humans did in medieval times – building towns and villages, trading, farming, fishing and hunting. There was sunlight, animals and birds. And it was peaceful except for occasional skirmishes between the different provinces. Then everything changed. Deathhound discovered through magic how to control the portal and carried his evil into Wolf Land."

Talia halted and closed her eyes. She looked heartbroken.

"And you say the day will come when I have to cross over into that terrifying world, Mother?"

Her eyes opened. She looked at him and sighed. "That is what the crystal ball predicts, son. I wish it were otherwise but that is your destiny. So I must tell you all I can." A frown appeared on her brow. "The portal shimmers like a large mirror, Blaise. It is full of stars. Once you cross through and enter Wolf Land you will know that you're in another world. You will not hear birdsong and night-time is eternal. The sky seems so much closer than it does on Earth. Millions of stars twist and turn against the black abyss. Like beautiful diamonds, they fall from the sky. There are two moons – a egg-shaped blue moon and the moon that we see from Earth – and they seem so close. You will see the ancient abbey and the Tower of Wolves. Over to the right will be the scriptorium. That is where the monks used to work on copying and illustrating their manuscripts."

Blaise looked at her in surprise. "But the abbey and the Tower of Wolves are in this world, Mother?"

"Yes, Blaise. Those things on the border of the two

worlds appear in both, like a mirror image. However, beyond the settlement is a town and that is nothing like a town in Ireland. That is where the evil werewolves live. You will have to tread carefully there."

"You're frightening me, Mother."

"I'm sorry, son. But I need you to remember everything I have just told you. It will be important to you in the future. Do you understand me?"

"Yes, Mother."

"And remember this important fact, Blaise: I was told by those from Wolf Land that when the portal opens it only stays open for roughly twenty-four hours in Earth time – they couldn't measure the time precisely because there is no division of day and night in Wolf Land and no clocks. Remember that, my son."

Blaise would never forget the determined look in his mother's eyes.

"*Listen!*" said Albert.

They heard the sound of voices in the distance.

"They're coming this way!" said Blaise. "We have to move fast. Follow me!"

Lottie turned and looked at her little brother. He was a pitiful sight. His face was puffy and tears streamed from his eyes. His entire body was covered in soot. He fell into her arms and sobbed.

"I'm scared, Lottie!" Albert cried. "I can't go with you to Wolf Land. I'm not brave after all!"

Lottie hugged him and buried her nose in his soft blonde hair, which smelt of smoke.

"You'll be brave when you need to be, little man," Blaise said. "Just you wait and see." He placed his hand on Lottie's arm. "We need to go now, Lottie. Before people come – goodness knows what they might do to Günther."

Albert lifted his head from his sister's shoulder and wiped his eyes with the back of his hand.

"Albert, you hold Snowdrop steady," said Blaise. "Just hold the reins like this and stroke her nose." He felt that distracting the little boy might help.

Albert happily stepped up to the horse and took the reins.

Lottie and Blaise hauled Günther to his feet. Then Blaise made a stirrup of his hands and Günther put the foot of his good leg into it. With a supreme and painful effort from Günther they managed to get him onto Snowdrop's back. Blaise swung Albert onto the horse behind him.

Blaise led them on through the forest. There was an eerie silence. It felt as though they were in an old abandoned graveyard. There were no birds or animals to be seen anywhere. Lottie got the strangest feeling. It felt as though she were being watched. She turned her head and shuddered when she saw a pair of red eyes peering at them through the trees. Lottie was about to tell Blaise but when she looked back the eyes had gone. It must be my imagination playing tricks on me, she thought.

"How far away is the Tower of Wolves, Blaise?" she asked.

Blaise could sense her trepidation. And he knew why.

Something was following them. Something with eyes that burned like coal. Blaise had seen it earlier but he hadn't wanted to alarm Lottie and Albert. He needed them to remain calm.

But Blaise realised that if an otherworldly creature was roaming around the forest then the portal to Wolf Land must have opened again.

Chapter Twenty-eight

The Sorrow Bird

"We're nearly there, Lottie. We'll see the Tower of Wolves once we emerge from the forest."

Lottie heard a rustling in the trees and the snap of a branch. She didn't dare look back and edged closer to Blaise. So close that she could hear him breathing. Instinct told her that she could trust Blaise and that he would protect them no matter what happened. Truly she did. However, there was something out there in the forest. It was following them and watching their every move. Could it be one of those Thought Monsters Blaise told them about? And then there was the curse that was put on anyone who crossed the gateway into the abbey. Did she really want to bring a curse on herself and her brother? They already had enough bad luck in their lives with the war. They didn't need any more.

In fact, the closer that they got to the ancient

settlement and the Tower of Wolves the less Lottie wanted to go there. She felt as though they were being led to their deaths. The more she thought about it the more she wondered if a teenage boy only a couple of years older than herself was someone that they could rely on? A hard lump formed in her throat as she followed Blaise.

Blaise knew that he should tell Lottie everything. It wasn't fair to keep things from her. But he didn't want her to run away again as she had done earlier. However, after a while, he beckoned to her to step up beside him.

"What is it, Blaise?" Lottie knew by the look on his face that it wasn't good news.

"I need to tell you more about Wolf Land. As I told you, it's a very dangerous place, Lottie. Deathhound will stop at nothing to kill anyone who enters. People have disappeared over the years – people who stumbled upon the portal by accident. And then there are the missing children."

"Do you mean Cuán?" Albert enquired.

Blaise hadn't realised that the little boy could hear him. He forced a smile as he looked at Albert. He hoped he wouldn't be too frightened.

"Yes – Cuán," he said. "But there were others too."

Lottie hunched her shoulders. The muscles in her neck tensed as she tugged at Blaise's waistcoat and whispered into his ear. "I'm not sure that we should go there, Blaise."

"We must – it's the only place where we can hide Günther from the villagers." He didn't mention that the portal must be open and that this might be their only chance of getting through it. Time enough for that when they arrived there.

Lottie frowned but she realised that it was too late to turn back. She didn't have a clue where they were and she didn't fancy her chances of being alone in the forest with a werewolf.

As they emerged from the mouth of the forest, the sky turned pink like candyfloss. Clouds floated across the sky and turned it purple like a bruise. It looked as though there was a storm brewing. Lottie could not understand it as it had been sunny moments earlier.

"There!" said Blaise. "The Tower of Wolves."

The ancient crumbling round tower rose up from behind the abbey walls. It was built of stone. It looked frightening. It looked as though it could be haunted by ghosts and inhabited by witches. Lottie imagined werewolves surrounding the tower in packs while the people hid inside. She wondered how long they could have stayed in the tower. Even if they had food supplies with them, they would have had to leave it eventually.

They approached the granite arches that marked the gateway.

Then Lottie noticed something moving from the corner of her eye. She looked in the direction of a large oak tree. On its thick, outstretched branches sat a lone magpie. Lottie recalled the magpie that she saw at the train station when they were being evacuated. She recalled the words that the old woman had whispered into her ear. *"One for sorrow."*

Then the bird flew past her and she swung around just as Albert cried, "It's gone! Like magic. It flew into *that!* Then it just vanished."

A large square-shaped shimmering mirror of stars had appeared in the gateway in front of them.

"Where did the bird go to, Blaise?" Albert enquired, his large eyes open like whirlpools.

"To its death," Blaise replied.

"And what is *that*?" Albert asked.

"That is the Portal of Starlight."

He stepped forward and placed his hand into the shimmering starlight. His hand disappeared from sight just as the bird had moments earlier. Tears streamed down his face as he pulled his hand back. He knew that Cuán was on the other side.

"It's just as Mother said it would be," he said.

Somehow, Lottie didn't feel scared any more. She knew that they had to enter.

Chapter Twenty-nine

The Mirror Made of Stars

"We need to cross now," said Blaise. "In case the portal shuts again. This could be our only chance."

"What's happening?" Günther said. "I don't understand."

Blaise looked up at Günther, slumped on Snowdrop's back. How could he possibly explain to him? He tried to state it simply.

"Günther, this is where you have to make a choice. And quickly. We have to go through this portal which leads into a dangerous world called Wolf Land inhabited by werewolves. And we have to go now, immediately. There are people on the other side depending on us. But, you see, we never intended to take you there. We meant to hide you in the abbey but, as you see, now we can't. The entrance is blocked by this portal." He swung Albert down from the horse. "So, Günther, either you let Snowdrop take you back to my caravan where you will have to cope alone, or you come with us into Wolf Land – where we may not survive."

Albert was looking up at him, white-faced, the realisation that Wolf Land was truly a dangerous place hitting him as suddenly as a bolt of lightning on a sunny day. Blaise was sorry to be so blunt but he felt he had to make the situation clear to Günther.

"But how can he manage alone?" said Lottie. "He's very ill. What if he gets a fever? He could die. And what if the villagers find him? Who knows what they might do?"

"It's a tough choice, Lottie," said Blaise grimly. "That's why only Günther can make it for himself."

"I don't understand, Blaise!" Günther cried. Then he gasped as a searing pain shot through his entire body. Beads of perspiration lined his forehead. He didn't understand what Blaise was saying about another world. He must be mistaken. He put it down to the language barrier and his fever. But as he stared at the shimmering mirror of starlight that had appeared right before his eyes, he wondered if Blaise was some sort of magician or wizard. He had never seen such a thing before. He felt as though he was staring into the reflection of a sky full of stars in a river.

This is no time for questions, he said to himself. He had no choice but to trust Blaise and the boy and girl. They were his only hope.

"I will go with you," he said, "whatever the dangers."

"So be it," said Blaise. "Lottie, help me to get Günther off the horse."

"Surely he would be more comfortable on

horseback?" she said.

"No – we can't take Snowdrop with us. It is too dangerous. She would be eaten alive by werewolves. In any case, she won't survive in Wolf Land. No animals can live there since Deathhound's curse."

"I am not leaving Snowdrop here! She's my friend!" Albert cried. Then his nuzzled his cheek against the horse's nose.

"Hey, don't worry, Albert," Blaise said gently. "Snowdrop knows her way home from here. Don't you, girl?"

He patted the horse three times on the back. She nodded her nose and raised her head. It was as though she understood every word Blaise said. Then she swished her tail and galloped off in the direction they had come. The children watched until they could see her no more.

Albert wiped his snotty nose on his sleeve.

Lottie smiled at Blaise. He really cared about Albert. He was more than a friend, he was like a brother. He was kind and thoughtful and he had a special way with animals too.

"Lead on, Lottie," said Blaise. "I feel that it is open because you are here. It never opened for me."

"No! I don't want to cross the portal alone." Lottie trembled as she spoke.

Blaise nodded. The silver earrings he wore jangled. His dark eyes flashed and he moved like a cat towards Lottie and Albert.

"Neither do I, Lottie. Since mother died I learnt to fend for myself. Without survival skills I wouldn't last a night alone in the forest. I've got used to doing everything alone. Only this time I don't have to. I have you now."

"We should hold hands and enter Wolf Land together," Lottie said. "Whatever awaits us we will face it as a team."

She reached out her hand to Blaise who took it. Then he in turn reached out for Albert who took Günther's hand.

"Are we like an army then?" Albert asked.

Lottie frowned. She did hope that they would not be going to battle. "Sort of," she said.

"Whatever you want to call us, we will be stronger together." Blaise squeezed Lottie's hand.

And they entered the Portal of Starlight side by side. It glistened like a million stars. It felt cool on their skin. Then it turned warm. It reminded Lottie of being in a warm bath. The whooshing sound of shooting stars whizzed past their ears and they each felt weightless. It was as though they were floating through time and space. They held each other's hands tightly and did not let go as brightly coloured lights flashed before their eyes. Although it could only have taken a few seconds to cross the portal, it felt like a lifetime.

Then it was all over and they fell onto stony ground at the other side of the portal, inside the abbey walls.

Lottie screamed. Blaise scrambled towards her and placed his hand over her mouth. "Hush, Lottie, we don't want to attract attention." Then, removing his hand, he looked about, astonished at what he saw.

Chapter Thirty

A World of Wolves

The sun was extinguished like a candle whose wick had burnt low. The sky appeared to be very close above their heads. It was blanketed in glistening stars which shimmered and lit up the sky. Two large moons shone down on them. One was closer to them. It was as blue as the ocean and egg-shaped. The other moon was pale in comparison. This moon was the one visible from Earth.

They were surrounded by trees that were bent like hooks. But they weren't ordinary trees. They appeared to be made from bone. They were smooth, alabaster-white.

"Lottie, look!" Albert pointed at the lifeless body of the small magpie that only minutes earlier had flown through the portal.

"Birds can't survive in Wolf Land, Albert," said Blaise. "Nor animals, as I told you. That's why we couldn't take Snowdrop."

Albert nodded. He felt sorry for the small black-and-white bird. He dug a little hole in the ground and buried the magpie in a small grave. He placed stones over the tiny grave as a marker.

Lottie turned towards the cobbled path and walked towards the ancient crumbling Tower of Wolves. A large wall surrounded the tower, which could only be accessed through an iron gate. The gate had the fierce face of a wolf engraved on it. The tower looked like the tower in the real world, although in the darkness it appeared more menacing. It was its mirror image. It looked like the type of place that could be haunted by ghosts. Perhaps it's a witch's lair, Lottie thought.

Then she looked down at the ring her mother had given her. The amber eyes on the wolf were glowing brightly. Suddenly beams of rainbow-coloured light were projected up into the air.

Lottie's eyelids snapped shut and she froze. She was suddenly in a trance.

"Lottie! The ring! Take it off!" Blaise cried.

Lottie could hear Blaise calling to her through the darkness, but could not see him. She was in another place. She was in a medieval-looking town, inhabited by werewolves. It consisted of rows of wooden houses that jutted out above meandering canals. There was a Town Hall and a bell tower. There was a castle in the distance. The canals weaved their way past bustling streets and were occupied by long, narrow boats that transported boxes of fine linen and goods to the landing slip in the centre of the town. It was market day and the town was full of people.

Then the scene shifted and Lottie saw a terrifying image. There were glass cages hung from bone trees. They were on the edge of a dark menacing forest, the kind her mother warned her never to enter. Inside the cages were children. She recognised one of the children straight away: it was Cuán, the girl from the photograph, her mother's friend. Then another image flashed before her eyes. It was Cuán again. Only this time she wasn't in the glass cage. She was in a dense, dark forest and a wolf-like creature with glowing red eyes was chasing her. It was the most terrifying creature Lottie had ever seen. It ran upright, like a man. Its entire body was covered in mangled fur. Silver battle scars lined its flesh. It breathed fire and sharp teeth like blades hung from blood-red gums. Its claws were as sharp as needles and it was at least ten feet high. Its body was powerful and muscular. Unlike normal wolves, it did not possess a tail.

Lottie screamed and fell to the ground. She thrashed about, kicking her legs. Strands of her long red hair blew around her face. She was covered in sweat. Goosebumps erupted like molehills on her skin. It was as though she had a fever.

"What's wrong with her?" Albert cried. He had never seen his sister in such a terrible state before and he was petrified. He hoped that she would not die like the magpie.

Lottie clawed at her eyes. The horrors that she was seeing in Wolf Land were too much to bear.

"Help me, Blaise!" she gurgled, then her jaw locked and she was unable to get more words out.

"Lottie, the ring is affecting you!" Blaise called as he tried to grab her hand. *"We must get it off now!"*

Blaise had recognised the ring straight away. He had an identical one himself that belonged to his mother. And, besides, there was the one in the photograph which Lottie hadn't seemed to notice. He guessed that crossing the portal into Wolf Land had activated something ancient and powerful within the ring.

He gripped Lottie's finger and pulled the ring off. The beams of rainbow-coloured light disappeared immediately.

Suddenly Lottie found herself lying on a bed of stones. She turned her head towards the shimmering portal. The entrance from her world to Wolf Land. Thousands of stars looked down on her like eyes from the sky.

Lottie reached out towards Blaise. Then she threw her arms around his neck and sobbed. Everything he'd told her was true. She should have trusted him all along.

"Blaise, I was in a terrifying place! I saw children in glass cages. There were other things too, terrible things. And packs of snarling werewolves. One of them was the most terrifying of all. It must have been Deathhound. He was a hideous creature. He was chasing Cuán through a deep, dark forest. Evil lurked around every corner."

Blaise cupped her face in his hands. She was worn out. Black rings like half-moons appeared under her eyes and her cheeks were stained with tears.

"That vision is the same as one that appeared in my mother's crystal ball, Lottie. She showed it to me."

His mind raced as he handed the ring back to Lottie.

"This ring, Lottie, where did you get it?"

"My mother gave it to me. She said it had belonged to a friend."

Suddenly everything was starting to make sense to Blaise.

"This is Cuán's ring, Lottie. She was wearing it in the photograph. The one with your mother in it. Didn't you notice? She must have given her Wolf Ring to your mother."

Lottie blinked back her tears. It was another secret that her mother had kept from her.

"But why didn't she say so? Surely she would have?"

Blaise shook his head. "Not if someone who was in great danger swore her to secrecy."

Lottie clutched Blaise's arm. "Blaise, this Wolf Land is full of horrors. I saw it with my own eyes! We should go back!"

"Don't you see, Lottie?" Blaise said urgently. "It's a sign. I have crossed the arched gateway and visited the settlement a thousand times. Yet I have seen nothing there. The portal was closed. I was beginning to lose faith. What you've just told me about the glass cages, the children and Deathhound – those are the things that my mother saw too. They need our help, Lottie. We have been chosen to save them. They are close by. I can feel it. We can't turn back now. It might be their only chance to escape."

Instinctively Lottie knew this was true. She released Blaise's arm and turned away.

Standing in front of the round tower, she heard the unmistakable sound of someone screaming in the darkness. She hoped that it was her imagination playing tricks on her. She flinched as she imagined the bones of thousands of wolves buried beneath their feet.

The temperature suddenly plummeted and Lottie looked up at the sky. It was as black as coal. There were no stars to be seen now. They had all disappeared. But the two moons shone on. Within seconds a cold wind gathered around their ankles. It blew Lottie's skirt. Then snowflakes fell steadily from the sky. In a soft, white drift they landed on the cobbled path. And within seconds the entire land was covered in a pristine white blanket of snow.

"Why is it snowing, Blaise?" Albert said. "It's summer not winter. The sun was shining only minutes ago!" Then he remembered Blaise's story and how it was always winter in Wolf Land.

Lottie shot a look at Blaise as she heard the sound of howling in the distance. She shuddered at the thought of being prey for wolves. Then she remembered that there were no animals in Wolf Land. Only werewolves . . .

Blaise had longed for this moment for so long. However, now that he was finally in Wolf Land he felt scared. "I can't believe I have finally entered Wolf Land, Lottie. Now that I'm here it feels like a dream."

Lottie looked up at the snowflakes that fell like teardrops from the sky and she knew what Blaise meant. She too felt as though she were dreaming and could wake up at any moment. She looked back at Blaise and could see the uncertainty in his eyes.

"We will save the Wolf Children, Blaise. Don't worry. You are not alone now."

Blaise was so grateful to Lottie. She had been sent to him. He felt it in his heart. As her red hair blew gently in the breeze like a flickering candleflame, he thought that Lottie Hope was the most amazing girl he had ever met.

Lottie blushed as he stared at her and she turned away from him. She pointed at Günther who was leaning against a bone tree.

"We need to hide Günther, Blaise."

"Yes, but where?" He looked about.

"Why is there a blue moon here, Blaise?" Albert asked.

"Albert, this is no time for such silly questions," said Lottie.

"No, Lottie, it's not a silly question," said Blaise.

Lottie felt her cheeks flush. She didn't like being told off by Blaise and felt embarrassed.

Blaise pointed up to the larger of the two moons. "Albert, the blue moon we can see is the Wolf Moon of legend. Mother said that it appeared with the arrival of Deathhound and his evil werewolves. As long as there are wicked werewolves in Wolf Land the blue moon will shine. Mother believed that if the day ever came that they were gone, then the other moon, the one that is visible from Earth, would become brighter and that then the portal between the two worlds would remain open forever."

A thought suddenly occurred to Lottie. She wondered why she hadn't thought of it before now.

"Blaise, if Cuán and the other children are werewolves, how can we trust them?"

"Lottie, they are not like Deathhound. I suppose I haven't made it clear that not all werewolves are evil. There have been rebellions against Deathhound's evil reign over the centuries, all of which he crushed. There was one that almost succeeded about thirty years ago, led by a famous female warrior called Saoirse. He crushed that too in the end. So, you see, there are many good werewolves but they are suppressed by Deathhound and his followers. Remember, too, that the Wolf Children are more human than the other werewolves because they were born in Wolf Land but grew up on Earth as members of human families, before they were lured back here."

"Look at Günther!" Albert suddenly shouted.

Lottie and Blaise turned to see Günther slumped on the ground beside a bone tree.

Blaise ran over to him. "We will get you to safety now, Günther," he said, helping him to sit up. He glanced towards the round tower.

"No, Blaise. I can't climb into the tower – it is too high," Günther said as he leaned his weight against the tree made from bone.

"None of us can," said Blaise, "without a ladder to reach the door which is high off the ground. Come with me, Albert."

Blaise and Albert did a rapid search of the area surrounding the tower but there was no ladder to be found.

Coming back, Blaise surveyed the abbey. It was no more than a shell. The stones had eroded over the years. The roof had gone. All that was left was the outer walls. It appeared exactly as it did in the human world. Except that it was now covered in snow.

He made a decision. "We need to get you into the scriptorium. It is over to the right-hand side of the tower."

"What is a scriptorium?" Albert asked.

"It's where the monks went to write and illustrate their manuscripts."

"Like a library?"

"Yes, I suppose it was but there will be no books there now."

They walked past the abbey and through an overgrown graveyard, Blaise and Lottie supporting Günther as best they could. Each of the gravestones was covered in ivy. Lottie noticed that one of the graves was protected by a statue of a snarling wolf. She imagined werewolves in her mind's eye, digging underground tunnels, uttering deep guttural howls inaudible above the ground, filling the underworld with their wicked ways, breathing fire until one day they would rise again from the dead.

They reached a small stone building with a cleverly crafted stone roof. There was an arched wooden door. It had studs on the front and images of frightening wolves were carved on it. Lottie was relieved once they were inside and she discovered that an iron bar could be drawn across the door to bolt it shut. There were two tiny windows, no more than slits in the wall. They let in a slither of silver moonlight. It was peaceful inside, a haven from the terrors of Wolf Land.

Blaise helped Günther to lie down on the hard stone ground. Then he pulled a match from his pocket and struck it against the wall. It fizzled as Blaise gazed down at Günther's leg. Blood was seeping through the bandage.

Lottie took her cardigan off and placed it under Günther's head for a pillow. It wasn't much, but she thought that it might provide a little comfort. Lottie wondered if they would have been better off handing Günther over to the authorities back home. It would have been a rotten thing to do. But at least he would be in a hospital bed, instead of lying on a cold, damp stone floor in another world.

A squeaking sound above their heads told them that they must have disturbed a family of bats. Lottie listened as they flew away. She wished that she could join them and go up, up into the sky, far away from the ground where werewolves roamed.

Fear moved through Lottie's veins like a river to the sea.

Blaise looked at Günther who was barely breathing. The pilot was running out of time. He needed heat and fast. There was a small fireplace in the building – they must light a fire.

"Lottie, I will go out and fetch some wood to light a fire – we need to warm Günther up."

"No, Blaise! It's not safe. What about the

werewolves?" Lottie whispered. She was afraid that even the slightest mention of werewolves might summon them.

"We don't have any choice, Lottie. He'll die of the cold otherwise. Lock the door after me. I will knock three times on the door to get back in and you will know that it is me."

Albert hugged Blaise.

"Stay safe, little man. Take care of your sister. You are in charge while I am gone."

Tears fell from Albert's eyes as he let Blaise go. Those were the words his father had used when he had gone to war – and he never returned.

Chapter Thirty-one

The Fiendish Cry of Wolves

Blaise ran out of the scriptorium like a rabbit released from a trap. His heart pounded as he thought of the creature with the red eyes that had followed them. He knew it was a Thought Monster, one of Deathhound's spies. The entire place would be crawling with snarling werewolves in no time. Having Günther with them was holding things up and the werewolves would smell his fresh blood for miles around. If it wasn't for Gunter they could be on their way to find Cuán and the others. Yet, he knew he had to help him. In a strange way, he felt a connection to Günther, which he couldn't understand as he had never met him before.

As Blaise ran through the bone trees, he thought of his mother's diary in his pocket. He knew every inch of Wolf Land. He had studied the map in preparation for the day when the portal opened once more. Then suddenly he felt her presence there with him, darting through the trees. Her spirit animal was there by his side. Guiding him through the wilderness.

Suddenly he was staring into the dark eyes of a beautiful silver wolf. Her right paw was bent, her ears pricked, her eyes large and bright, like whirlpools.

"Mother, it's you!" he cried.

"Yes, my precious son," said Talia. "But we haven't got long. My spirit will leave you soon. I have been waiting here for you in Wolf Land. I longed to see your face one last time before I left for the spirit world."

Blaise reached out his hand to stroke her beautiful grey fur, but it went straight through her. He could see the bullet hole in her side.

"Mother!" he cried. It was as though he was losing her all over again. Grief twisted like an arrowhead in his heart.

"You must be brave and fearless, Blaise, just like I taught you. So much is depending on you. Lottie, Albert, Günther, Cuán and the Wolf Children need you now."

"I am sorry, Mother!" Blaise cried as he wiped his eyes with the back of his hand.

"Do not be frightened, my precious son. You have travelled a great distance through the arched gateway and the ancient Portal of Starlight. Wolf Land is a very different place to Earth. You must tread carefully through the town. It is full of wicked creatures. Beyond that is the Forest of Non-Existence. That is where you will find Cuán. I have to leave you now. But know I am always with you."

As she spoke, she gradually faded away until she was no more than a memory.

"*Mother, come back! I can't do it on my own!*"

But it was too late. Talia had already gone.

Blaise fell to his knees in the cold white snow and cried. His heart ached, then he remembered that he was not alone any more. He had Lottie, Albert and Günther. He remembered Lottie's words to him as he pulled himself to his feet. "*Whatever awaits us we will face it as a team.*" He would never be alone again. His mother had led him to a new family. They were his pack now.

However, there was one vital piece of information that Blaise had yet to tell Lottie and Albert, and that was the fact that once the Portal of Starlight was open, they were in a race against time – as his mother had told him, the portal would remain open for only twenty-four hours in Earth time.

The moonlight glistened on the snow as Blaise ran towards the town. The Wolf Moon was as blue as the ocean. He ran amongst the bone trees. Their twisted branches pointed up to the sky. With every breath he took, the ice-cold wind filled his lungs. Each step brought him closer to danger.

"*Be brave and fearless, Blaise!*" He could hear his mother's words echoing through his mind.

He did not stop until he reached the outskirts of the town. He saw a cottage there. From the outside it appeared normal. Its walls were covered in trailing ivy and a candle burned in the window. A scrawny wolf cub with black eyes was looking in. Blaise noticed a pile of chopped firewood left on a cart at the side of the cottage. He crept over to the cart and filled his arms with as much wood as he could carry. He hid behind the cart as he heard the front door of the cottage swing open.

Four large, muscular werewolves appeared. They growled and snarled viciously at each other. They had glowing red eyes and sharp yellow teeth. Their menacing howls could be heard for miles around. One of the werewolves, the most fiendish creature Blaise had ever seen, moved towards the young wolf cub and swiped him with his large paw. Then another of the werewolves opened his large jaw and went to bite the cub. He narrowly missed the small creature who howled as he ran away in the darkness. Within moments the four evil werewolves were battling with each other. They tore at each other's flesh and roared. Their powerful bodies shook snow from the roof of the cottage.

While they were distracted Blaise decided that he should slip away. Bent double, he turned to go but tripped over a rock that was hidden beneath the snow and fell. Luckily the snow muffled any sound. But some of the wood that he was carrying fell from his arms and thudded as they hit each other. He lay there frozen with fear as he waited for the wolves to come and get him.

Chapter Thirty-two

The Book of Starlight

"What is taking him so long?" Albert cried as Lottie paced up and down the room.

Lottie was thinking the same thing. Terrifying thoughts entered her mind. What if Blaise was captured by werewolves and they ever saw him again? To distract herself from the harrowing thoughts, she knelt down beside Günther and placed a hand on his brow. Then she noticed that he didn't seem to be breathing. Fearfully, she opened his flight jacket and shirt and put an ear to his chest. She was hugely relieved to hear the thud of his heart and feel that his chest was gently moving up and down.

Albert screamed as a loud knock came to the door.

"Hush, Albert!" Lottie hissed.

"Blaise!" Albert cried.

"Wait – there was only one knock. Blaise said that he would knock three times."

They waited in trepidation. When two more loud knocks sounded on the door Lottie jumped to her feet and drew the iron bar across. Blaise stumbled in, a flurry of snow followed him. He was as pale as a ghost. Lottie quickly bolted the door again.

"We thought something terrible had happened to you!" Albert cried.

"Don't worry about me, little man. I told you I'd be back." Blaise reached over and ruffled Albert's hair.

Lottie could see that Blaise was trembling. And her instincts told her that something terrible had happened.

Blaise placed the wood in the grate and lit a fire, beginning with some twigs as kindling. When they were burning well he added some firewood.

"We must pray there isn't an ancient bird's nest in the chimney," he said. "Or anything else blocking it."

Albert immediately closed his eyes and began to pray.

After a while Blaise said with a laugh, "Your prayer has been answered, Albert. You can open your eyes!"

Albert opened his eyes to see flames licking at the wood and climbing up the chimney.

"No smoke coming back at us," said Blaise. "I think the chimney is clear."

When the fire was roaring. Blaise took his mother's diary from his pocket and handed it to Lottie.

"I need you to look at this."

"What is it, Blaise?"

"It's my mother's diary."

Lottie gasped in amazement as she flicked through the worn pages of the book. There were diagrams of stars and charcoal drawings of children standing beside wolves.

"There is a map of Wolf Land," said Blaise. " I have memorised it. You need to memorise it too."

Lottie studied the diary as Blaise reached out and placed his hand on Günther's forehead.

"Blaise!"

"Yes?"

"It says here that the portal only remains open for about twenty-four hours at a time." She spoke in an undertone, hoping Albert would not hear her.

"Yes, Lottie," he answered quietly. "After that the portal closes. Whoever is in Wolf Land then will remain there. We are in a race against time."

"You knew that all along?"

"Yes."

"So why didn't you tell me?"

"Lottie, forgive me – I thought it would be too much for you to take in, together with all the other frightening things about this place."

"You mean," she said with a steely look, "you were afraid that I wouldn't agree to come here if I knew."

"That too," he whispered.

Lottie stared into his earnest eyes and forgave him. She understood he was compelled to do all he could to rescue Cuán and the others. He believed it was his fate to do so. Hers too.

She shrugged. "Then we have to move fast," she said. "Several hours have passed already." She frowned. Unfortunately, neither of them had a wristwatch. And

Günther's had stopped, possibly damaged in the crash – or maybe human watches didn't work in Wolf Land.

"Thank you, Lottie," said Blaise. "You are amazing."

"Don't deceive me again, Blaise. I won't forgive you the next time."

He looked shamefaced. "Well, let's see … we need to get food and drink and fresh bandages for Günther, and some kind of disinfectant for his wounds. And some blankets. He won't survive for much longer without these things."

"Here in Wolf Land?"

"No. I went to the edge of the town – we might have found something there – but what I saw there was truly terrifying, Lottie – ferocious werewolves battling each other. I thought they had seen me and I nearly died of fright. But they were too focused on tearing each other apart to notice or smell me." Blaise closed his eyes and recalled the menacing cries of the werewolves and their bloody claws. His eyes sprang open. "We'll have to go back the way we came, Lottie, to the outside world."

"But we can't leave Günther here!"

"We have to. He is too sick to be moved – and we can't carry him. We should never have brought him here. Can we get food from the house that you are staying in?"

"The Dunlivins' house?"

"Yes."

"I suppose so. But if they catch us sneaking around they will lock us in the cellar and we won't be able to get back to Günther."

"That's a chance we'll have to take, Lottie."

Lottie hated to leave Günther alone in Wolf Land, but Blaise was right. He would die without those supplies. And the clock was ticking. They had less than twenty-four hours to save him and the Wolf Children before the portal closed.

Chapter Thirty-three

Cuán
1920

As Nancy clambered out of the window, her nightdress snagged on a shard of broken glass, and she fell awkwardly onto the ground beneath. A pain ricocheted through her body as her ankle twisted.

Rain poured down relentlessly as she hobbled onwards and followed the grey wolf as she ran through the pine trees. Terror overwhelmed her as she tore through the brambles, limping on her painful ankle in a desperate attempt to save her friend.

"Cuán, come back!" she screamed.

Nancy felt as though she had failed her friend. All she had to do was to make sure that she didn't escape in the night. Her heart was beating like a drum. Her head was spinning. Cuán was her friend. She would never hurt her. Nancy knew this even if Cuán didn't.

The tip of the wolf's grey tail shone in the moonlight.

Then it stood on top of a rock, silhouetted against the moon and howled. Nancy crouched down amidst the trees and watched the beautiful creature. She was scared to breathe in case she scared her away.

"Please, Cuán, come back," she mumbled, and for a split second the wolf turned and looked in her direction. It was as if she had heard her. But then she was running again harder than before.

Nancy followed her, even though intense pain seared through her ankle. She stumbled over rocks and picked herself up again. She could smell the damp grass in the air. The birds were huddled in their nests. It felt as though the entire world was holding its breath.

The arched gateway to the monastic settlement came into view. Nancy had heard the stories about the place. She was told it was home to the Banshee and that it was cursed.

"Please, Cuán, it's not safe there!" Nancy cried but it was too late.

Cuán disappeared through the gateway and Nancy never saw her friend again.

Chapter Thirty-four

The Cage of Lies in Everlasting Darkness
1940

The everlasting darkness was punctuated by the two moons which shone like eyes in the sky. Lottie, Albert and Blaise left Günther alone in the scriptorium and made their way through the snowstorm back towards the Portal of Starlight. In the short time that they had been inside the snow had come down fast. They shivered with the cold, their clothes inadequate in such a harsh climate. A climate made for wild creatures. A world fit for wolves. As they trudged through the relentless snow Lottie had the unnerving feeling that something terrible was about to happen. She could feel it in her bones. It was as though the bomb which fell from Günther's plane, a moment before it crashed, had conjured something up. It had opened up the gateway to Wolf Land and in doing so it had released something powerful and warped.

Blaise could feel it too, although he didn't tell Lottie. Now that he had seen the werewolves on the outskirts of the town he realised they were cruel and vicious creatures and far more wicked than he could ever have imagined. He was lucky to have escaped with his life.

He was hugely relieved to discover that the shimmering Portal of Starlight between the two worlds was still open. Although it appeared slightly smaller than he remembered it. Was it shrinking?

"Quick, we haven't got much time!" he cried as he gripped Lottie by the hand.

Lottie reached out to Albert. "It's all right, Albert. Hold my hand and we'll enter the portal together just like last time."

Once more the children entered the portal of shimmering light. It glistened like a million stars. At first it felt cool on their skin. Then it turned warm. The whooshing sound of shooting stars whizzed past their ears and they each felt weightless. It was as though they were floating through time and space. They held each other tightly and did not let go as brightly coloured lights flashed before their eyes. When it was all over they fell onto a blanket of soft, green grass at the other side of the portal and outside the abbey walls. The low orange sun had begun to set in the distance and melted into the horizon. The brightness of the light hurt their eyes. It took them a moment to adjust from the dark gloomy atmosphere in Wolf Land.

Albert was disappointed to discover that it had stopped snowing once they crossed back through the portal. Although he was relieved to feel the heat of the sun on his skin.

"We'll go back for Günther, won't we?" he panted as he ran alongside Lottie and Blaise.

Lottie felt a rush of love towards her brother. He must be bewildered. She knew she should take care to explain things clearly to him.

"Yes, Albert. We will. And we're going to save Cuán and the Wolf Children. But we don't have long."

When the children reached Kilbree, they stopped in the field overlooking Hugh and Ida's house. They needed time to catch their breath. The hay had recently been cut. Large bales were dotted around like yellow teeth that had fallen from the mouth of a giant.

"What will we tell the Dunlivins?" Albert asked.

"You mustn't say a word about Günther to them, under any circumstances," Blaise warned him. "Do you hear me?" Blaise felt bad for being stern with Albert but he needed him to understand. Günther's life depended on it.

Albert felt scared. Blaise seemed angry with him. "Why can't I?"

"People will take him away and lock him up if they find him," Lottie said. "That's why we hid him in the first place!"

"I forgot," said Albert in a small voice.

Lottie felt ashamed. She had only just promised herself to remember to explain things clearly to him – and here she was snapping at him already.

"Let's go," Blaise instructed, and they made their way through the field and on towards the Dunlivins' house.

Albert didn't like telling lies. His mother had told him that lies are like seeds that grow into a tree inside you. Eventually the branches will form a cage around your heart until it stops beating.

The warm glow from the Dunlivins' windows looked inviting and smoke rose from the chimney despite the fact that it was a warm summer day. It mingled with the early evening mist that had gathered like a translucent cloak spread across the hilltops.

"I don't want to go back to the Wolf Land, Lottie. I want to stay here in our own world," Albert huffed.

Lottie was surprised and shocked. "We must go back, Albert. You said so yourself. Günther needs us. He will die if we don't help him." She came to an abrupt halt in front of her brother – she needed him to understand the importance of what they were doing.

Albert sighed, then he kicked a stone across the path "I know, it's just that . . ."

Suddenly it dawned on Lottie. All the questions that Albert was asking meant something.

"Did you see something that scared you, Albert?"

Albert shrugged his shoulders as nonchalantly as he could. "I saw someone or something with red eyes following us," he said as he stood on a leaf which crunched under his foot.

Lottie looked at her brother squarely in the eyes. "Why didn't you tell me this before?"

Albert shrugged his shoulders and picked his nose.

"Never mind – we'll talk later," Lottie said as she took his hand.

They hurried after Blaise who was beckoning them impatiently.

"We need to hurry!" he said. "Günther needs those supplies."

Fear ripped through Albert's body, like a hurricane through an unsuspecting town.

"Do you think that the creature with the red eyes will hurt Günther?"

Blaise's voice was quiet as they were now close to the house. "I don't know, Albert, but we need to get back there fast before another disaster strikes."

Chapter Thirty-five

Wolf Children

Cuán screamed as she woke from another nightmare. She sat bolt upright in her glass box which was suspended from a tree made of bone. Its branches stretched high above the forest floor. She shivered with cold as snow fell from the black sky. Her hand fell on the wolf cub that lay beside her. Its mother, Silver, was killed in a battle and Cuán had rescued the small creature. As she stroked the animal's soft grey fur it nestled close to her body for heat. However, Cuán felt weak and hungry. She needed caring for herself and didn't know if she would survive another Battle of Wolves. She wished with all her heart that someone would rescue her from this vile land. She peered through the glass box and searched the shadows for signs of Deathhound and his wicked werewolves. They lurked like monsters in the forest below her. A thick grey mist slipped through the trees like a slithering snake. The branches of the bone trees stirred. Yet there was no birdsong in Wolf Land. Just the howling of wolves and the rumble of thunder. In the distance she could just about see light coming from the windows of cottages in the town.

She thought of the extraordinary event that had occurred before she fell asleep. The rumble in the distance that seemed like a giant explosion. For a moment it seemed to rock the world. Then a fireball fell from the sky like a meteor.

What did it mean, Cuán wondered just as a flash of lightning lit up the black sky. Cuán had never seen lightning in Wolf Land before. It illuminated the blue mountains. The wolf cub was scared. It whimpered and moved closer to Cuán for comfort as the two moons peered out from behind dark storm clouds.

"It's all right, girl," Cuán soothed.

The grey cub raised its nose and sniffed the air. She could smell danger.

An explosion, the fireball and now this lightning, thought Cuán. There was change in the air. She knew it. She felt it. Her head ached but she had to remain strong. If not for herself then for the other Wolf Children.

Cuán wished with every bone in her body that she had not run through the forest on that fateful night and crossed through the Portal of Starlight. She could still see her friend Nancy pleading with her not to go, her long blonde hair flowing over her shoulders. *"Please, Cuán, come back!"* However, the call of Wolf Land was too strong and the Thought Monsters had succeeded in luring her away from Kilbree.

Cuán's only companions in Wolf Land were the other Wolf Children, all of whom had lived for some years on Earth before they were lured back to Wolf Land. They slept in glass boxes which were suspended from the trees. There had been many of them over the years. Each of them had been drawn towards the Portal of Starlight which linked the two worlds, by the evil Deathhound.

"Did you really feel it too, Cuán?" Madigan asked one more time. "The explosion? And see the fireball?"

Cuán placed her hand against the glass cage and smiled at her friend. "Yes, Madigan, I did."

Tears sprang from Madigan's steel-blue eyes. Her long black hair fell in curls across her shoulders. Madigan was twelve years old and she was shorter than the other Wolf Children which made her weaker in battle. Her shoulder bones protruded through the fabric of her blue linen dress. Her features were dainty and elf-like. Madigan shivered in the cold. The endless night meant that it snowed for most of the year. Icicles hung like silver daggers from the roof of her glass box. She crouched on her knees and placed her face against the glass. Her breath fogged it up and condensation ran like small rivers down it.

"Something is happening, Cuán. I know it. Someone is coming for us."

Madigan's wolf cub padded across the glass box and placed its paws on the glass. As terrible as being locked in a cage was, Madigan was grateful to be high above the forest floor. She peered down through the bottom of her glass box. And she saw the Thought Monsters roaming around, searching for prey. Madigan huddled beneath her brown blanket and tried to recall home. At times she could hear her father's voice warning her not to go out alone at night as it wasn't safe. But something had called her away. It was the same voice that had called Cuán and Faolán.

At first Madigan felt guilty for leaving home. However, over time she realised that she couldn't help it, none of them could. The first time that she changed into a wolf, she killed all of the sheep on her farm. Her parents were devastated but they never suspected her. Not for one moment – why would they? What kind of girl would be capable of such a barbaric act? But Madigan wasn't a normal girl. She was a wolf too. And the people who raised her were not her real parents – just like Cuán no-one knew who Madigan's real parents were. Her father found her on the doorstep of his cottage one night. There was a pale blue moon in the sky, a Wolf Moon. A beautiful she-wolf was there too but she ran away when the man opened the door.

"You two are fools. No-one is coming for us." Faolán scowled. He banged his fist against the glass and then slid down onto the floor. At fourteen years he was the oldest of the Wolf Children, and the strongest and fiercest of the werewolves. He was tall and slender. He had long brown hair which hid a wolf-shaped birthmark which ran down his skull.

Whenever the Growling took place, Faolán changed into a large black wolf with a silver streak down his back.

He had a fierce temper which served him well in battle.

Wolf Land was split into four provinces, like Ireland. And during the Growling, which was a battle organised by Deathhound, they had to fight against Wolf Children from other provinces. And each province had many Wolf Children.

The Wolf Children were released from their glass boxes twice a day, morning and evening, to exercise and train for the Growling. Even though it occurred only once a year, they needed to practise their fighting skills every day. Only the strongest would survive the battle. There was no room for weak wolves in the Growling.

Faolán hated it all. He often wondered what the children from the other provinces were like. He only ever met them in battle. He wished that there was some way of communicating with them so that they could plan a revolt and overthrow the wicked Deathhound once and for all.

"You are wrong, Faolán!" Cuán said. "You heard the explosion too. I know you did! It sounded as though it came from the heavens!"

Faolán could not deny it. He had heard it and had felt the reverberations in his box. And he had seen the flashing flaming object falling from the sky. But they had got their hopes up many times before, only to have them dashed.

"There is no escape for us – the sooner that you realise that, the better it will be for all of us!" he snarled.

"Keep quiet, someone is coming!" Cuán warned them.

For the first time in a long time, Cuán felt hopeful, regardless of what Faolán had said. The explosion and fireball in the sky signified change, she could feel it in her wolf heart. Someone was coming for them. If there was even the slightest chance that she could escape and return home to Ireland she was going to take it.

Chapter Thirty-six

Oisín the Healer and the Girl Who Ate the Starlight

The Wolf Children had no way of knowing what time it was. There was no dawn chorus of birds to start the day. No golden sunset to soothe them to sleep at night. Their routine began when Oisín the Healer visited their boxes each day to feed them. They counted that as morning time.

Oisín pounded through the forest. He had heard the explosion and seen the flaming object flash through the sky. And then there was the lightning. Excitement rose in his gut. Change was coming. He could feel it. Maybe the change he had been expecting for centuries.

Very few people ventured so deep into the forest. However, Oisín was a healer. The trees spoke to him. The other werewolves feared him. He heard the high-pitched screech of the Thought Monsters as they ran for cover. Even they feared him.

Oisín accepted his role in Wolf Land. It was part of who he was and it had kept him on the path of goodness and caring for others. His goodness was like a shield that protected him, living among evil creatures as he did. He was the only werewolf apart from Deathhound who was immortal. However, he achieved immortality through his knowledge of medicine unlike Deathhound who did it with evil magic. Oisín had no real desire to keep on living but he did it for the sake of keeping some goodness alive in this evil place.

However, his gift came with a price. He was made to work for Deathhound. His knowledge and healing power meant that he was invaluable to him and this meant that he was the only werewolf who dared to resist Deathhound's orders at times. He hated Deathhound as much as the Wolf Children did. However, he valued being in charge of caring for all of the Wolf Children.

When Oisín reached the heart of the forest, he was relieved to see that the glass boxes were still intact. They swung from the trees made of bone. He pulled the golden lever which lowered the glass boxes to the ground.

Oisín, though immortal, looked like a human of thirty winters old. He had a large muscular frame, eyes which were the colour of emeralds and short blonde hair. He deliberately chose to keep his human form at all times, in protest against Deathhound who had often in the past tried to force him to live in werewolf form. He wore a silver helmet on his head and a wolfskin covered his shoulders to keep out the cold. Beneath it he wore a red tunic as was fitting for one of Deathhound's warriors.

The first glass box he opened was Cuán's. She was sitting at the back of the box, clutching her wolf cub. Her knees were bent and she looked sad, her face paler than usual. This meant that she was sick. Although the Wolf Children ate the stars each night, the human part of their existence required food to stay alive.

Oisín had learned over the years not to trust the Wolf Children, regardless of how innocent they looked. At any second they could shift into wolves and sink their sharp teeth into his skin. He had the scars to prove it. He moved tentatively towards Cuán and filled her trough with food. Red and blue pellets contained vitamins and minerals. Orange and yellow pellets contained protein, carbohydrates and fat. They were essential for keeping the children alive, especially in a world without sunlight. The green pellets were the most important as they prevented the Wolf Children from growing older.

Oisín had kind eyes. They wrinkled in the corner like the skin on a bowl of custard when he smiled.

"Good morning, Cuán," he said.

Cuán covered her face with her hands. She refused to talk to Oisín, even if he did have the appearance of being kind. Cuán had been tricked on many occasions into trusting people in Wolf Land. And she had suffered the consequences. Faolán had warned her that in order to remain strong she must not get close to anyone except her own group of Wolf Children. Making friends in Wolf Land would only make her weak and vulnerable to attack.

Oisín rummaged in the pocket of his tunic and surreptitiously pulled out a small green vial containing starlight. He slipped it into Cuán's trough as quickly as he could. He knew that the Wolf Children weren't supposed to eat starlight during the day. But Cuán was fading fast and she needed to gather her strength for the Growling. Oisín knew that he was risking his life by giving her starlight in this way. However, he cared deeply for Cuán and didn't want anything to happen to her.

Oisín took his helmet off and held it in his right hand. Then he licked his bottom lip and looked around to check that none of the red-eyed Thought Monsters had followed him through the dense forest.

"Eat up all of your pellets, Cuán, and drink the starlight fast. You are coming to the town with me." The potion Oisín needed to heal Cuán was in his cottage. He knew that he could keep a closer eye on her there.

Cuán had been to Oisín's cottage before. All of the Wolf Children went there if they became ill or if they required treatment following the Growling battle. Cuán didn't mind going there. She knew that Oisín would take care of her and she could take her wolf cub with her. Although she hated leaving Madigan and Faolán behind. Cuán guessed that each province had their own healer as she had never met a Wolf Child from another province while she was there. Cuán's treatment usually involved lying in a bed with bright lights shining above her head. Classical music from the human world was played through a gramophone. It was usually music by Mozart or Chopin, Oisín told her. And scenes of nature from back home in Ireland were painted on glass slides and projected against a white wall by a magic lantern.

It wasn't so bad really. It was better than being in the glass box. The worst thing about it was that she would recall her home in Wexford. She would think of Ma and her friend Nancy. She felt sadness like a great weight crushing her soul whenever she thought of home. She would never forget the look in Nancy's eyes the last time she saw her. She hoped that her friend would come to rescue her one day. Although deep down she knew that it would never happen.

Cuán knew that Oisín was a good werewolf. She wondered why he always appeared as a human but had never asked him. Perhaps he felt it was easier to win the Wolf Children's confidence that way.

Now he had risked his own life to bring her the starlight. She turned her back on the other Wolf Children, removed the cork from the glass vial and quickly drank the starlight. It tasted like honey and felt hot as it slipped down her throat. She could feel it taking effect right away and she felt stronger and more ready for battle than she had when she first woke up. The dull, lifeless air that had run through her lungs now felt charged with energy. She had a power that she hadn't felt in a long time.

What Madigan said was true. Change was coming. Cuán could feel it within her bones.

Cuán picked up her grey wolf cub and stepped out of her box. The cub whimpered. It sensed danger in the forest. Evil werewolves hiding in the trees. Red-eyed monsters following their every move.

Madigan was filled with horror. *"Cuán, don't leave us!"* she cried. *"I'm afraid!"*

Part of Cuán wanted to stay with her. But she knew they would never escape that way. The answers she needed were not in the forest.

"Don't be frightened Madigan," she said. "I'll be back soon."

Cuán's eyes met Faolán's and he nodded at her. She knew what she had to do. This was her one chance. The last time Faolán had been injured in battle he had found a book in Oisín's house. It contained a map which led to the other side. Oisín caught him and hid the book somewhere. Cuán knew that she needed to find it in order for them to escape.

But maybe Madigan was right. What if someone had come to save them? Could it be possible? Whoever was coming would have to be brave enough to survive a battle with the wolves from the other provinces, as well as the Thought Monsters, the wicked demons with red eyes who fed off negative thoughts.

Even if they were fortunate enough to survive everything, if Deathhound discovered them he would sentence them to immediate death.

Chapter Thirty-seven

The Undertaker's Kitchen

Lottie was overcome with relief when she discovered that no-one was home. She pushed the front door and was glad to find it open. She shoved her brother inside and followed with Blaise.

"Quick, Albert, we need to get as much food as we can for Günther. Then we need to get out of here before Ida and Hugh get home. I'll find some blankets and bandages." She ran up the stairs.

"See if there is any disinfectant anywhere!" Blaise called after her.

Albert and Blaise ran into the kitchen.

There was ham on the table and some golden scones cooling on a wire rack. Brown currants protruded like eyes from them. Albert stuffed one of them into his mouth. Then he looked around for something to carry the rest of them in.

Blaise laughed as crumbs fell from Albert's lips. "Here, Albert, use this." He put a large wicker basket on the table.

Blaise sliced the ham roughly and wrapped it in some brown paper. Then he plunged into the pantry and came out with a large cheese and a big loaf of bread. He put them into the basket, then added some apples from a bowl. After all, he thought, they would all need to eat something to keep their strength up.

Lottie ran in with two small blankets and a sheet. She shoved them into Blaise's arms and rushed over to the kitchen dresser. She opened the bottom door and found a bottle of Ida's homemade lemonade. She put it into the basket along with three cups.

"That should do the trick, Lottie," Albert said as he swallowed the last of the crumbs. He was starving as they hadn't eaten since breakfast and it was suppertime now.

"Wait!" Blaise cried. "He will need some water." He ran over to the sink and filled a large glass bottle with water and put it into the basket.

"Let's go!" Lottie cried. Then she took the heavy basket from Albert.

"Not so fast!"

The children nearly jumped out of their skin. Lottie swivelled on her heels and saw Prudence Dunlivin standing there, like a bolt of lightning on a summer's day.

Blaise dropped the blankets behind a chair. As Lottie faced Prudence, a false smile erupted on her lips.

"Prudence, what are you doing here?" Lottie said. Then she stepped backwards and tried to hide the basket behind her back.

"*I live here or have you forgotten that?*" Prudence screeched. The tiny red veins in her eyes grew larger. Then she frowned and raised her left eyebrow, which resembled a caterpillar crawling across a leaf.

"Of course," said Lottie. "It's just that we thought you were out with your parents."

"What have you got there?" Prudence asked.

"It's nothing," Lottie lied.

As she stepped back Prudence stepped forwards. If a passer-by had glanced into the window the girls would have looked as though they were dancing.

Prudence glared at Lottie and shook a clenched fist at her. "*Show me your hands if it's nothing!*" Then she swiped at Lottie who stumbled and lost her footing.

The contents of the basket fell out onto the floor. Albert stepped out of the shadows. Then he fell to his hands and knees. Blaise scuttled around and helped Albert to pick everything up again.

Prudence was livid. Her pigtails swung from side to side. She placed her hands on her hips. "I knew it! You are a pair of petty thieves! Mother and Father are next door. A meeting that has been called to discuss the plane crash. Mother thought that you had been killed by the blast. I wish you had! If I scream loud enough Mother and Father will come running and catch you red-handed. Then they will send you straight back home. Or maybe to gaol!"

Lottie sighed. "Please don't, Prudence!" she begged.

Prudence opened her mouth wide to scream.

Lottie held her hands out in front of her as if to catch Prudence's scream when it came from her quivering lips.

Prudence's mouth snapped shut. *"I want answers – fast!"* she said.

Lottie knew that Prudence meant business. Her pigtails swayed at the side of her head and she tapped her toe on the floor tiles.

Albert took a deep breath. "We were going to the woods to have a midnight feast."

"Don't lie to me, you little brat!" Prudence screeched then she licked her lips and opened her mouth wide again to scream.

Lottie knew there was no time to waste. She ran over and placed her hand over Prudence's mouth so that the only sound that came out was a squeak.

"Albert, open the cellar door!" Lottie cried. "Blaise, help me!"

Prudence's cheeks were crimson. She kicked Lottie's legs as she held on to her.

"Lottie, what are you doing?" Blaise cried.

"We must lock her in the cellar! We don't have any choice. Ida and Hugh could be home any minute – then we won't be able to help anyone and Günther could die!"

Lottie took her hand off Prudence's mouth and she spluttered and coughed.

"Please don't put me in the cellar with the coffins!" she croaked. "I promise I won't say anything."

"I am sorry, Prudence, but we have no other choice," Lottie said.

Blaise and Lottie pulled Prudence over to the cellar door and down the cellar stairs. Then they ran back up the stairs and out of the cellar. Blaise slammed the door behind them and bolted it.

Prudence was furious. She ran back up the stairs and pounded on the door with her fists.

"*Let me out!*" she screamed.

"Let's get going, we have very little time," Blaise said.

Then Lottie picked up the basket and the three children ran out of the house and on towards the horror that awaited them in Wolf Land.

Chapter Thirty-eight

The Chamber of Hearts

Deep within the forest, danger lurked around every tree. It was no place for children. Cuán's wolf instincts were strong – they had to be in order for her to survive. However, she was a lone wolf without a pack and this made her easy prey. Cuán kept pace with Oisín. She was safe as long as she stayed by his side. Snow fell from the black sky. Stars twisted and twirled above her head like silver coins. She was grateful for the starlight that Oisín had given to her earlier. It coursed through her veins, warming the chambers of her hearts. The grey cub in her arms pricked its ears and sniffed the air. Cuán placed her fingers into its fur, which was soft like wool. The heat from its tiny body reached her fingers. The gentle murmur of its heart, like the tick-tock of a pocket watch was reassuring to her. It was alive too.

Oisín walked ahead, a bow and arrow slung over his

shoulder, a spear in his hand. He was not only a healer, but a brave and fierce warrior also.

A breeze rippled through the trees like a secret. It caught Cuán off guard and she shivered. The cub in her arms growled. Danger was near.

Oisín turned to Cuán and looked into her large, bright eyes. She was getting stronger. She was only a Wolf Child. Someday soon she would be a great leader like Saoirse her mother was.

"Why are you so kind to me?" Cuán asked.

Oisín froze. Her instincts were stronger than he thought.

"I am kind to all the Wolf Children."

Cuán shook her head. "No, you treat me differently to the others."

"Nonsense! You are imagining things."

Cuán's heart thumped in her chest as panic took hold. "You know things about me, Oisín. I can see it in your eyes."

The wind stirred the branches on the trees and there was a rustling of leaves and a screeching sound. A pair of red eyes appeared in the darkness, sharp white teeth gleaming below them.

Oisín gripped Cuán by the arm and pulled her behind a rock as a Thought Monster slithered past. It had eight legs and slime dripped from its body. Red eyes stared back at them.

Oisín took his bow and arrow and shot the hideous beast. It ran into the undergrowth. Oisín pulled Cuán to her feet. The cub yelped in her arms.

"It's not safe here, Cuán. We need to get you to my house and fast."

Cuán nodded as fear took hold. Her boots sank into the snow. Her toes felt numb with cold. Her breath left a trail on the air. They ran past trees, jumped over ditches and followed the path of moonlight that flowed from the sky through the spindly branches of the bone trees. Eventually the ancient, medieval town appeared like a bad dream through the mist. It consisted of winding streets, arched alleyways and canals which were sailed upon by extravagant canal boats. Beautiful wooden houses jutted out and were reflected in the glistening water. Each of the ornate buildings was decorated with wooden carvings of wolves. It was a spectacular sight to behold. The narrow, cobbled streets were lit by gas lamps and filled with shops. There was a market square in the centre of the town which was overlooked by a soaring bell tower. It was market day and the entire place was bustling with werewolves.

"Stay close by my side, Cuán, and don't talk to anyone," Oisín warned.

Cuán edged closer to Oisín as they meandered past street sellers and market stalls. Deathhound's warriors were everywhere. Cuán knew that they were not like Oisín and they would kill her in a heartbeat.

They walked past a row of shops. It looked like an ordinary town. Except for the fact that all of the people there were evil werewolves. They hissed and howled as Oisín led Cuán along the winding narrow streets. Cuán peered into a brightly lit shop. The window was decorated with brightly coloured wooden figurines of toy soldiers. It was a toy shop. A woman and a small child stood at the counter. The woman was wearing a green velvet dress, the bottom half of the dress covered in ostrich feathers. The child wore a yellow dress. They looked like ordinary humans until the little girl swivelled her head and looked at Cuán. When she did she revealed a wolf's face with the sharpest wolf teeth Cuán had ever seen. She hurried along after Oisín. Two boys and a girl in dishevelled clothes sat on the street. They had no shoes on their wolves' feet and their faces were covered in hair. Sharp teeth protruded from their hungry mouths and their eyes were yellow. They snapped at Cuán and tried to bite her. She realised that the wolf cub she was holding would make a tasty meal. One of them tore at her dress.

Oisín gripped Cuán's arm and growled at them.

"*Away with you!*" he ordered.

The three children scampered along an alleyway. Cuán felt sorry for them. They were just children after all.

"This way," Oisín said as he led Cuán past the canal and along an alleyway until they came to his house.

A wooden sign swung outside. It had the image of a potion bottle on it and the word *HEALER* was carved into the wood. Werewolves arrived at his door, day and night. They sought cures for ailments, which ranged from ingrowing toenails to fever. The house was five floors high and towered above all of the other houses in the town. Inside, it had fine, stone windows and high wooden beams. Tapestries depicting the town's history and paintings hung from the walls. The vaulted ceiling was decorated with wooden carvings and there was a labyrinth of rooms, some of which Cuán was forbidden to enter.

Oisín led Cuán into the main living room, which he also used as the infirmary. The floor was made of stone and an oval-shaped wooden table with two chairs was placed before a roaring fire. Cuán left the wolf cub down. It wagged its tail and ran around the room, before settling down in front of the fire.

There was ghastly picture of Deathhound on the wall. It was obligatory for each and every household in Leinsteria to have a painting of him on display and his warrior wolves went on weekly inspections to ensure that his orders were obeyed. Spies were planted all around the town and they reported back to Deathhound. No-one knew who the spies were so Oisín was suspicious of everyone.

The walls were covered in bookshelves. Cuán had enjoyed reading when she was at home with Ma. Thoughts of home made her feel sad. Think about Madigan and Faolán and finding the book with the map, she told herself. She needed to stay strong and focused. She looked around at the sea of books. The last time she was in the cottage was after a Growling. She was badly injured and her back needed stitches.

Against a wall was a pharmacy. An old wooden counter was piled high with an assortment of glass bottles of different shapes and sizes. Each bottle contained a magical potion that Oisín used to heal the injured Wolf Children. On a stone shelf behind the counter, Oisín kept the hearts of the Wolf Children who died in battle. Each heart was in its own jar and the name of the child that the heart belonged to was formed by butterflies in the air above it. A thousand fireflies lit up the shelf, which appeared more like a shrine. Cuán did not know why Oisín kept the hearts of the Wolf Children. And she shuddered to think of her own wolf heart ending up there one day.

Oisín took off his wolfskin and laid it on a bed in the corner of the room. Then he lit an oil lamp and placed it on the table.

"Would you like a drink, Cuán?"

"Yes, please."

Oisín walked over to the dresser and took the cork from a green bottle. Then he poured red liquid into two goblets. He handed one to Cuán and drank from the other.

Cuán coughed and spluttered. "What is it?"

"It is a potion to heal you and make you stronger."

Cuán sat down in front of the fire.

"Your animal instincts are growing stronger now, Cuán," Oisín remarked as he studied Cuán's pale skin and amber eyes.

Cuán jumped to her feet. As she thought about the hearts of the Wolf Children it became clear to her. Oisín knew the origins of every wolf in Wolf Land.

"Please, Oisín, tell me who my real mother is! Why was I left in the forest as a baby? I need to know."

Oisín bit his bottom lip and clenched his jaw. He owed

it to Cuán to be honest with her. She was more than a Wolf Child. Cuán was special.

"You're right, child," he said. "It is time."

He walked over to the stone shelf containing the jars of hearts, then he lay his hand gently on a small gold lever on the end of the shelf which opened a small red velvet-lined drawer. Cuán hadn't noticed the drawer before as it was hidden beneath the shelf. Then a golden envelope flew out, carried by two purple butterflies. It landed in Cuán's hand. She usually enjoyed Oisín's magical illusions – however, on this occasion it had no impact on her. This time she was more concerned with finding out the answers to questions she had about her past in order to find out about her future.

"Read the letter. It will tell you everything." Oisín walked back over to warm his hands by the fire.

Cuán carefully opened the golden envelope which was sealed with wax. The image of a wolf was stamped into the red wax. The letter was written in the ancient language of werewolves which long ago she had realised she could read and understand without ever having to learn it.

My darling daughter,

If you are reading this letter, then I am dead. And you are here in Wolf Land. A fate I did all I could to spare you, our only hope. You know of me by this time if you have been given this letter by Oisín. I risked all to lead a rebellion against that cursed Deathhound who had oppressed us for centuries. We almost won, my dearest one, but then the tide turned against us and he crushed the revolt like an egg beneath his foot.

But the year before that, you were born. I took you to Ireland through the Portal of Starlight and left you there to save your life should the rebellion we had planned go wrong. It nearly broke my heart to leave you but I was full of hope that soon we would win a better world for you to grow up in – a new Wolf Land free of the vile Deathhound. I didn't leave your side until I saw you being rescued from the forest by a kind human woman. Then I knew that, even if our revolt failed, I had given you the chance of a happy life. You would learn human ways and belong to a human family. I knew that some children from Wolf Land settled well into the human world. Their human natures became dominant and they were never bothered by their wolfish natures. This is what I hoped for you – not that I wanted you to reject your magnificent wolf self but there was no choice in the matter. To be free and happy, you had to become wholly human.

But now, if you are back here in Wolf Land, I fear the worst has happened – your wolfish nature has conquered your human side and you have been lured back to this terrible life.

This is what I need to tell you now, my precious daughter: there are many Wolf Children like you, all secretly taken to Ireland by their loving parents who hope to rescue them from this vile place. Each of them has a Wolf Ring – I hope you still have yours. On the day that the Great Warrior Wolf comes from the sky, join forces with him. Defeat Deathhound and set the Wolf Children free.

The future of Wolf Land depends on you.

Your loving mother,

Saoirse

Tears sprang from Cuán's eyes. Her hands were shaking.

"Oisín, is it true? Was my mother Saoirse, the brave rebel leader you have told me so much about?"

"Yes, Cuán. This is your mother's house. All of these books belonged to her. She was a remarkable person, Cuán – intelligent, caring and very brave. Werewolves had rebelled against Deathhound's evil reign before over the centuries, but none were as loved by her followers as Saoirse was. Those rebellions all failed and hers did too, though it looked for a while that it would succeed. As I have told you, it was crushed brutally by Deathhound and all the rebels horribly tortured and killed. But Saoirse was loved and there were many who risked their lives by hiding her. I am sure she hoped to go through the portal to search for you but Deathhound had the portal guarded by Thought Monsters. His soldiers found her in the end, but she died like the warrior she was, surrounded by attackers. Deathhound's rage was terrible to see when he heard – he had given orders that she was to be taken alive. He tortured and executed every werewolf present at the scene of her last battle."

Tears poured down Cuán's face as her heart ached.

"She had entrusted me with that letter for you, should you return here."

"Why are you only telling me this now?"

"Because you weren't ready before. I have watched you grow. Your animal instincts are powerful now. Each time you eat the stars you become stronger. You are now ready to fight alongside the Great Warrior Wolf and there are signs that his coming may be at hand. In *The Book of*

Wolves it says that the Great Warrior Wolf will come from the sky – just as your mother's letter says. When this happens the Wolf Children will run free once more."

Cuán felt sick. She could not believe what she was hearing. All these years she had wondered who her mother was and why she had left her in the forest with the wolves. There were times when she hated her for abandoning her. Now she knew the truth. And that the future of Wolf Land was in her hands.

"The explosion that shook the world and the flaming thing that fell like a meteor through the sky last night – could that be the Great Warrior Wolf?" Cuán asked.

"What do your instincts tell you, Cuán?"

Cuán thought back to the feeling of hope that she felt when she heard the explosion and saw the fireball in the sky. She felt strongly that someone had come for them. Could it be true?

"I feel it was him," she said.

"Yes, so do I."

"Does anyone else know about this, Oisín?"

"No, Cuán. You must stay here. I have to go to the monastic site. To the ancient gateway. I have to see for myself if the Portal of Starlight is open."

"The Great Wolf is there."

"Yes, Cuán. I feel that you could be right. If he is, I will find him. I will smell his blood."

"I am coming with you, Oisín."

"No, Cuán, it is not safe. As you know, I often go there to gather herbs for my potions. Deathhound's warriors won't suspect anything. However, if they see us together, they will follow us and hunt you down. And you are still weak. It is important that you rest and gather your strength."

"When will you go?"

"I must go now, Cuán. The Portal of Starlight only remains open for a certain length of time."

"Oisín, what did my mother look like?"

"She was beautiful, Cuán, just like you. She had long black hair and large brown eyes. Wait, I have something to show you."

Oisín walked over to one of the bookshelves and pulled out a small piece of paper. It was a watercolour painting of a woman in a red dress. He handed it to Cuán.

Cuán gasped and blinked back her tears.

"Mother!" she cried. The grey wolf cub jumped up onto her knee.

Oisín placed his hand on her shoulder.

"I know that this is a lot for you to take in, Cuán, but you need to be strong now. A weak wolf is vulnerable to attack. Now I really must go."

"Of course." Cuán knew that Oisín was right. For the first time in her life she knew who she was. She was the daughter of Saoirse, the Rebel Leader of Wolf Land. Cuán felt dizzy. She watched as Oisín drank the remainder of his drink.

Then he placed his wolfskin over his head and hurried out of the cottage.

Cuán walked over to the door. The room started to spin. She tried to call Oisín back, to tell him that she needed help. But it was too late. She hit her head off the table as she fell to the floor.

Chapter Thirty-nine

A Stampede of Wolves

Günther was petrified as he waited for the others to return. His leg had stopped bleeding but he still felt weak. He knew that there were wolves outside. His eyes shifted slowly towards the door. If a pack of wolves came for him there was nothing he could do. He was defenceless. The flames from the fire flickered and cast shadows on the wall of the scriptorium. He could hear the menacing, bloodthirsty howl of wolves. They were closer now. Günther looked around the room. He needed a weapon. A sharp stone or rock. Something to defend himself with. He spotted a piece of wood over by the door. He crawled over and grabbed it. In doing so he used up most of his strength and his entire body trembled with pain. As the wolves jumped on the roof of the building, Günther placed his right hand into his jacket pocket and pulled out a photograph of his twin brother Wilhelm. It was taken when they were eight years old. The two boys stood arm in arm outside their family home in Germany. They smiled at the camera. They didn't have a care in the world. Günther held back the tears that threatened to stream from his eyes. If he was about to face the wolves he had to remain brave. Günther missed Wilhelm who had died a year earlier in battle, and he longed to see him again, although he was not ready to die yet.

Within seconds he heard a thundering and clawing at the door. He thrust the piece of wood into the fire and set it alight just the iron bar gave way before a stampede of wolves.

But they were not wolves. They wore clothes and brandished weapons, and they stood upright like humans. Clearly they were werewolves. And Blaise's talk of other worlds was no more than the truth.

"Get back!" Günther yelled as werewolves circled around him.

The hair on their backs stood on end. They were ready for battle. Their eyes were red like demons. Their howls turned to snarls. Günther waved the piece of wood in the air each time one of the werewolves approached and they pulled back.

Then the most evil-looking creature appeared in the doorway. He had glowing red eyes and his entire body was covered in mangled fur. Silver battle scars lined his flesh. He breathed fire and sharp teeth like blades hung from blood-red gums. His claws were as sharp as blades and he was ten feet tall. His body was powerful and muscular, a single dark eyebrow lined his forehead. However, unlike a regular wolf this creature did not possess a tail. Around his neck hung a piece of rope. On it were the teeth of the werewolves he had killed in battle.

Günther gulped. He was petrified. His mother had told him stories of werewolves as a boy. She said that they lurked in the forest and that their piercing cries could be heard for miles around. She told him that they were human during daylight hours and wolves at night. Günther had thought they only existed in fairy tales until now.

"Retreat!" the fierce-looking warrior snarled. Flames erupted from his mouth as he spoke. The rest of the pack of werewolves backed away.

The evil werewolf knelt down in front of Günther and stared into his eyes. He grabbed his hair and pulled his head close. Günther could see the veins protruding from his forehead where his mangled fur had fallen out. His teeth were black.

"How dare you enter Wolf Land without my permission!" he snarled.

"Please don't kill me!" Günther cried.

"Shut your mouth. I am Deathhound, Ruler of Wolf Land. How did you arrive here?"

Günther felt as though he was trapped in a nightmare and couldn't wake up. "I was hiding from my enemies. I found this building and came here to rest."

Deathhound threw his large, vicious head back and laughed wildly. His advisors, the chief wolves, had told him that the explosion and the fireball in the sky meant that the Great Wolf had arrived as predicted in *The Book of Wolves*. But this was no Great Wolf. It was an injured boy werewolf from one of the neighbouring provinces. This fool was no match for the great and powerful Deathhound.

"*Guards! Enter!*"

Two guards entered.

"Take him away and kill him."

"I beg you to spare my life!" Günther pleaded. "I have done you no harm and I am no threat to you. I came here by accident." But he knew that pleading was no use. He could tell that Deathhound took great delight in his distress.

"*Wait!*" a voice shouted.

Deathhound snarled, arched his scar-lined back and stood. "*Who dares question my authority?*" he roared. The air throbbed with tension as he swivelled his head. He was about to pounce when he saw the man standing in the doorway.

"Oisín, what brings you here, my healer?" he snarled.

"I was out gathering herbs and leaves when I saw the Warrior Wolves. Who is this boy?"

"Nothing to worry about, Oisín. He is just a wanderer from another province. I have just ordered his death."

"No, you mustn't kill him," Oisín said forcefully.

Deathhound glared suspiciously at Oisín with his blood-red eyes.

"Why not?"

Oisín knew he had to think fast. Although the injured

boy didn't look like the Great Warrior Wolf, Oisín knew it was him straight away. He needed to protect him at all costs.

"The Growling battle takes place tomorrow. Let me heal him. We could use more Warrior Wolves in our province. Or he could well be a bargaining tool with the other provinces."

Deathhound gave a monstrous roar. Then he smiled to reveal his sharp black, dagger-like teeth.

"You are a wise wolf and a good friend, Oisín. Take this fool and heal him. He will battle for us in the Growling."

With those words he strode from the scriptorium. The pack of snarling wolves followed him through the snow.

Günther stared at Oisín. "You are mistaken – I am not a wolf," he said.

"Don't concern yourself with that now. You are badly injured and need help. You are lucky that I found you in time." Oisín almost laughed. It was so clear that the boy was a wolf. His skin smelt like wolf. His ears twitched like wolf and his eyes shone bright like wolf.

"Who are you?" Günther asked.

"Oisín is my name. I am a healer. I live in the town. You must come with me now."

"I can't. My friends will be back soon. They won't know where to find me."

Oisín's heart leapt with joy. "Dear Wolf! There are more of you?"

"Yes, three more. Lottie, Blaise and Albert. They have gone to fetch supplies."

"Then the ancient *Book of Wolves* is correct. Don't worry about your friends. I will return for them but first I must take care of you."

Günther nodded gratefully.

"I will carry you on my back. You can hide under my wolfskin. My house is in the town. It is only a short distance away. I have potions to heal your wounds. Do you agree?"

"Yes," Günther nodded. He knew that he had no other option. It would only be a matter of time before more werewolves would smell his blood.

A sharp pain raced up Günther's leg as Oisín hauled him onto his back.

He was heavier than he looked but Oisín was strong and determined. He needed to get back to Cuán.

Chapter Forty

The Secret Lives of Wolves

Blaise snapped a branch of a tree. He knelt down at the entrance to the Portal of Starlight and in the soil drew a diagram of his home in the forest and the spot where Günther's plane had crashed.

"I can't know for certain but I think it was the bomb-blast that activated the portal between this world and Wolf Land," he said to Lottie and Albert.

As strange as it all seemed, it made perfect sense to Lottie. "I'm sure you're right, Blaise."

Darkness descended like a shroud. Lottie glanced over her shoulder. She knew the risk that they were taking. There was a very real possibility that they would vanish and never see their own world again. That she would never see her mother again.

Then it dawned on her.

"The ring!" she cried.

"What?"

"The ring, Blaise! I have Cuán's ring. I have to get it back to her. It's a magical ring. Perhaps it can help them to escape!"

Blaise inclined his head towards her and spoke gently. "Perhaps, Lottie. But before we cross the portal again there is something else you need to know."

Lottie bit her bottom lip. She could sense that what Blaise was about to tell her was about to alter her life forever. And she resisted it with every bone in her body.

"There is no time, Blaise," she said hurriedly.

Blaise clasped his right hand on Lottie's shoulder. He could see his own reflection in her glassy eyes as he spoke. Her flame-red hair looked like a halo around her face under the fading light.

"My mother wrote about her visions in her journal, Lottie, and recorded what others told her. But she also wrote about things that she remembered about it herself."

Then Lottie understood. It was as though someone had flicked on a light switch. It was all clear to her now. "Your mother was from Wolf Land, wasn't she?"

A smile curled at the edge of Blaise's lips. As he nodded his silver earrings jingled. "Yes, she was born there just like Cuán but she didn't leave until she was six years old."

Lottie leant in close to Blaise. She placed her hand in his. It was obvious that speaking about his mother was painful for him. And she wanted to show him that she cared.

269

Blaise paused. Then he rubbed his forehead. "My mother was a Wolf Child just like Cuán. Half wolf, half human. With two hearts. A human heart and a wolf heart. But, unlike most Wolf Children, she always knew she was a werewolf because she was older when she came here and remembered her previous life."

Albert frowned. "But how did she end up here?"

"My grandmother brought her through the portal, then left her with the gypsies to be raised by them. The gypsies gave a home to many Wolf Children. They understood their nature. My grandmother knew that her child would have a good life with them. All the Wolf Children here on Earth were brought here by their mothers or fathers who risked everything to remove their children from Deathhound's terrible regime. They hoped that they would not later be plagued by their wolf natures and would grow up as humans and have a peaceful life. Sometimes it worked and their werewolf nature was suppressed. Some did transform into wolves at night, especially at full moon, but they managed to conceal their wolfish natures from their families and others. My mother was among those. Others were tracked down and lured back into Wolf Land by Thought Monsters."

"Is that what happened to Cuán?"

"Yes, Lottie, it is."

"What happens to those lured back into Wolf Land?"

"They are locked in glass boxes which are placed all around the edges of the forest. They are fed pellets. As long as they eat the magical pellets they never age."

Albert wrinkled his nose in disapproval. Then he

stuck out his tongue. "That sounds disgusting."

"That explains why Cuán is still a girl even after all these years," said Lottie.

"Yes, Lottie."

Lottie jumped to her feet. Her heart thumped and nausea rose like a wave in her throat.

"If your mother was a Wolf Child then you are one too!" she cried.

"Yes, I am, Lottie."

Blaise had never admitted to anyone that he was a Wolf Boy before. He was deeply ashamed of his dark secret. All he wanted was to be a normal boy like everyone else. Instead he was a freak of nature. A boy with two hearts who could change into a wolf.

Blaise had never been to school like other children. He had never had friends before. His mother had always kept him away from society. Whenever he got sick she gave him natural remedies. They were made from the herbs of the forest. She had learnt such things from her mother in Wolf Land and she expanded on that knowledge all her life. Blaise never visited a doctor for fear that they would find out that he had two heart beats. Through her psychic powers his mother had managed to hide from Deathhound's Thought Monsters – and the fact she was constantly on the move with the gypsies helped.

But Blaise could feel his body starting to change lately. He knew it wouldn't be long until he became a wolf and was in danger of being lured to Wolf Land.

Lottie and Albert were the only people that he had

ever got close to. But, now they knew the truth about him, he was sure that they would leave him. And who would blame them? He was a wild beast after all. If he changed into a wolf in their presence he could kill them.

Tears streamed from Lottie's eyes. It became perfectly clear to her now. Blaise needed her help as much as Cuán and Günther did. Deep down she had always known that there was something different about him. The way his dark brown eyes drew her in. And his speed when he bounded through the forest. Even his way of sneaking up on her. These were all traits of a predator. Blaise was a wolf. There was no denying it. Lottie felt foolish for not seeing it before now.

She held out her hand to Blaise. But he pushed her away. He had betrayed her and he didn't need her pity.

"Get away from me, Lottie. I am no good for you. Just by being here you are risking your life and Albert's. I can't be trusted. I should have told you this before now."

"No, Blaise. You are wrong. We have to stick together!" Lottie was exhausted. It was all too much to take in.

"Are you stupid? Didn't you hear me! I can change into a wolf and kill you."

Albert ran and hid behind his sister's back. "I'm scared, Lottie! I want to go home to Mother in England!"

Lottie turned to Albert. Then she bent down, locked eyes with him and smiled.

"Everything is going to be all right, Albert. Blaise would never hurt us."

Blaise was shocked. He grabbed Lottie by the arm.

"How can you say such a thing?"

Lottie pulled her arm free. She pulled the photograph of Blaise and his mother from her pocket. Then she handed it to him.

"Because I believe in this little boy, Blaise. I know that he has a kind heart. Maybe two of them. And he is all alone in the world with no family."

Blaise broke down. He slid down onto the forest floor, and pressed his back against a tree.

"I am so sorry, Lottie," he sobbed. "I should have told you the truth. I was just so desperate to save Cuán and the others from their terrible lives, as my mother wanted me to do."

"What's it like to change into a wolf, Blaise?" Albert asked eagerly.

Blaise shook his head. "I haven't changed yet, Albert. But I can feel it starting to happen. I can't sleep at night. Sometimes I wake up and go outside to sleep beneath the stars. I hear my name being carried on the breeze."

Lottie gulped back her tears. Then she moved a strand of her flame-red hair from her eyes. "My mother was with Cuán on the night that she disappeared – it said so in the newspaper article. She was staying with her and Cuán didn't harm her."

"Your mother was lucky, Lottie."

"No, Blaise, you are wrong. Cuán cared for my mother deeply. She was her friend. Just like we are friends."

"That was when she was still just a girl, Lottie. A wolf isn't capable of feeling love towards anyone."

"You are wrong, Blaise. Animals are gentle and loving creatures. You only have to look at your beautiful horse Snowdrop to know that. They are capable of caring for others, just like humans. Wolves live in packs and have strong family bonds. It is only when they are scared or trapped that they attack. My goodness! Your mother was a Wolf Child! You know she was gentle and good and never harmed anybody!""

Blaise nodded and arched his eyebrows. What Lottie was saying made perfect sense. It lifted his spirits.

"Then you are not going to leave me?" he asked.

"We are not going anywhere!" Albert cried.

"You see, Blaise," said Lottie, "we know what it's like to feel alone and scared. Back home in England we were in great danger every night. But it wasn't from wolves. It was from bombs being dropped by Hitler's air force."

"Children need to stick together," Albert chipped in. "You can be my big brother."

Blaise smiled. Then he wiped his eyes with his sleeve.

"So, Blaise," said Lottie, "is there anything else you need us to know about Wolf Land?"

Blaise opened up his mother's diary. On the front page was a map.

"This is the map of Wolf Land I told you about, Lottie. The land is split up into four provinces: Ulsteria, Munsteria, Leinsteria and Connaughtia."

"They are like the provinces in Ireland!" Albert cried.

Blaise nodded. "The map only tells us about Leinsteria. This is the province that we entered, the one ruled by Deathhound. Each province has its own Wolf

Children. They are made to battle against wolves from the other provinces in what is called the Growling. It takes place here in the Forest of Non-Existence." He pointed at the map. "Many are killed each time."

"How awful! The Wolf Children have to battle to survive?" Lottie asked.

"Yes. I suppose it is a kind of punishment for attempting to escape from Wolf Land – or a punishment for their parents who were actually responsible. Most Wolf Children are killed eventually. Those who survive a battle but are wounded are taken to the town to be treated by Oisín the Healer. The provinces are separated by four waterfalls. They are known as the Waterfalls of Children's Tears. Once you step through the waterfall you are entering enemy territory."

Blaise paused and looked at Lottie.

"Yes, Blaise? What is it?"

"There is something else that you must know. After twenty Growlings, if the Wolf Children survive, their human hearts die and they stay as wolves forever. They become what is known as Elder Wolves and live in the forest in packs – as natural wolves do – but of course they still must eat the stars to survive."

"But, Blaise! This is the twentieth year for Cuán!" said Lottie. "That means that the next Growling is Cuán's last battle!"

Blaise nodded. "If we don't save her, Lottie, her human heart will die."

"We need to go back there immediately!" Albert piped up.

"One more thing," said Blaise. "This is my mother's wolf ring." He pulled a green velvet ribbon out from inside his shirt.

Lottie gasped when she saw the wolf ring. It was made of pure gold and had emerald eyes. "Blaise, it is beautiful!"

"She gave it to me on the night that she died."

"How did she die, Blaise?" Albert asked.

Blaise hung his head. "It was all my fault. She got pneumonia. I tried to care for her myself. She refused to go into a hospital because she wanted to protect me."

"In what way?" Lottie frowned.

"If she went into hospital they would discover her wolf heart. It was too late for her, but she knew that if they found me they would lock me away and experiment on me. They would treat me like a piece of meat. A freak of nature."

"Couldn't you have just left her at the hospital? If she didn't tell them she had a son they would never have found out."

"But people knew of me. Besides, she wanted to die at home with me."

"You must miss her terribly, Blaise."

"Not a day goes by that I don't think of her. I cared for her until the very end. We made a bed beneath the stars. On the night that she passed away I held her in my arms. I promised her that I would do everything I could to stop myself from going to Wolf Land. Eventually her human heart gave up. She changed into a beautiful grey wolf with amber eyes."

"So she survived as a wolf!" Lottie gasped.

"Yes, she did."

"Do you still see her, Blaise?" Albert asked. His eyes were wide with expectation.

At first Blaise didn't reply. He turned his head away and then he said, "At first I saw her every day. She would come up into the caravan with me. I would sing to her and play music. At night-time she would sleep outside. I always felt safe with her there guarding me. It was as though she had never left."

"Where is she now?"

"Word got out amongst people in the village of Kilbree that there was a grey wolf roaming through the forest. Late one night as I slept I heard the sound of a gunshot being fired. Then there was a piercing cry. I knew that it was her straight away. I lit a lamp and ran outside. I found her lying there in a pool of blood. The farmer that had shot her stood there too. Smoke rose from his gun. I lay beside her and placed my head against her chest and listened to the steady beat of her heart. It got slower and slower until eventually it stopped beating. And I realised that my beautiful mother had died for the second time. I was overcome with grief. I still am."

Lottie placed her hand on Blaise's arm. She was taken aback when he suddenly threw his arms around her neck.

"Your mother will always be with you, Blaise," she said. "Love that strong never dies."

Albert turned his face towards the full moon which

hung like a silver penny in the black sky. He sobbed as he thought of his own mother back home. Her kind eyes. Her blonde hair tied up in a pony-tail. And his heart broke for Blaise.

"Enough about me," said Blaise, releasing Lottie from his embrace. "We need to go and rescue the others."

"All right, Blaise," said Lottie. "But may I have a look at the journal first?"

"Of course." Blaise handed Lottie the diary.

Lottie began to leaf through it. It was more like an instruction manual about life in Wolf Land. At the front of the diary was the map. This was followed by a list of children's names. There were over forty of them. Blaise's Mother had drawn two pictures beside each one: one of a child and one of a wolf.

"Are all these Wolf Children?" she asked.

Blaise nodded and bowed his head as he spoke. "They were all there with Cuán in the glass boxes in my mother's visions. They were all from Leinsteria."

"Where are they now?"

"Some may have died in battle. A few may have survived twenty Growlings, turned into wolves and roam around the forest as Elder Wolves."

There were other pages in the diary too. There were detailed explanations about the properties of starlight. And how the werewolves needed to eat the stars in order to survive. There was also a page about the Growling and the tactics to use in battle.

"Here. This is what I wanted you to see."

Blaise turned the page. There was a picture of a man

with a long blonde beard. He looked like a Viking. He had a large smile and was standing outside a wooden house. He was wearing a wolfskin coat.

"The image is of Oisín the Healer," Blaise explained. "He is a werewolf too though he sticks to his human form – this is forbidden by Deathhound but he depends on Oisín's expertise as a healer to keep the Wolf Children alive. He is the only one besides Deathhound in Wolf Land to be immortal. And he is the one who helped my grandmother to sneak my mother out of Wolf Land."

"Didn't he get punished for it?" Lottie enquired.

"Mother told me that no-one ever suspected him. And it would never have crossed Deathhound's mind that any of his loyal henchmen would have dared to defy him. Oisín had helped others in the past too."

"So where are they? Your mother met them, you said, on your travels."

"They live around ancient sites. They can be found all over Ireland. One is at Glendalough, another is the Giant's Causeway. But there are many more. Some, of course, still live in human families. Some travel with the gypsies. And some have left Ireland never to return. Günther's ancestors no doubt."

"Günther isn't a Wolf Child – he is a soldier," Albert announced.

"He is both, Albert," said Blaise. "I knew it the moment I saw him. Call it intuition or my animal senses. It is written in *The Book of Wolves* that the Great Warrior Wolf will come from the clouds. He will help to save the Wolf Children. I believe that is Günther. Besides, doesn't his name Günther mean 'warrior'?"

"It makes perfect sense," said Lottie. "Günther was never meant to drop bombs on Ireland. He couldn't help himself. It was like being drawn here by a huge invisible magnet." Lottie snapped the diary shut and handed it back to Blaise. Then she tossed her long red hair over her shoulder. It glistened under the moonlight which peeped like a thief through a cloud.

"Let's go!" Albert cried.

Lottie took his hand and walked to the Portal of Starlight. Then she paused. She looked up at the moon and breathed the cold night air into her lungs.

Blaise bit his lip. "What are you doing?" A knot twisted in his stomach like a dagger.

"This may be the last time that we see our world. I want to take one last look before we go."

Then Blaise took her other hand. And together the three children ran into the portal and on to face the battle of a lifetime.

Chapter Forty-one

Danger beneath the Glowing Moons

Under the watchful gaze of the shining silver moon Lottie, Albert and Blaise moved through the portal of shimmering light. It glistened like a million stars. At first it felt cool on their skin. Then it turned warm. The whooshing sound of shooting stars whizzed past their ears and they each felt weightless. It was as though they were floating through time and space. They held each other tightly and did not let go as brightly coloured lights flashed before their eyes.

When it was all over when they fell onto a blanket of soft, white snow. The air was cold. So cold that Lottie could see her breath in the air and tiny snowflakes landed on Albert's eyelashes. The snow continued to fall. A clap of thunder that sounded like a monster's roar rumbled above their heads.

"Come on!" Blaise called as he ran towards the scriptorium.

Then his worst fear was realised. The wooden door had been torn from its hinges.

Lottie ran after him and was about to enter the small stone building when Blaise unexpectedly grabbed her arm.

"Wait! It might be a trap!" he warned, and he tentatively walked towards the small stone building. It was dark inside and the fire had gone out. He stepped in, unsure of what or who he would meet.

"Blaise, what can you see? Is Günther there?" Lottie asked. Her heart thumped in her chest. She feared the worst. What if Günther was dead? She would never forgive herself for bringing him there.

Blaise waited for a few seconds for his eyes to adjust to the dark. His hands trembled as he reached out in the darkness, not knowing what he would find. But Günther was gone. It had been a mistake to leave him alone. Blaise realised that they had to keep moving. Whoever or whatever had taken Günther could return at any moment.

"We need to go now!" Blaise cried as he reached out and gripped Albert's hand.

"Where's Günther?" Albert asked. His blond hair fell into his eyes as he spoke.

"He's gone, Albert," said Lottie.

"Gone where?"

"I don't know," said Blaise. "But we need to get out of here and fast."

"Wait – we can't just leave!" Lottie gripped Blaise by the elbow and stared into his eyes.

"Günther is gone, Lottie." Tears sprang from Blaise's eyes. He knew he sounded harsh. But he needed her to understand. There was nothing that could be done to help Günther now.

She knew what he meant, when he said Günther was gone. It meant that he was dead. The werewolves had killed Günther.

"The smoke from the fire must have sent out a signal, attracting werewolves from miles around," she cried. "How could we have been so stupid?"

"There's no time for that now, Lottie," Blaise said reassuringly. "When my mother was killed I asked myself the same questions. I blamed myself for not doing more to protect her. I asked myself questions like – what if I had seen the farmer approaching with his gun? Or, what if we had moved away? Over time I forgave myself. None of this is my fault, or yours, Lottie."

Blaise was right. Lottie had seen it back home in Manchester. So many innocent lives were destroyed due to the war. People died every night as bombs fell from the sky. And there was nothing anyone could do about it. At least here they could try to save Cuán and the Wolf Children.

A horn sounded in the distance. Lottie sensed that it signalled danger.

"Which way should we go now, Blaise?" she asked urgently.

Blaise took his mother's diary from his pocket and studied the map. It was hard to see in the darkness.

"We have to go to the edge of the forest and begin to

search for the glass boxes where the Wolf Children are imprisoned."

"Lottie, I am scared – maybe we should go back through the Portal of Starlight!" Albert cried.

Lottie hunkered down like a cat and looked her brother squarely in the eye.

"You need to be brave now, Albert. Like a real soldier going into battle. Like Father."

Albert nodded and tried to look brave.

Suddenly the distant sound of men shouting and wolves howling echoed through the trees made from bone. Deathhound and his wolf warriors were out hunting. But who or what was their prey?

"This way!" Blaise cried.

They ran past the Tower of Wolves and on through the trees. They leapt over rocks and scurried through brambles. A cool breeze brought a fresh drift of snowflakes

They came to a deep stream, too wide jump across, and were forced to run along its bank. The howling of wolves and the sound of horns were now closer behind them.

Suddenly Albert fell. His caught his leg on the sharp edge of a rock and it was bleeding.

"Quick, Albert!" Lottie cried as she helped her brother to his feet.

They ran on. Lottie felt sorry for Albert when she saw his bright-red blood against the white snow.

The hunt was close behind. Yes, they were the prey.

When Blaise saw a small boat moored to a post by the

stream, he had an idea. They could put the hunt off their scent.

He leapt into the boat, almost upsetting it. "Get in!" he yelled.

Lottie and Albert scrambled in. Blaise untied the boat and the current of the stream carried it away.

They rounded a corner and Blaise called out: "*Keep your heads well down!*" They were approaching some low-hanging branches. He grabbed the mooring rope with one hand and, as the boat swept beneath them, he grabbed the branches with the other.

The boat halted with a jerk and swung around to the bank.

"Get out, Lottie! Albert!"

He followed them and let the boat float swiftly on.

Now they were on the opposite bank from the hunt.

"*Follow me!*"

Blaise led them away from the stream until he came to some rocks. He crouched down behind them and the others joined him.

Blaise peered out through a crack between two rocks.

Deathhound and the hunting party stormed along the bank of the stream until they halted at the point where the boat had been. Deathhound bent and sniffed at the mooring post like a bloodhound. Blaise had never seen such a fierce warrior before. He breathed fire and sharp teeth like blades hung from blood-red gums. His claws were vicious, and he was muscular and hugely tall. He howled and pointed downstream with his huge spear.

Then he and his warriors rushed off down the stream.

"*Yes!*" said Blaise. "They fell for it! They lost the scent at the water and think we're still in the boat ahead of them. They'll keep going until they find that boat!"

He got to his feet and began to run again, beckoning to the others to follow him.

Lottie's heart lurched in her chest when she realised that he was heading back towards the Tower of Wolves.

"You're going the wrong way, Blaise!"

"Trust me, Lottie, I know what I'm doing."

When they reached the settlement they moved more cautiously in case any warriors had been left there.

"*Ow!*" Albert had tripped and fallen again.

"*Albert!*" hissed Lottie. "*Be careful!*"

"I've found the ladder, Blaise!" Albert said.

A rickety wooden ladder was lying in the grass.

"Excellent! Well done, Albert!" said Blaise. "We need to hide in the Tower of Wolves until we work out a plan. I just hope that door is not locked."

Blaise set the ladder against the tower and held it for the others to climb up to the doorway. The cold wind chilled their bones as they scrambled up the ladder.

"Keep going, Albert! Think of how proud Father would be of you!" Lottie called out. She knew that Albert was terrified of heights. Just one wrong move and he would tumble to the ground.

When they reached the doorway Lottie was hugely relieved to find the metal door was not locked. They entered a small round room with a stone floor and Blaise pulled up the ladder and bolted the door behind them.

They climbed a spiral stone staircase that led to the

top floor of the tower.

Blaise looked out one of the narrow windows. The view was breath-taking. Two moons shone down on Wolf Land. The silver moon that was visible from Earth and the large egg-shaped blue moon. It looked like a scene from a fairy tale, or a beautiful painting. From this vantage point he could see the mountain tops and the Forest of Non-Existence. Everything was exactly as his mother told him it would be.

Chapter Forty-two

The Great Warrior Wolf and The Leader of Wolf Land

Cuán blinked as she opened her eyes. The light above her head was bright and she could make out the shape of someone standing over her. For a moment she thought that she was back at home, in her own bed with Maeve watching her. She took a deep breath and smiled. She could almost smell the sweet scent of her ma's baking. She reached out her hand to touch her face. Instead she found the soft grey fur of her wolf cub. He yelped with delight and licked her face. He was glad that she was alive.

"You gave me a fright!" a voice boomed.

It was not Maeve. It was Oisín the Healer. She was in his house. Then it all came back to her. She remembered Oisín bringing her there and how he had told her that her mother was Saoirse, the famous rebel leader of Wolf Land. After that it was all a blur.

Cuán tried to wrench herself up but did not have the strength. "What happened to me?" she croaked. Her vocal cords were damaged and the words scratched her throat as she spoke.

"Not enough light. You have something that humans call anaemia, Cuán. You have been exposed to twenty years of darkness. It's taking its toll on your body. I had to leave and when I got back here you were in a coma. Don't worry – I'm taking care of you now."

Cuán's mind was racing she had so many thoughts. So much to catch up on.

"What about the Growling?"

Cuán knew that if her wolf heart stopped then she would be of no use to Deathhound. He would send her to the forest to die.

"There is no need to worry, Cuán. I've had to stop your wolf heart temporarily. Your human heart is keeping you alive. Once you are feeling stronger I will inject your wolf heart and it will beat again."

Oisín patted Cuán affectionately on the hand. He cared for the Wolf Children as if they were his own. He was genuinely heartbroken when a Wolf Child died. Besides, Cuán was no ordinary Wolf Child. Her mother was the great warrior Saoirse.

"You have company," Oisín said.

Then he spoke to someone else as he left the room.

"I have to have to go but I will be back soon," he said.

He went out and Cuán heard the rattle of keys as he turned them in the multiple locks that were on the door. There were bars and shutters on the windows. He had to ensure that the werewolves were kept out. They were always lurking around outside his house and were quite capable of slaughtering any injured Wolf Children if they got inside.

Cuán glanced across the white room. Her head felt fuzzy. She saw a boy in the bed opposite her. His leg was covered with a bandage. He wore a uniform that consisted of a dark grey jacket with a brown belt and light-grey trousers. They were torn and stained with blood. Cuán's heart leapt for joy. For a moment she thought that she was still dreaming but then she realised that her instincts were right. The boy opposite her was the Great Warrior Wolf. The Chosen One. Perhaps there were others with him. Maybe even an army of wolves who could help them to escape. While she was unconscious she had dreamt of a girl with flame-red hair. Her heart raced and her cracked lips forced a smile.

"Are you the Great Warrior Wolf that came from the clouds?" Cuán asked. Her voice was weak and she had to strain to be heard.

The boy sat up. "What do you mean? My name Günther does mean 'warrior' and I did come from the clouds as my plane crashed. But where does 'wolf' come into it?"

Cuán didn't recognise his accent. For a moment she wondered if he was one of Deathhound's evil Thought Monsters playing a cruel trick on her. It wouldn't be the first time she had been snared by their wicked ways. Tears fell like marbles from her eyes. She had not seen someone from home in such a long time. She longed to crawl across the room. To touch his skin and smell his clothes.

"Where are you from?" she asked instead.

Günther had never seen such a strange-looking creature before. Her eyes looked as though they belonged to a wild beast, not a little girl.

"I am from Germany. I am a fighter pilot. As I said, my plane crashed but I survived and some friends brought me to the abbey. I don't remember exactly how that happened. I was in pain and I think I blacked out ..." He shook his head in puzzlement.

Cuán gasped in delight. "There are more of you?"

"Yes, but they do not know I am here in this town. They hid me in the scriptorium." Günther lay back on his bed and stared at the ceiling. "They went to get food and drink and blankets but while they were gone a wicked beast called Deathhound arrived and wanted to kill me. But Oisín insisted on healing me instead so he brought me here."

"Does Deathhound know that you are a Wolf Child?"

"What do you mean?"

Cuán realised that Günther didn't know what she was talking about. There was no easy way to say it. "I am a Wolf Girl, Günther. I change into a wolf. I have two hearts – one human and one wolfish."

A smile exploded on Gunter's lips. "You don't expect me to believe that, do you?" He was beginning to think that Cuán had something wrong with her mind as well as her body.

Cuán shrugged her shoulders and stared into

Günther's eyes. "Believe what you want. It is a fact. They use me and the other Wolf Children as a form of entertainment. They make us fight each other to the death."

Günther didn't want to upset Cuán. She looked as though she had been through enough. So he changed the subject. "How long have you been here?"

"In Wolf Land?" Cuán asked.

Günther looked puzzled. "Yes, if that is where we are."

Cuán swallowed hard. "What year is it now?"

Günther found it hard not to laugh. "Don't you know? It is 1940."

Cuán coughed and her chest rattled. "Then I have been here for twenty years. Since 1920."

Günther thought that she was having a joke at his expense. "That is impossible – you are still a child."

Cuán needed him to understand. "Listen, Günther, we have no time to lose. Deathhound won't keep you here for long. As soon as you recover he will send you to the forest to fight."

Günther turned on his side. His leg was aching "How do you know?" he gasped.

"There have been other prisoners over the years. Wolf Children like me who are lured here by some invisible force that calls our names each night. Others just accidentally arrive here like you."

"Where are the other prisoners now?" he asked.

"Most of them are dead." Cuán thought of Niamh. It pained her to remember her friend. She recalled how the

Thought Monsters had treated her so cruelly in the last few days of her life.

"Now I remember … he said something about a battle tonight." Günther panicked. His eyes darted all around the room. "We need to escape."

"We can't, Günther. I know because I have tried to escape. There is only one way out. Through the Portal of Starlight. The portal was open and you came through. However, *The Book of Wolves* says that it only stays open for twenty-four Earth hours at a time."

Günther remembered the shooting stars but . . . a Portal of Starlight? Earth hours? He winced in pain as he adjusted his leg. His suspicions were clearly right – this girl had lost her mind.

Cuán looked sad. She could tell that Günther didn't believe her. She opened her yellow eyes wide. "Believe me, Günther, we have all tried to escape. My friend Niamh lost her life trying to escape from this evil place."

Günther hated to be in such as hopeless position. He had survived the plane crash. But now he was locked up with some strange girl who thought he was a wolf. "So all we can do is wait?"

"For now." Cuán smiled reassuringly.

Günther smiled back. Whatever her state of mind, he liked her.

"You are the first new person to arrive in Wolf Land for a long time. Faolán, another one of the Wolf Children, thought that the gateway between the two worlds was shut forever. But then we heard an almighty blast. It sounded like something had fallen from the sky. This was followed by something shooting from the sky like a meteor. Then you arrived, Günther. It is written in *The Book of Wolves* that the Great Warrior Wolf will come from the clouds to save us."

Günther could not believe Cuán. "Before my aeroplane crashed I dropped a bomb. That must have been the sound that you heard. The blazing light was my plane. It caught fire in the sky."

A single tear fell from Cuán's eye. "If it was the plane then the two worlds are closer than we ever imagined. Of course I do know that somehow we share the same stars . . ."

She lay back and stared at the white wall in front of them on which the magic lantern flashed images of Ireland. There were rolling valleys, mountain tops and rivers. The sky was blue and the sun shone.

"What is this?" Günther asked.

"This is part of our treatment, Günther. Night is eternal in Wolf Land. But the human side of our brains needs light to survive. The projected images are a form of healing. There is also artificial light which helps our bodies to function."

The rattle of keys being turned in the locks alerted them to the fact that someone was coming.

A look of fear crossed Cuán's eyes. "Don't speak of this to anyone, Günther, except for me and the other Wolf Children. Do you understand me?"

Günther nodded. He had never felt so terrified before. Not even when his plane was a somersaulting ball of smoke and fire hurting through the clouds. At least he understood then what was happening. This world that Cuán called Wolf Land was alien to him and she herself seemed deranged.

The wooden door swung open and Cuán's jaw dropped in amazement while Günther cried out with joy as Oisín, Albert, Blaise and Lottie entered and stood in front of them.

Smiling, Oisín stood back while Lottie rushed to Cuán's bed and Albert darted over to give Günther a big hug. Blaise followed him and embraced Günther, smiling. Cuán's wolf cub sniffed the air and jumped off the bed. He ran over to Albert who stroked his soft fur.

"Cuán, you are alive!" Lottie said.

"Nancy! You came for me!" Tears leapt from Cuán's eyes. She could not believe it. Her friend had found her after all this time.

"No, Cuán, I'm not Nancy. I'm Lottie, Nancy's daughter."

Cuán reached out and hugged Lottie. She recalled the last time she saw Nancy and how she had shared her secrets with her. It was hard to believe that this was Nancy's daughter.

"Of course! Nancy is twenty years older than me now. How is your mother, Lottie? She was very kind to me."

"Mother is fine," Lottie said. Although she had no real way of knowing. Every night more bombs were dropped in England. But Lottie felt it was best not to mention any of this to Cuán.

"Did she tell you about me, Lottie?"

Lottie bit her bottom lip. She hated to admit to Cuán

that her mother had never mentioned her. Although she thought that her mother was simply protecting her. She hoped that Cuán would understand.

"No, my friend Blaise told me about you." She pointed at Blaise.

"Nancy is a good friend," said Cuán. "She promised that she would never tell anyone that I was a Wolf Child."

"Oh! So that was why! I wondered why she never told me about you."

"We have come to rescue you both," Blaise said.

He looked at Cuán and smiled, then blushed as she met his eyes. She was even more beautiful than he had imagined her to be. Her dark hair framed her face. Her skin was pale and her eyes were large and round. His mother had told him that Cuán was born to be the leader of Wolf Land. Together with Günther they made a strong force. However, they were both injured.

"We don't have much time," he said. "The portal only stays open for about twenty-four hours."

"But Cuán is not well enough to leave yet," Oisín said. "Her heart is too weak."

The sound of a loud bang coming from outside the house alerted Oisín to danger. It was followed by the frightening sound of wolves howling. It was enough to chill the blood. Oisín knew it meant danger.

"Deathhound must be here. We have to hide you children. Come here!"

Lottie, Albert and Blaise followed Oisín over to his bookcase. He pulled out an ancient leather-bound book.

The bookcase swivelled open to reveal a small room.

"Wait in here and don't make the tiniest sound," Oisín instructed. "Wolves have sharp hearing and so do werewolves." He grabbed what looked like a large perfume bottle from a shelf just inside and quickly sprayed the children with a strange-smelling liquid. "To block your scent."

Then he stepped outside, placed the book back on the shelf and the bookcase shut.

"*I command you to let me in right now!*" Deathhound's voice boomed.

"*I am coming, Great One!*" Oisín cried as he opened the door and let the werewolves in.

Chapter Forty-three

The Revelation of Wolves

Deathhound hunched his shoulders, clicked his knuckles and sniffed the air. The scent of wolf blood was strong inside the house, too strong to be just Cuán's. It was proof there were two Wolf Children present.

"I called to see how our new Wolf Boy is," he said. With each word he spoke he came a step closer to Günther.

Günther fixed his gaze on Cuán, refusing to look into Deathhound's evil red eyes. His heart thumped in his chest.

"Sly one, aren't you, Wolf Boy?" Deathhound snarled. Then he pulled a knife from his belt and placed it on Günther's throat. As he spoke, his lips stretched back and his teeth appeared sharper. "How did you find us?"

Günther forced himself to look at Deathhound. "After my plane crashed, I needed somewhere to hide and stumbled across the abbey," he said as calmly as he could. He must not mention the other children. He felt indebted to them for all the kindness that they had shown to him.

Deathhound could almost hear the sound of Günther's thoughts ticking over in his brain, like cogs in a wheel. He knew that the Thought Monsters would be able to infiltrate his mind in a heartbeat during the Growling.

"How long have you been a Wolf Boy?"

Günther flinched like a deer caught in headlights. Cuán had been telling him the truth about changing into a wolf. He glanced at her and she turned away, like the tide retreating from the shore.

"You are mistaken," he said. "I am not a Wolf Boy. I am human."

"Is that so?" Deathhound said with a hideous grin. "That had better not be true for your own sake. Your wolf blood will be put to the test tonight at the Growling." He thrust his face close to Günther's, his fiery breath so hot it almost scorched his skin.

"*No!*" Cuán cried.

Oisín ran to her. "Pardon me, sir, but Cuán is too weak to take part in the Growling battle tonight. Her wolf heart is still frozen. She will need time to heal." He placed his hand on Cuán's wrist and felt for her pulse. It was beating too fast.

"There is no time. Heal her!" Deathhound ordered.

Oisín feared that Cuán would have a heart attack. "I am not sure that I can heal her."

"Would you prefer a trip to the Wolf Pit?" Deathhound shrieked.

"No, sir!" Oisín cried, though he didn't believe his master would ever fling him into a pit to be mauled by werewolves. He was too valuable to him for that.

He hurried across the room towards a shelf which was full of ancient manuscripts and books of potions. There was an oak cabinet in the corner of the room. The faces of two wolves were carved into the doors. They opened when he said the magic words *"Wolf Blood"*.

Inside the small cabinet, wooden shelves were lined with red velvet. There was an assortment of glass bottles of different shapes and sizes. He picked up various tinctures and potions in his quest to find the one which would keep Cuán alive.

"Where is the heart-reviver potion?" he muttered to himself. He hesitated for a moment then sighed with relief. He picked up a brown bottle off the top shelf.

Then he ran back across the white tiles, carefully carrying the potion in his hand. A small golden ladle with a handle made from pearl was in a kidney-shaped metal tray beside Cuán's bed. Oisín reached for it. Then he took the cork out of the bottle. It hadn't been opened in a long time. The foul stench of rotten eggs and sour goat's milk wafted through the air. With no time to lose, he poured a thick treacle-like substance onto the golden ladle. Then he pressed it against Cuán's chapped lips.

"Drink, Cuán!" he ordered. His large watery eyes pleaded with her while his hand trembled with fear.

Cuán slowly opened her mouth and allowed the black

liquid to slide down her throat. She coughed as it landed like a rock in her stomach.

Oisín flinched as Deathhound lurched forward. For an awful moment he thought that his wicked master had discovered that he was hiding the children.

A hideous scowl spilled across Deathhound's face like milk from a jug as Cuán gasped and her body jerked. *"What is happening to her?"* he demanded, grabbing Oisín by the throat.

Cuán stretched her fingertips out and touched Oisín's quivering hand. She needed him to know that she would play her part at the Growling. She would eat the stars and with the help of Günther the Great Warrior Wolf she would face the battle of her life.

"I will fight!" she choked out.

Deathhound released Oisín who fell to the floor.

Günther watched the healer stagger to his feet again. He didn't understand what was happening. But he knew that he would do battle in the Growling. Even if it meant pretending to be a Wolf Boy. Even if it meant risking everything.

Deathhound turned to him. "Let's see how you perform at the Growling, new boy!" he sneered. "The stars are perfectly aligned which means that the Wolf Children and the Thought Monsters will give you the battle of a lifetime."

Thought Monsters? Günther didn't know what those could be. Heart beating hard, he lay very still and watched as Deathhound strode out of the house, slamming the door behind him.

Günther looked over at Cuán. She looked weak. He realised that they were both in great danger. He had escaped one war back home. And another, far more dangerous one was about to begin.

Chapter Forty-four

The Forest of Non-Existence

That evening the cages were lowered to the ground. The glass doors sprang open.

Faolán was the first out of his cage. He stretched his long limbs and walked calmly to the edge of the Forest of Non-Existence. All the Wolf Children had gathered. Faolán recognised some of them from previous battles. Deathhound's evil warriors were also taking up position to guard the perimeters of the forest in case the children tried to escape.

Now the Wolf Children had to exercise as they did every evening. The Growling would be later that night. Before it, they would return to their boxes to rest and eat. Deathhound needed his Wolf Children to be in peak condition, if they were to win.

Faolán waited for Madigan to join him.

Madigan's long brown curls covered her shoulders.

She was dressed in a dress made of black petals. It stretched to the ground. Her wolf ring was on a chain around her neck, its sapphires sparkling. Faólan wore trousers made of black petals and a cloak made from wolfskin. His wolf ring had diamond eyes.

"Today is a good day – someone is coming for us," Madigan whispered to Faolán as they darted through the trees, alongside the other children.

They had to run around the forest for forty minutes to get their blood moving. If at any point the children stopped running the Thought Monsters would be released from inside the trees, which were made of bone. They would chase the children until they could run no more. Then they would devour them. The younger and weaker Wolf Children were the most vulnerable. Madigan watched a young girl with mousy brown hair. The girl stopped to catch her breath and a Thought Monster slid out from inside a tree and gobbled her up. It was as though she had never existed. Madigan looked away. She had to keep going.

Faolán panted breathlessly. "I can feel it too. The explosion and the fireball in the sky, it's got to mean something. But Cuán is yet to return." He ran ahead, around a group of teenage boys.

Madigan lurched forward to follow him, almost banging into one of the boys.

"*Hey, watch it!*" he shouted.

Madigan smiled to herself as she caught up with Faolán. All of the Wolf Children respected him, as he was a strong wolf.

She turned her head to him. "It is written in *The Book of Wolves*. The Great Warrior Wolf will come from the sky. We have to get a message to the Elder Wolves."

The Elder Wolves were the only wolves who could wander freely between the provinces. They could alert all the wolves in Wolf Land.

Faólan felt light-headed. Madigan was right. The Elder Wolves were Wolf Children once. They had survived twenty Growlings. This meant that they were wolves forevermore. He would never admit it, but he cared for Cuán and Madigan more than anything. They were family to him and he didn't want anything to happen to them. He knew that Madigan was right. It was their only chance of survival. They needed more wolves to join with them at the Growling.

Madigan watched a pair of twins running amongst the trees. They had bright blue eyes and long blonde hair. Then she sprinted forward to keep pace with Faolán.

"I know what we can do," he said. "We can contact the group of Elder Wolves that live beside the Waterfall of Children's tears – if we are quick we can make it there before we're called back to our boxes." They had often seen those wolves from a distance but had never approached the waterfall as the sound of children's voices crying which came from it distressed them. They had heard that the presence of the Elder Wolves helped to lessen that mournful sound.

Madigan's black curls were stuck to her forehead with sweat. She struggled to find the words to reply to Faolán. She needed to save her strength. They had waited for many years for this moment. This was their only chance. She knew what she had to do. One foot in front of the other. It sounded so simple and straightforward. Yet her chest ached as her two hearts thumped like a drum.

Faolán circled her like a bird of prey while other children overtook them. He was willing her to keep moving.

"We need to sneak off now, while the coast is clear," he said. "If we are quick we can reach the Elder Wolves and be back before they even realise that we are gone."

It would be risky, Madigan knew, but it was a risk she was willing to take. She had one last surge of power. Faolán reached out and held her hand. And when no-one was looking they slipped through the trees. They both knew that they had to do this. Their lives depended on it.

Chapter Forty-five

The Girl with Two Hearts

Cuán was unable to stop crying.

"Hush, child. It will all be all right," Oisín soothed. He placed his hand on Cuán's forehead to check her temperature.

There were times when Cuán strongly felt the struggle taking place inside her. Between Cuán the girl and Cuán the wolf. Only one would be victorious. Only one would survive.

"Will it hurt when you restart her wolf heart?" Albert enquired.

Cuán was terrified. She knew that her body would have to be strong to survive the Growling. And even if she did survive, tonight was her twentieth Growling. After this she would be an Elder Wolf. Cuán the Wolf would be victorious.

"I will make sure that it is as painless as possible for

you, Cuán. I have a special tonic that will strengthen you." Oisín gave a watery smile. It didn't quite reach the corners of his mouth. He knew that the chances of Cuán surviving were small. They both did. Even with his potions and tinctures there simply wasn't enough time for her heart to heal. And even if there was, after tonight it would all be over. She would be a wolf forever.

Günther sat on the edge of the bed with his legs on the floor. He needed to be able to walk if he was to have any chance of escaping.

"What exactly is the Growling?" he asked.

Oisín was administering an injection into Cuán's arm to help ease the pain. Her vein throbbed and she immediately relaxed.

"The Growling is a battle between Wolf Children that takes place at a sacred time when all the stars align, Günther. It happens once a year when the Blue Wolf Moon appears in the sky. Then the children eat the stars and turn into wolves."

Günther's jaw dropped: what Oisín was saying was unbelievable.

Blaise sat on a stool reading from *The Book of Wolves*. It was incredible. The words were scribed in ancient werewolf language. Yet he could read it perfectly. It was every bit as beautiful as his mother had told him.

"Is it true that I have wolf blood?" Günther asked.

Blaise put the book down on the table and looked at Günther. "You do, Günther. And it is particularly strong."

Günther scowled furiously. "You are wrong. I have

never changed into a wolf."

"Not yet. But you will, boy – mark my words," said Oisín as he prepared an injection for Cuán.

"How can you be so sure?" Lottie asked.

"The scent of Günther's wolf blood is strong," Oisín explained. "It is carried in the air like the scent of roses on a summer's day."

Günther rubbed his chin and sighed. "You are all crazy."

"Believe what you want, boy," said Oisín. "But there was a reason why your plane fell from the sky. The best way to describe it is that it is like a magnetic force."

"You mean I was fated to come here to Wolf Land?"

"Yes, in a nutshell," Blaise replied.

Then they all fell silent as they watched Oisín administer the injection to kick-start Cuán's wolf heart.

Suddenly Cuán's entire bed began to shake.

"What's happening to her?" Günther cried.

"Her wolf blood is being pumped through her veins. There is great resistance from her human heart. It wants to reject it."

Cuán's eyes rolled around in their sockets. The veins in her hands and neck looked as though they were about to burst through her skin. Her lips turned blue. Her skin turned a deathly pale grey colour.

"Do something!" Günther shrieked. He put the full weight of his body on the floor. As he hobbled over to Cuán's bed his leg began to bleed again. Blood trickled through his bandage.

"There is nothing more that I can do," Oisín said,

rubbing his beard with his hand. "We just have to wait now and hope that she survives." His eyes narrowed and his throat felt dry.

Oisín wished that he could take Cuán's pain away. He had loved her from the moment she arrived back in Wolf Land, and he knew that the fate of Wolf Land lay in her hands. It said in *The Book of Wolves* that a girl with ivory skin would arrive. She would join forces with the Great Warrior Wolf from the sky. If Cuán died it was all for nothing.

While the children waited by Cuán's bedside, Oisín walked over to his bookcase and took the leather-bound book from the self. Once more the bookcase swivelled open and Oisín entered the dark room.

Albert tiptoed over and peered in after him, then jumped back as Oisín emerged out of the gloom with a large box in his hands.

Oisín placed the heavy box on the floor. He put the book back on the shelf, and like magic the door shut again.

"What's in the box?" Albert asked, admiring the faces of wolves carved into the wood. They were the same as those on the doors of the cabinet.

Oisín bent down and opened the lid. Inside the box were the most beautifully decorated carnival masks that Lottie had ever seen. Each mask was made in the image of a wolf. There were also green and red velvet cloaks with hoods that fastened with a ribbon around the neck.

Oisín carefully took the masks out of the box and handed them to the children.

"The Growling will start in a few hours' time. You can go and watch the proceedings as long as you wear a disguise."

"Do you have a mask small enough for me?" Albert enquired.

"Yes, Albert, I have the perfect mask for you."

Oisín handed Albert a wolf mask that was covered in thick brown fur. Two large teeth protruded from the open mouth. Albert held the wolf mask up to his face and Lottie was astounded by how real it looked.

Lottie took a beautiful red cloak from the box and put it on, pulling the hood up over her head.

"There is just one other thing that you need," Oisín said as he fumbled with a cork on top of a yellow glass bottle.

"That smells disgusting!" Albert cried as Oisín poured some of the green liquid into the children's hands.

"What is it? Lottie enquired as she sniffed the strange potion.

"It is wolf scent. Whenever you are wearing this the wolves won't sense your human blood. They will think that you are wolves and are less likely to attack."

"This is so exciting, Lottie!" Albert cried.

Blaise glanced at Lottie. He knew that they would be in great danger roaming around the forest with the wolves, but they needed to help the Wolf Children escape and this was the only way.

"Now you are ready for the Growling," Oisín said as he stood back and admired the three children. He was proud of the clever disguises that he had created. "When the Wolf Moon is at the highest point in the sky go to the forest, hide amongst the crowds and wait for the Growling to begin."

Blaise turned to Oisín. "What about Cuán and Günther?"

There was something familiar about Blaise to Oisín. It was as though he had seen him before. He had the darkest brown eyes. Oisín knew a young she-wolf child many moons ago who had the same piercing eyes. He had helped her to escape. Oisín wondered if she was the boy's mother.

"If Cuán recovers in time, I will prepare her for the Growling," said Oisín. "She will travel with me. Günther, you will come too."

Günther nodded. The more he heard about the Growling, the more frightened he felt. Although he knew deep down in his heart that he had to be the brave warrior that he was born to be.

Chapter Forty-six

The Elder Wolves

"Hurry, Madigan, we don't have much time!" Faolán warned as they approached the edge of the forest. He was nervous because they were dangerously close to the border.

Madigan was relieved to see a pack of Elder Wolves resting by the Waterfall of Children's Tears. The water was crystal clear as it cascaded over the edge of a cliff.

Faolán had never seen so many Elder Wolves together before. They were a magnificent sight to behold.

The leader of the Elder Wolves was a beautiful white she-wolf called Thorn with piercing blue eyes. She was the first to sense the children's presence. She stood on the edge of a huge rock, her silhouette visible against the two moons.

"Come here, young wolves, don't be frightened. I am Thorn."

Madigan was always amazed that the Elder Wolves retained the human ability to talk after their human hearts had died.

Madigan and Faolán approached the wolves. She knew that she and Faolán were safe – the Elder Wolves were gentle creatures. They had participated in enough Growling battles over their lifetime to know that fighting doesn't solve anything.

Faolán was struck by all the injuries that the Elder Wolves had sustained in battle. Each of them was wounded. One poor wolf had lost all its fur and its skin was scarred. Another only had one eye.

Thorn leapt down from the rock, landing in front of the children.

"We are sorry to disturb you, Elder Thorn." Madigan said as she looked into the she-wolf's gentle eyes.

"You must know that it is not safe for you to venture so far from your pack, child. The Growling will commence tonight, when the great Wolf Moon turns purple. You both should be back in your cages resting."

Sorrow filled Thorn's heart as she looked at Madigan and Faolán. She knew what it was like to battle in the Growling. She wished that she could protect them.

As if they read her mind, suddenly all the Elder Wolves formed a circle around the children.

"We need your help, Thorn," said Faolán. "The Great Warrior Wolf is amongst us. He came from the sky as was prophesied in *The Book of Wolves*."

"I sensed a powerful presence, when the lightning flashed in the sky."

Tears filled Madigan's eyes. She was relieved that the Elder Wolves had sensed it too.

"Yes, that was him," she said. "He has come to save us all."

Thorn brushed her head against Madigan who threw her arms around the Elder Wolf's neck.

"We have come because we need the Elder Wolves to cross into the other provinces to alert all of the Wolf Children of his presence," Faolán said.

Suddenly all of the Elder Wolves began to howl. It was a thrilling sound and a beautiful sight.

Thorn placed her soft white paw into Madigan's hand.

"Have no fear, child – we will spread the word far and wide. Now hurry, go, you don't have much time."

"Thank you, Thorn – you are the kindest wolf I have ever met," Madigan cried as she turned and left.

"Go, child, and stay safe – we are thinking of you."

Seeing so many Elder Wolves together left Madigan feeling optimistic about her future. She looked at Faolán, who didn't look quite so sure, so she reached out and touched his hand.

"Whatever happens tonight, Faolán, know that I will always be there for you," she vowed.

Chapter Forty-seven

The Growling

A cold wind whipped up the snowflakes that fell from the opaque sky. Stars shone above the trees which were made from twisted bones. Two black wolves with teeth as sharp as daggers led Faolán and Madigan from their cages to the edge of the forest where they were joined by many other Wolf Children. There were boys and girls of all different ages, waiting to battle. For some it was their first time. Others had been there many times before. They had the scars to prove it.

Madigan still couldn't believe that they had made it back to their cages on time earlier. They had risked their lives visiting the Elder Wolves. But it was worth it. Every time she closed her eyes, she saw Thorn with her beautiful white coat and piercing blue eyes. Knowing that she was out there somewhere, beneath the Wolf Moon, made Madigan feel safe, despite the desperate circumstances that she found herself in and the ache still in her heart since she said goodbye to her wolf cub, perhaps forever.

The air throbbed with tension. Deathhound stood at the edge of the forest in front of a roaring bonfire. The fire crackled and hissed as flames rose up against the black sky. A large crowd of werewolves had made their way from the town to observe the deathly proceedings. Like wicked phantoms, they meandered through the forest, walking on their hind legs like humans. Their souls were evil and they longed for the battle. Many other werewolves had also gathered. They had come from the four corners of Leinsteria to witness the Growling. They wore green and red cloaks and each wolf had made a Growling mask, which was a mask painted with the face of an angry wolf. There was great competition amongst the werewolves to see who could create the most terrifying masks. In their sharp claws they held candles and each had a belt with a dagger on it. Drums pounded and their raucous laughter filled the air.

Deathhound was ready for battle. The crowd gasped in amazement as he cricked the bones in his neck. Then he smiled and showed his sharp black teeth.

"Tonight is the night. Victory will be mine!" he howled and all the werewolves howled back at him and danced frantically around the bonfire.

Oisín blinked back the tears as he led Günther and Cuán from his house and on towards the forest for the Growling. He had healed them well. There was no sign of weakness or injury. However, he had no way of knowing if the attempt to escape would work.

"Remember what I told you," he said. "Stay calm and you will both survive."

"What if you are mistaken, Oisín?" Günther shivered as he stood in the snow. He wore trousers and a waistcoat. They were made from the petals of black roses. He did not have any shoes on his feet and his back was covered with a wolfskin cloak. His face was painted with black stripes to make him appear like a warrior.

"There is no time for doubt, Günther. Believe in yourself and the great warrior you are."

As they arrived in the forest Günther gasped. He had never seen such a sight. Crowds of children stood ready for battle. Boys like him and girls like Cuán.

Oisín nodded at Günther who took off his wolfskin cloak and threw it into the snow as instructed.

The crowd of werewolves howled up at the Blue Wolf Moon which shone down on them like a torch.

Cuán stood beside Günther. She was as pale and delicate as the snow that fell from the sky. Black hair framed her face. Her dress was made entirely from black petals and her yellow eyes shone like amber in the darkness. Günther held Cuán's hand and together they walked through the trees alongside all of the Wolf Children from Leinsteria.

Deathhound looked up at the stars. They hung like diamonds in the black sky. The heat from the bonfire followed him as he stepped onto a wooden platform and addressed the crowd.

"*The time has arrived. The stars are perfectly aligned. In a few moments the Growling will commence. Tonight our great army of Wolf Children we will be joined by a new wolf!"*

Günther stepped forward as Oisín had instructed him to do.

"The White Wolves of Winter will now lead the Wolf Children deeper into the forest."

From the dark depths of the forest white Elder Wolves bounded through the trees. They pulled golden carriages. It was a magnificent sight to behold.

Each of the carriages was accompanied by werewolves. They wore golden brocaded coats and white wigs sat on their heads beneath black hats. The werewolves opened the carriage doors. Madigan and Faolán stepped inside the carriage that was closest to them. Then Cuán and Günther got in after them,

The carriage was adorned in opulent purple silk. The door handles were crafted from sparkling green rubies. Cuán placed her face against the small square window. It had green velvet curtains. She longed to say to goodbye to Lottie and the other children, but knowing that they were out there in the crowd was reassuring. The carriage shook from side to side as it made its way deeper into the Forest of Non-Existence. The crowd of evil werewolves watched in awe as the golden carriages moved like a dream through the tall trees, which were covered in snow. Then they followed them to catch a glimpse of the Growling battle.

Madigan placed her hand in Cuán's.

"Cuán, you are alive!" Tears fell from her eyes like raindrops from a storm cloud.

Faolán stared at Günther. "Are you the Great Warrior Wolf?" he snarled.

"Yes! Günther has come to save us!" Cuán said and she smiled at Günther.

"He doesn't look like much of a warrior." Faolán was envious of Günther. He looked strong and fearless. Up until now he himself had been the strongest male wolf in Leinsteria. However, he knew he'd be no match for the Great Warrior Wolf.

Günther turned to Madigan. "I am a pilot. I dropped a bomb and it seems it has activated a portal between Earth and Wolf Land. This much I do accept. But I don't consider myself to be a warrior or a hero come to save you."

Cuán smiled at Günther. "Oh but, Günther, you are! The word 'warrior' means soldier or fighter. You have fought in a Great War back home on earth and you are fighting alongside us now. And your name itself means 'warrior.'"

Madigan gasped and looked at Faolán, catching the look of jealousy in his eyes as he studied Günther. She touched his hand. "We were right, Faolán. This is our chance to escape!"

"We don't have long," said Cuán. "*The Book of Wolves* says that the portal to the other world stays open for only twenty-four Earth hours."

"That means we have to go tonight," Günther said.

"Yes, but Deathhound's evil werewolves are everywhere," said Cuán. "They may be guarding the portal. Even if we make it there on time, they will kill us before we cross it."

"Are there others with you, Günther?" Faolán asked.

"Yes, my friends Lottie, Albert and Blaise. They are the young people who helped me when my plane crashed. They are out there in the crowd."

"Only three!" said Faolán. "And just children! That won't help us much."

"But some higher power has sent them here," said Cuán. "How else could they even be here? They must be sent to rescue us. And it was they brought Günther to us. Don't you see? They are no ordinary children."

The others remained silent, thinking about this.

The snowstorm was heavy and it was bitterly cold. After a while Cuán couldn't see anything outside of the carriage window. Except for her own reflection in the mottled glass.

"We will arrive soon. There is no way of knowing if we will survive the Growling," she said sadly, suddenly feeling hopeless. "This is my twentieth year. I will become an Elder Wolf tonight."

"We met with a band of Elder Wolves this morning in the forest," said Madigan. "They are going to spread the word so that every wolf in Wolf Land knows that the Great Warrior Wolf is here."

Günther blushed. He could see Faolán staring at him.

Cuán hugged Madigan. "That is great! There is something else I must tell you. Oisín told me that my Wolf Mother was Saoirse."

"*Saoirse!* They Leader of Wolf Land?" Faolán gasped.

"Yes, Faolán."

Faolán bowed his head reverently before Cuán.

Madigan smiled. Her large eyes sparkled. "This is destiny. It's written in *The Book of Wolves*. The stars have aligned. Tonight is the night. I just know it!" She clasped her hands together and lay her head on Cuán's shoulder.

"We have to survive the Growling first," said Faolán.

The gentle rocking motion of the carriage made Cuán feel sleepy. Her eyelids were heavy. She drifted off to a dreamless sleep and when she woke she realised that they had stopped moving and she was alone.

Cuán turned the ruby handle and stepped outside. The wind whipped her ankles and snowflakes landed on her eyelashes. The ice-cold air took her breath away.

Günther stood at the front of the carriage with a perplexed look on his face.

"Why have we stopped?" he asked.

"This is the Growling, Günther," Cuán explained.

"It is freezing cold. We will perish out here in the snow," he said.

Cuán looked at her new friend. "You need to remain strong to survive."

"Where have Madigan and Faolán gone?" he asked. "They were here a moment ago."

"The rules of the Growling state that we work in pairs," Cuán explained. "If we are to survive we need to work together."

Madigan and Faolán walked farther away from the carriage. It had stopped snowing but the snow was at least two feet deep in places. There were tiny prints in the snow. They looked like they were made by birds.

Sparrows or robins perhaps. Madigan knew that this was not possible. Birds could not survive in Wolf Land. They would perish under the harsh conditions that they all had to endure. The Thought Monsters were playing with her mind again. They often tried to trick her by reminding her of her life back on earth. She had to stay strong. If she weakened now she would never survive the Growling. Madigan was grateful for her wolfskin cloak. It covered her shoulders and kept her warm. The silver satin boots that she wore on her feet were soaking wet. They did little to keep the cold out.

She wondered where Cuán and Günther were now. She wished that they could have stayed together.

The trees stretched up their branches like knitting needles. They scratched patterns in the white sky. At the top of the trees were large nests made from branches. Madigan knew that was another trick.

She walked between the pine trees until she could no longer see the carriage. It was as though something was drawing her deeper and deeper into the forest. Although she had no way of knowing what it was. She listened for the familiar cry of the Wolf Children from other provinces. There were no sounds to be heard, except for the crunch of the snow beneath her feet. She knew that the Thought Monsters hid in the hollow of the trees, like bloodthirsty beasts.

Be brave, Madigan, she told herself.

Then she turned to face Faolán but he was nowhere to be seen.

"Faolán, don't leave me here!" Madigan cried as she fell

to her knees. Where was he? How had she lost him? The Thought Monsters must have led her astray. Or led him away from her. Now her fear would make them flock to her.

The sky above her turned purple and then black like a bruise. She heard a tremendous rumble of thunder. The air around her was stifling. The sky above her head was black. She could see the stars. Four of them gathered around the great Blue Wolf Moon.

Out of the corner of her eye she spied a figure emerging from the hollow of a tree.

Then she heard a voice shouting her name. It was Faolán.

"Run, Madigan! Run!" he yelled.

"I am coming, Faolán!"

But in an instant she decided to run further into the forest as she didn't want to lead the Thought Monster to Faolán.

A shrieking sound came from behind her. There were more Thought Monsters following her. Hunting her down. Madigan knew not to look into their red eyes. That would mean immediate death.

The Thought Monsters surrounded her like a cloak. So this is what it is like to die, she said to herself as she fell backwards into the snow.

Chapter Forty-eight

The Star-Eaters

Cuán bounded through the hollow trees with Günther by her side. She had a plan. In order for it to work she must appear strong and fearless at all times. Like the strong wolf that she knew she could be. Just one crack in her calm veneer, one moment of self-doubt and the Thought Monsters would be all over her.

She turned to Günther. It was his first experience of the Growling. Despite everything that she had told him he was still in denial of his Wolf Blood. The change would come as a shock to him, just as it had for her all those years ago.

She recalled the terror that she felt the first time it happened. Pain consumed her as she clawed at her own flesh. Cuán sighed. Günther was a wolf even though he didn't know it yet. She craned her neck upwards and looked at the sky. The stars were falling fast. A ferocious hunger gnawed at her insides. Like it always did before she ate the stars. Günther felt it too. He was shuddering and almost buckled under the pressure. Cuán glanced around. She was terrified that the Thought Monsters were lurking. If they saw how Günther was reacting to the starlight they would kill him.

Günther fell to his knees in the snow.

"What's happening to me, Cuán?" he cried out in pain.

Cuán knelt down in front of him. Then she placed her hands on his shoulders. She produced a small blue bottle from a pocket inside her cloak. Oisín had prepared a potion to ease the pain of the change. Günther's eyes narrowed. Sweat lined his brow despite the fact that there was a chill in the air. A reluctant mist rose off the snow like a ghost from a corpse.

Cuán gazed into Gunter's green eyes and smiled at him reassuringly.

"Keep looking into my eyes," she said as she uncorked the bottle and handed it to Günther.

He drank the contents down in one gulp. His hands trembled and his face turned pale.

"That is disgusting!"

"It will make the change easier. What you are feeling is perfectly normal, Günther, Don't resist it or it will tear you apart."

Günther was used to the horrors of war but transforming into a wolf was something that he was not prepared for. He was never as terrified of something in all his life. It was as though he was unravelling. As his wolf heart became stronger his human heart weakened.

Günther grasped Cuán by the arm. "Help me, Cuán! I can't do this!"

Cuán shot him a warning glance. "There is no way back, Günther. You need to accept what is happening to you."

"I am starving, Cuán!" Günther growled. Then he peered upwards towards the black clouds. He watched as two stars hurtled towards them like comets. They spun and twisted through the air like golden kites on a summer's day.

Cuán stood up. "Do as I do, Günther," she instructed. Then she held her hands up towards the sky and opened her mouth wide. Günther watched in amazement as the yellow orb slid down her throat like a piece of meat. Then she reached up again and caught the second star. She handed it to Günther. He allowed his insatiable appetite to control him. His wolf instincts kicked in, sending him into a feeding frenzy. He bent over the star and devoured it in a heartbeat. Blood pumped through his veins like ink through a pen. The moonlight shone down on him and the snow glistened. Cuán didn't take her eyes off Günther for one second as he wriggled across the snow. Cuán knew exactly what he was going through. She wished she could take his pain away. Even Oisín's potion was no match for this. Cuán knew that the first time you change into a wolf was the worst.

Günther's human side was resisting it. Each and every cell in his body was fighting for its life. Intense pain ripped through his body. His muscles stung as his face stretched and contorted and his jaw grew larger.

Günther's skin was replaced with thick grey fur. Hair sprouted all over his body. Red veins protruded from his bulging eyeballs. He closed his eyes and when he opened them again his yellow eyes were shaped like half-moons. One by one the black petals fell from his clothing. He winced in pain as his fingers were replaced by dagger-like claws. Amber eyes shaped like half-moons swivelled in his skull. Sharp teeth shot like tiny swords from his blood-red gums. Finally he dropped to his knees and howled. The transformation was complete.

Günther turned to look for Cuán but in her place was a beautiful grey wolf who howled in the moonlight.

Chapter Forty-nine

The Waterfall of Children's Tears

Deathhound ordered Oisín to return to his house in the town. To wait for injured wolves. Lottie, Albert and Blaise watched him go. Albert clung to Lottie's blue cotton dress. The thin fabric was no match for the bitter cold. They hadn't expected Oisín to leave. That was no part of the plan.

"I am scared, Lottie."

"Hush, Albert, the wicked werewolves will hear you!" Lottie whispered.

While the crowd of ferocious werewolves banged their drums and danced around the bonfire the children hid amongst the dense trees. Suddenly a pack of bloodthirsty wolves howled. Lottie knew that they were in danger. The howling grew louder and more terrifying with each second. They knew that werewolves were close, waiting to pounce. Lottie recoiled in terror. Her flame-red hair fanned around her face.

"*Run!*" Blaise cried.

Then they rushed like lightning-bolts through the trees. The snow made visibility difficult. Lottie hoped that this was a good thing. If they couldn't see the pack of hungry werewolves the werewolves couldn't see them. Although she knew they would smell her fear.

I am not scared of werewolves, I am not scared of werewolves! Lottie told herself over and over again. Her arms and legs trembled. Her teeth chattered loudly. She regretted her decision to return to Wolf Land.

Blaise snapped his head in her direction and frowned. "Lottie and Albert, be brave or the Thought Monsters will appear!"

They ran on until Blaise halted and pulled out his mother's diary.

Albert's blonde hair framed his face. His large eyes looked like whirlpools. Snowflakes fell on his shoulders like confetti. He was terrified.

"Don't worry, Albert – I will take care of you," Lottie promised.

"Think brave or comforting thoughts, Albert," said Blaise. "We have lost the Thought Monsters and the wolves but if they feel your fear they will find us." He didn't want to terrify the little boy further but everything depended on Albert conquering his fear.

Albert gulped and nodded. He began to think of a white Christmas at home, throwing snowballs with his friends, his mother waving at him from the window telling him to come in for tea at the fire.

Lottie sighed and looked around. The moon shone down and illuminated the snow-capped mountain tops. She wondered what was on the other side. Her eyes darted around the forest like tennis balls.

All was quiet for a moment.

Blaise flicked through the worn, yellow pages of his mother's diary until he found the map of Wolf Land. His eyes glistened as he peered at the map "It says that there is a waterfall around here somewhere. This is bad, Lottie, as it means that we are dangerously close to the border of the Province. We don't have long. Soon the Wolf Children from the other provinces will arrive and we will be an easy target for them."

Blaise traced the map with his finger as a cold wind froze their bones. The howling got louder.

"It is all going horribly wrong!" Lottie whispered, not wanting to frighten Albert.

"Yes, Lottie. We could get caught up in the Growling battle."

Lottie's heart sank. Be brave, Lottie, she told herself.

Suddenly she could see the outline of wolves flickering through the trees. She could hear them snarling.

Suddenly Blaise's face lit up with hope. "I remember my mother's journal said that a pack of Elder Wolves live near the waterfall! They probably would protect us. Let's go!"

They tried to quell their fear as they ran through the snow. Eventually they arrived at a waterfall. It gushed over the edge of a glass mountaintop. From a distance it looked beautiful. However, as they approached it they could hear the sound of children's voices crying.

Lottie walked towards it slowly in fear of what she would find. She noticed a sign pinned to the branch of a tree. It read:

The Waterfall of Children's Tears
This waterfall is powered by the tears of all the unhappy children in the world. Enter at your peril.

There was no sign of any Elder Wolves.

Blaise voice shook as he said, "They must move away during the Growlings."

Lottie covered her ears as the sound of the children crying grew louder and louder.

Blaise stepped closer to her. "We need to get back out of this forest fast. We are in terrible danger."

"What about Cuán and the others? We are here to save them!" Lottie cried.

"We should never have gone to the Growling, Lottie. We didn't think things through. And we should at least have brought weapons to protect us."

"But we didn't plan on getting separated from Oisín. Now is no time for regrets, Blaise!"

A shrill scream pierced the air. It was Albert. Lottie and Blaise ran through the trees. Three wolves stood growling at Albert who was fixed to the spot. He was unable to move as the wolves crept towards him. They snarled and hunched their backs.

"Go back in the direction we came and stand right under the waterfall, Lottie!" Blaise yelled.

"Why?"

"The wolves in Wolf Land don't like water!"

"No, I won't leave Albert!" Lottie cried.

Blaise lurched forward and scooped Albert into his arms. Then he hauled Lottie by the collar of her dress and ran as swift as the wind towards the waterfall.

They plunged in seconds before the wolves pounced.

The water was freezing cold and their clothes clung to them like a second skin. Images appeared in the waterfall of children crying. It was a terrible sight. Lottie had never seen so many unhappy children before. She guessed that the war had caused there to be more unhappy children in the world than usual. She wished with all her heart that she could do something to help them. She studied the children's faces. There were boys and girls from all over the world. Some were younger than Albert. Others were older than her.

Albert covered his ears with his hand. Their cries were deafening.

Albert saw Douglas Proud, the boy from the train. He was attending a funeral in a small graveyard. The sky was dark and he was crying. A tall woman dressed in black, who looked as proud as he did, stood beside him. Albert guessed that the woman was his mother. Although Albert didn't like Douglas he hated to see him so sad. There were other children there too. They looked like they were in a prison. They were so thin that they looked like skeletons and their heads were shaved.

At last the wolves turned and left, and the children were able to step out of the waterfall. They were astonished to discover that there was not a single drop of water on their clothes. They were bone dry.

Blaise knew that they didn't have a second to lose. It wouldn't be long before more wolves came. They could sniff out prey from miles away.

"*Come on!*" he shouted.

Together they bounded through the forest, Lottie holding Albert's hand.

Albert saw a figure emerge from one of the trees. It had its finger pressed against its lips. Red eyes shone out of its hollow skull. Albert squeezed Lottie's hand.

"What's the matter, Albert?"

"I saw a monster with red eyes! He's following us."

Lottie bit her lip. Her hair swayed in the breeze. Goose-bumps appeared on her freckled skin.

"Albert, you must not look into his eyes – he is a Thought Monster," Blaise said urgently. "Like I told you, he is here *because* you are scared. Do you understand me?"

Albert nodded. He gathered his courage together and thought of Christmas again and the Thought Monster disappeared like a whisper into the forest.

The children clung to each other as they stumbled on through darkness. Snow glistened on a row of oblong-shaped stones. It led them down a narrow path.

"There is nothing to worry about as long as we remain courageous and calm," Lottie told Albert.

The Forest of Non-Existence was dark and forbidding, despite the moons that shone down from the black sky and reflected off the snow.

Albert stiffened. "What was that sound?" he gasped.

"It's your imagination playing tricks on you," Lottie warned as they edged further and further into the damp night. Although she had heard the noise too.

It was a low growling sound. She yanked her brother by his shirtsleeve and pulled him even closer. The sound came again. Louder this time and more shrill. It sounded like an injured animal. A fox caught in a trap.

Albert frowned and two lines converged in the centre of his forehead. *"You must have heard it that time!"* he cried.

"I heard it, Albert." Lottie turned towards Blaise.

"We need to keep going," he warned.

They clambered over rocks and stones. There was no way of knowing what direction they were heading. They seemed to be moving closer to the terrifying sound with every step that they took. Lottie had never felt so frightened. Whoever or whatever Albert had seen out there in the snow had followed them. She imagined monsters and wolves chasing her. Hungry for her blood. With a huge effort, she quelled her fear.

She turned towards Albert but he wasn't there.

"Albert!" she screamed.

But Albert was running ahead as swift as a fox. In the direction where the sound was coming from.

She screamed and sprinted towards her brother. He was no more than a shadow. She plunged through the snow, desperate to catch him, Blaise by her side.

Chapter Fifty

The Death of Wolves

Faolán carried Madigan's injured body towards the town. He needed to find Oisín. He was the only one who could help them now. Madigan looked peaceful. It was almost as though she had been sleeping for one hundred years, although her lips had turned blue and dark rings had formed beneath her eyes. Her ribcage hardly moved beneath the black petals on her dress. Dark red blood trickled from her head. Her long curls fell in front of her face. Her large blue eyes were shut. She felt weightless. She resembled a small bird who had fallen from its nest.

Faolán was terrified. He should have taken better care of her. If he had stayed with her and noticed when she wandered off then none of this would have happened. He halted and kissed her gently on the cheek. It was as cold as the snow that fell from the sky.

"Don't worry, Madigan, my beautiful angel – we are

going to get help," he assured her as he shifted his weight from foot to foot. Oisín had told him that when a person was about to die, their hearing was the last of their senses to leave them. Faolán knew that it was important to speak to Madigan in case she could hear him.

Ghostly cries filled the air. He must move on. Each step took him closer to Oisín and the hope of finding a cure for Madigan. He tried to move his foot in the snow and realised with horror that his foot wouldn't move. He looked down. A small outstretched hand gripped him by the ankle. He saw that there were hands reaching up through the snow. Long knotty fingers like the branches of the trees. They were everywhere. The hand that had a firm grip on his left ankle looked as though it belonged to a child.

"*Let me go!*" he yelled.

The sound of the wolves coming from the next province grew louder. Up until now they had been a distant moan like that of a soul reaching for heaven.

Faolán knew that he would never survive this Growling. He had not turned into a wolf yet or eaten the stars. Then his worst fear became a reality. He spied a pack of red-eyed snarling wolves. They came from the neighbouring province and were approaching him. He knew that there was no escape. He was trapped.

Faolán nestled his head on Madigan's shoulder. "I am sorry, Madigan." he whispered into her ear. Then he squeezed her tight. He would never leave her. They had lived together and they would die together.

"It's not over yet, Faolán!" a strong voice cried.

Faolán peered through a veil of his own tears. A smile curled on his lips as he saw Oisín standing behind the wolves. He held a torch in his hand. The amber flames licked the air like angry tongues. Black smoke drifted through the air. He propped the torch between two rocks, plunged his hand into a leather pouch and produced a pistol. This he pointed in the direction of the wolves.

Faolán was astonished to see this. There were no guns in Wolf Land. How had Oisín acquired one? Had he gone and brought one in from Earth?

The wolves had their backs arched. Their teeth bared. Ready for battle.

Oisín fired the gun. Four shots rang out, making a pinging sound. He heard the shriek of a werewolf. Then finally a whimper as they retreated back into the forest. The werewolves were no match for the gun.

Faolán looked down at his feet. The hands that had gripped him had disappeared into the snow like a bad dream. They were replaced by the grey body of a Wolf Girl. She was six years old. Her name was Aoife. She came from the province of Connaughtia. Now she was lying in the snow, curled up like a puppy. The sight of her lifeless body caused Faolán to shudder. He had never seen such a young child in the Growling before. And Oisín had shot her. Faolán felt weak. He loosened his grip on Madigan. Oisín ran towards him and scooped Madigan from his arms. Faolán fell to his knees in the snow and cried. Oisín knew that he had taken a great risk shooting a Wolf Child. He had disobeyed the most important rule of all. No-one must intervene in the Growling. No matter how bad it got. And Deathhound would know that no-one in Wolf Land but he would have managed to acquire a pistol and keep it hidden. Now, even if Deathhound wouldn't want to send him to the Wolf Pit, each and every werewolf from the four provinces of Wolf Land would.

Oisín looked at Faolán. He hadn't expected him to crumble so easily. He had always been the bravest of all the Wolf Children. It seemed that without Madigan he was nothing.

"We must get to my house," Oisín said. "I need to treat Madigan before it is too late."

Faolán laid his head on the soft body of the wolf cub. Her tongue hung from the side of her mouth. And her ice-blue eyes stared vacantly at the forest.

"What about her?" he asked.

"I am sorry, Faolán. We must leave her here."

"Can't you heal her? She's so young! And, if someone finds her they will know that you shot her."

"My medicine doesn't work on wolves from the other provinces. Besides, they will have heard the bullets being fired from miles around. This is our only chance of escape. We must go at once, Faolán. Madigan needs medicine right away."

Faolán glared at Oisín. "You haven't even checked to see if she is really dead!"

Oisín hesitated then put Madigan back in Faolán's arms and bent to check the Wolf Girl's pulse. She was clearly dead but he wanted to appease Faolán.

"No, Faolán," he said. "There is no hope."

Faolán sighed deeply. Then somehow he found an inner strength. He had to keep moving for Madigan's sake. Carrying her, he began to run, Oisín at his side.

When they reached the town they followed the light from the flickering street lamps. The glowing flames led them down a flight of steep stone steps which ran alongside the canal. They ran down a narrow, arched path that was known as the Path of the Blind Wolf.

On the path was a large statue of a Wolf Child eating a star. It had been carved from the hollow trees in the Forest of Non-Existence many moons ago. Oisín led Faolán down ancient alleyways, across cobbled pavements and over stone walls. He was relieved that most of the wolves of the town were in the forest for the Growling.

"This way!" Oisín beckoned. He looked at Madigan's lifeless body. He hoped that they weren't too late or all of this would have been for nothing.

They arrived at his house and quickly went inside.

Oisín bolted the door and pulled down the blinds.

"Hurry, Faolán, lie her down on that bed. We don't have much time."

Faolán did as he was instructed.

Oisín removed a book from a shelf and the bookcase opened up to reveal the secret storeroom. A musty smell like rotten eggs swam into the outer room and Faolán gagged.

Oisín scratched his head. "Now where is it?" he cried. "Ah, there you are!" He picked a bottle off the shelf. The label said *Wolf Blood*. The red liquid sloshed around inside the green bottle. It appeared black like ink. He then placed his hand into another jar containing insects. Ants, spiders, woodlice, cockroaches wriggled in his fingers. He scooped up a handful of them and scurried back to the bed.

Faolán turned away as Oisín prised open Madigan's mouth and waited while he dripped the wolf blood onto her tongue. Then he placed a handful of insects and a large spoon of water into her mouth. He held her lips shut to ensure that the concoction slid down her throat.

Within seconds Madigan sat bolt upright, gripping her chest and gasping for breath. A bitter taste clung to the roof of her mouth. She coughed and spluttered. The insects nibbled at the lining of her stomach. Wolf blood surged through her veins.

Faolán ran over to her and hugged her. "Madigan, you're alive!"

"What happened?" she asked.

"You are safe for now, child," Oisín reassured her. Although he knew that it wouldn't be for long. Word would soon reach Deathhound that a Wolf Child had been shot. He would immediately know that only Oisín could secretly possess a pistol. Besides, his powerful sense of smell would tell him that Oisín and Faolán had touched her.

Their joy at Madigan's recovery would be short-lived.

Chapter Fifty-one

The Battle of Wolves

"Albert, where are you?" Lottie cried out in anguish. Though desperation surrounded her like a cloak, adrenalin surged through her veins and her heart nearly burst from her chest as she searched for her brother.

"*Lottie, help!*" It was Albert's voice.

The snowstorm was coming thick and fast. Lottie stumbled and fell.

"*Go to him, Blaise!*" she screamed.

Blaise ran through the forest amidst the hollow trees until he arrived at a clearing. Lottie arrived moments later.

Albert was sitting sat on a tree stump beside two wolves. It looked as though they were guarding him. A blinding light erupted from their eyes which were shaped like half-moons. Lottie and Blaise were stunned by its brightness. They fell to their knees and buried their faces in their hands.

When Lottie opened her eyes again Cuán was only a few feet away from her. She was a girl again.

"Cuán, it's you!" Lottie gasped.

"Günther is here too."

Lottie swivelled her head and saw Günther holding Albert's hand. Snow fell from the sky.

Cuán wore a dress made from the petals of black roses. Around her neck was a necklace made of thorns. She moved towards Lottie like a starving beast. Lottie thought that she should run but she found herself standing still. Cuán bared her teeth. They were as sharp as needles. Her fangs were blood-red.

"Please don't hurt me, Cuán!" Lottie cried.

Then she heard a low growling noise behind her. When she turned her head she saw a pack of grey wolves. So many thoughts ran through Lottie's mind. She had no way to escape. She thought that this was how her life was going to end. She would not be killed by a bomb on the streets of Manchester. She would be devoured by wolves in Wolf Land. The pack of hostile werewolves walked in circles around them. Albert moved slowly towards his sister.

Lottie didn't know if Cuán had the strength to fight a pack of wolves.

"What should I do?" she cried.

"Stay exactly where you are," Cuán replied. "Don't move a muscle. What you are about to see will scare you. But please know that I would never hurt you, Lottie." As she spoke her eyes remained on the pack of grey wolves that were breathing down Lottie's neck.

An ill wind blew. Lottie felt so cold that her feet were like blocks of ice despite the fact that her heart was beating like a drum.

One by one the black petals from Cuán's dress fell onto the snow. The body of a wolf was revealed. Fur and claws replaced her skin and nails.

Lottie gasped when she saw that Günther was also transforming. His skin was replaced with thick grey fur. Hair sprouted all over his body while red veins protruded from his bulging eyeballs. He closed his eyes and when he opened them again they were yellow and shaped like half-moons. One by one the black petals fell from his clothing. He winced in pain as his hands were replaced by claws, fingers by daggers. And sharp teeth shot like tiny swords from his blood-red gums. After a moment he dropped to his knees and howled.

"Blaise has gone!" Albert cried. *"He ran away!"*

Lottie looked around. She couldn't see Blaise anywhere.

"He ran away through the trees!" Albert cried.

A sickening feeling overwhelmed Lottie. Blaise had deserted them. After everything they had been through together.

"Don't move, Albert," Lottie warned quietly.

Cuán dropped to her knees and arched her back. The pack of wolves edged closer. Günther stirred beside her. Lottie counted the wolves. There were four of them. Cuán and Günther didn't stand a chance. The leader of the pack had black teeth. His fur was dishevelled. He had one blue eye and one yellow eye. He pounced on

Cuán and she whimpered as his teeth sliced through her flesh.

"*Cuán, no!*" Lottie cried as drops of blood fell into the white snow.

"*Do something, Günther!*" Albert cried.

Günther lurched forward. He dug his claws into the second wolf. But, injured as he was, he was no match for their strength. Günther was wrestled to the ground by the third wolf. He yelped out in pain as his injured leg was punctured with sharp teeth.

"*We're going to be killed!*" Albert screamed.

Lottie ran towards Albert. She clenched her teeth and braced herself. She knew that once the wolves were done with Cuán and Günther they would come for them. Herself and Albert would be their next victims.

A ripple in the trees alerted the children. They swung their heads towards the forest. Albert's face crumpled as the largest wolf he had ever seen bounded towards them. He was a black wolf and he was thirsty for blood. Lottie held her breath as the wolf soared past them. He was so close. If she reached out her fingers she could touch him. The black wolf snarled and revealed sharp claws that looked like blades. He lashed out at the four wolves, making contact and ripping through fur. With powerful blows of his paws he scattered them. Whimpering, they bowed their head in submission and backed away. Then they turned and sped off into the forest, leaving the black wolf standing there victorious. He raised his head and howled at the moon. Then he walked away.

Lottie knelt in front of Cuán and stroked her grey fur.

"Cuán, are you all right?" she cried.

Cuán nodded her head. Then she raised her paw to let Lottie know that she would be all right.

Lottie turned towards Günther. His leg was bleeding. He licked at the wound.

The black wolf stood on a jagged rock and looked back at Lottie. For a moment she thought that she could see a tear in his amber eye. She watched the beautiful creature as he leapt down and stalked off through the snow.

Suddenly she knew.

"*Blaise!*" she cried.

He was the black wolf. Guilt bubbled up inside her chest like a fountain. She took a deep breath and sighed with relief. Blaise would never abandon her. They were family now. He stopped, turning his head to look back at her.

Tears began to spill down her cheeks.

He lifted his head, gazed towards the sky and watched the stars glistening.

Cuán sensed his hunger. It would be unbearable by now. She walked over and stood beside him.

The children watched in awe as a golden star fell from the sky like a firebolt. It fizzled as it hit the snow. Lottie and Albert couldn't believe their eyes as Blaise ate his first star. He was a Wolf Boy now. His journey was complete.

"*Blaise!*" cried Albert, running to his side.

The black wolf lowered his head and nuzzled him.

"You saved our lives! Thank you!" Albert said. Then he buried his head in Blaise's thick black coat and cried.

Chapter Fifty-two

Race Against Time

"You must leave right away. The portal will close soon," Oisín said as he paced the floor. Lines of worry converged on his forehead.

Madigan pushed herself up by the elbows. Yes, they needed to go right away. There was no way of knowing how long the portal had been open or when it would close. The day that she had dreamt of for most of her life had finally arrived. They had a chance to escape. However, Madigan felt sad. As much as she hated Wolf Land, it was the only home she had. The repeated trauma of the Growling had almost wiped her memory of Earth completely. She could barely remember anything that happened before she arrived here. Sometimes she had glimpses of her parents in dreams. There was a lighthouse looking out to sea. She saw a woman with long blonde hair and a man with a brown beard. They were smiling at her and holding out their arms to welcome her home. At night she lay in her glass box and traced the outline of the moon with her finger and her heart ached. There was a family out there somewhere waiting for her to return to them. A mother and father who loved her dearly. However, returning to them scared Madigan more than she would ever admit to anyone.

"Where will we go when we get back home?" she asked.

"There are Wolf Children living all over Ireland," Oisín said. "They gather at the ancient sites. Go there, meet them and work out a way to reclaim Wolf Land. My dream is that one day wolves will roam freely in Ireland once more."

He pointed to a map of Wolf Land that was nailed to the kitchen wall.

"Study this map. You need to get to this arched gateway. The portal is there."

Tears sprang from Faolán's eyes. He cupped Madigan's face in his hands. "We can go home, Madigan. It is our chance to be free again after all these years."

Madigan inclined her head. Then she raised her hand and touched Faolán gently on the neck.

Suddenly they heard a tramping sound.

"Deathhound and his warriors are coming!" said Oisín. "You must go now, my children."

"Please, Oisín, come with us!" Madigan fell onto her knees and begged.

Faolán pulled her to her feet. "Is there another way out of here?" he asked as the werewolves pounded on the front door.

"Yes, there is a back door – it opens onto an alleyway.

Follow it and it will lead you out of the town. Where the alley ends go left across the open ground until you come to a wide stream. Then follow the stream away from the town until you see the Tower of Wolves rising up ahead. We must hope that Cuán, Günther and the others will meet you at the portal, if they have survived."

Faólan and Madigan ran through the house and Faolán opened the door. Ice-cold air swam into their lungs. Madigan felt light-headed and weak. But she knew that she had to keep going. They scurried out the back door at the exact same moment as Deathhound burst through the front door.

Outside a bitter cold wind howled as the children ran down the alleyway.

"Hurry, Madigan! It's now or never."

The blue and white moons shone down on Madigan and Faolán as together they ran along the dark, damp alleyway.

Madigan stopped in her tracks when she heard a bloodcurdling cry coming from ahead.

"What was that, Faolán?"

"I didn't hear anything – it's just your imagination playing tricks on you. Keep going."

After a few moments, the sound came again. Louder this time. It was a wailing cry.

Faolán turned to Madigan. "I heard it that time."

"Faolán, the sound is coming from the direction that we're going in." Madigan was shaking with fright.

Suddenly her name was whispered three times in the breeze.

"Madigan! Madigan! Madigan!"

Madigan screamed as she saw a large black werewolf with sharp white teeth running towards them.

Faolán and Madigan tried to run back down the alleyway in the direction that they had just come. However, another black werewolf appeared. The children huddled together and cried. They were trapped and this time there was no-one there to save them.

Chapter Fifty-three

Thought Monsters

The children scurried through the snow. The fog parted like a pair of scissors and the Wolf Tower appeared like a welcome guest at a party. Lottie, Albert, Günther and Blaise ran towards it frantically in the hope that they would be on time.

Lottie's red hair blew in the breeze like the flickering flames of a fire. A cold wind whipped at her ankles and sent a shiver down her spine. Change was in the air, she could feel it. She did not know if it was good or bad. A knot formed in her stomach.

They ventured tentatively past the scriptorium and the Wolf Tower and on towards the shimmering Portal of Starlight. It was much smaller and duller than Lottie remembered it to be. The air was still and threatening. Mist rose from the ground.

The children stood motionless. It was silent. But the

air was tense.

"What about Faolán and Madigan?" Cuán asked, her voice trembling.

"Something must have gone wrong for them." Günther looked at the Portal of Starlight. "The portal has shrunk in size. It won't stay open for much longer." He shuddered to think what would happen if it disappeared.

Lottie turned to Blaise. Fear danced in her eyes. "What should we do?"

"We can't just leave Madigan and Faolán here!" Cuán cried. They were her family now. She had spent most of her life with them.

"What choice do we have, Cuán?" said Günther. "If we don't leave soon we will all be trapped in Wolf Land and Deathhound will kill us."

Albert looked at Lottie. He didn't know why they were hesitating. He for one didn't want to be devoured by wolves.

"I want to go home, Lottie," he said. Large blue eyes peered out beneath his blond tousled hair.

Blaise reached out for Cuán's hand.

"It's over, Cuán. Time to go home to your ma."

"Is she still alive, Blaise?"

"Yes, Cuán, she is. She is waiting for you back home in Kilbree."

Tears fell from Cuán's eyes like silver coins. She could not believe that Maeve was still alive and waiting for her. She remembered how she had rescued her from the forest as a tiny baby. She had cared for her when she was all alone in the world. If there was even the slightest chance that she could see Maeve again she knew that she had to reach out and grasp it with both hands. They had to leave now, while they still had the chance.

But as they tried to step forward towards the Portal of Starlight they discovered that they couldn't move. They were frozen in time and space. It was as if they were trapped within an invisible sheet of glass.

"Lottie, what's happening to us? I can't move!" Albert whimpered.

Lottie could barely breathe. They were trapped within their own bodies. Only their quivering lips could move.

"*Help!*" she screamed. Her entire body ached as she tried to wriggle her fingers and toes. But it was useless. It felt as though all her bones were broken.

"Try not to fight against it," Blaise said.

Lottie knew he was right. The harder she fought the tighter the vice-like grip squeezed her.

Albert's heart hammered inside his chest. His entire body felt numb. He tried to squirm but it was no use. So he started to cry instead.

"*Silence, you wretched boy!*"

Deathhound appeared in front of them.

The menacing howls of werewolves pierced the air.

The children had unwittingly entered a trap.

Blaise's heart pounded. It was too late. They had lost their battle.

Four werewolves carrying swords moved towards the children, herding a defiant Faolán and a trembling Madigan before them.

Deathhound's lip curled wickedly. His red eyes

swivelled as he stared slowly and deliberately at each of them. He made a fist with his claw and snarled at Lottie. Then he slowly twisted his head so that the bones in his neck creaked and he breathed fire from his fierce, bloodthirsty mouth. The flames heated the children's bones and they were able to move again.

Deathhound grabbed Lottie by the hair with his claw, while the four wolves bared their large sharp teeth at the others and herded them towards the Wolf Tower.

Albert sobbed as he climbed up the rickety wooden ladder.

Lottie was petrified as she watched him and her friends enter the Wolf Tower without her. She trembled with fear as she realised that there was no way home. They were trapped forever. Dark, scary thoughts, the kind that normally rear their ugly heads in the dead of night entered Lottie's mind. She looked around at the trees made from bone and recoiled with horror when she realised that she was surrounded by evil, red-eyed Thought Monsters. They stepped out of the trees like nightmares. They were the most hideous-looking creatures that she had ever seen.

One of them had four crooked noses and sharp jagged teeth instead of eyeballs. Each time she blinked, her teeth chattered loudly. She wore a red velvet cape and cackled as she dripped beastly thoughts into Lottie's ear like poison.

"The portal will shut soon, Lottie, there is no going back – you will never see your parents again," she whispered, her beastly breath smelling of rotten eggs and boiled cabbage.

Within seconds more Thought Monsters tiptoed around her.

A terrifying young girl with green lips and skin made from ice played a black violin. She wore a long grey dress and came to announce Death. She made her presence known by playing a funeral song. Her voice was high-pitched and it could shatter glass. She sidled up to Lottie and shrieked monstrous and deathly thoughts into the hollow regions of her brain.

"Hitler will win the war. It will be your father's turn to die next."

Darkness surrounded Lottie as the next hideous Thought Monster appeared. Black slime dripped from eight spindly legs as he walked and all of his internal organs were on the outside of his large hairy body. His dirty fingernails went on forever and he flashed a wicked grin at Lottie.

She screamed at the top of her lungs like an animal caught in a trap. She had unwittingly entered a sort of nightmare. She covered her face with her hands and peeped through her fingers.

"*Lottie, look out!*" Günther yelled from the top of the tower.

Frozen with fear, Lottie turned slowly.

A large set of teeth grinned down on her and yellow eyeballs lit up the darkness. The Thought Monster's ghastly fingernails reached over Lottie's shoulder and grabbed her by the hair. Then he lifted her high up into the air.

"*Put me down!*" Lottie screamed.

"As you wish," the Thought Monster replied then he dropped Lottie vindictively onto the ground with a thud.

"*Lottie!*" Albert cried. There was nothing he could do to help his sister from inside the Wolf Tower.

Lottie picked herself up off the ground. Her clothes were torn. Her hands and knees were cut and they stung. She felt angrier that she had ever felt before. She wished with all her heart that she had never listened to Blaise. It was all his fault that she was trapped in this dreadful place. She just wanted a normal life away from all this fighting. She thought of her mother back home in England. Then there was Albert – she was his big sister, he trusted her and she had let him down.

"*What do you want with me?*" Lottie screamed at Deathhound.

His red eyes flashed with fury. Then he grabbed Lottie by the shoulders and dug his wolf claws into her.

"You had no right to come into Wolf Land," he growled. "I will destroy you and your Wolf Children friends. As I will destroy that traitor Oisín when I find him. I know he tried to rob me of my two Wolf Children – my champion Faolán and his girl! Now the coward has run away or used magic to hide himself – but he cannot elude me! He will die in the Wolf Pit! Take her away!"

A werewolf led Lottie towards the rickety ladder. Then she climbed into the tower to join the other children.

So Oisín was safe! Lottie prayed he would remain so. She must tell Cuán and the others. She knew that would lift their hearts a little. She herself was heartbroken. But it was too late for tears now. She sobbed as she began to climb the spiral stone staircase inside the tower, realising that she would never see her mother again.

Chapter Fifty-four

The Shimmering Portal of Starlight

Faolán thumped the tower wall with his fist. His eyes flickered around the tower. "I hate feeling so powerless!"

"There must be something that we can do!" Madigan cried.

"Oisín would want us to be brave and find a way to escape," said Cuán.

"What lies beyond the mountains?" Günther mumbled, his thoughts buzzing in his head like bees in a hive. From the top of the Wolf Tower they had a view of the entire kingdom of Wolf Land. The moons and stars illuminated the sky.

"No-one knows – we have never been further than the edge of the forest," Cuán explained. "We were told that the poisonous mist would suffocate us if we tried to escape."

"That might have been a lie!" Blaise said.

Lottie sighed, her eyes were puffy from crying and from sheer exhaustion. "Cuán, I need you to think," she said. "Is there anything that you can recall from *The Book of Wolves* that might help us to escape?"

Cuán shook her head. "I'll try to remember," she said. She put her head in her hands and thought hard, scanning through the pages of the book in her imagination.

The others watched her with bated breath. Albert was saying a prayer.

Minutes passed but Cuán didn't raise her head.

Then she lowered her hands and murmured, "No ... it can't work."

"What is it, Cuán?" Lottie asked urgently.

"It's no good ..." She shook her head.

"Whatever it is it could be our only hope," Blaise said.

"*The Book of Wolves* says that if five Wolf Children are together they can conjure up the bones of one thousand dead wolves. Or so I seem to recall."

"There are five of us here!" Blaise cried and a memory began to stir.

"But, you see," said Cuán, "we all need to be wearing our magic wolf rings for it to work. I don't have mine. I gave it to my friend Nancy – your mother, Lottie – back home in Ireland. Now that turns out to be a terrible mistake."

"But I have your ring here, Cuán!" Lottie took the gold wolf ring from her pocket and handed it to Cuán.

Cuán gasped. "My ring! I don't believe it!"

"My mother gave it to me and told me to take great

care of it – but she didn't tell me it was yours," Lottie told her.

"Wonderful!" said Cuán, clutching her ring.

"You're right about *The Book of Wolves*, Cuán!" Blaise suddenly exclaimed. "I remember now! In my mother's diary there was a picture of five Wolf Children wearing rings. They were holding hands to form a circle. I never understood what it meant until now!"

"But it needs five," Lottie said and her heart sank. "And Günther has no ring."

"Yes, he has!" said Albert.

"No, Albert," said Lottie sharply. "Don't tell lies!"

"But he has!" cried Albert. "He showed me!"

Günther stepped forward. He thrust his fingers into the breast pocket of his flying jacket and pulled out a gold ring. It had a wolf image with ruby eyes.

Smiling, he slipped it onto his finger.

"*You see!*" said Albert.

"Where did you get it?" Lottie asked.

"I've always had it, since I was a baby," said Günther. "It was an inheritance from my grandfather – or so I was told. It's my most precious possession."

Albert was running in circles around the curved wall of the tower. He stopped to look out the window.

"*They're coming! They're climbing the ladder carrying torches and wood!*" he screamed.

The others rushed to the window.

"My God," said Günther, "do they mean to burn us?"

"*No!*" Albert screamed, terrified.

"No, no, Albert," said Lottie. "The torches are just for

light." But she didn't believe her own words and a sickening feeling of dread gripped her heart.

"We have no time to lose!" said Blaise as he bolted the metal door of the room to delay the werewolves. "We can but hope that magic circle will save us!"

"What about us, Lottie? Who will save us?" Albert looked at Lottie with his big blue eyes.

Lottie hadn't thought about it until Albert mentioned it, but he had made a good point. They weren't Wolf Children like the others so how could they be saved? Albert threw his arms around her. She loved him more than anything. He was the best brother she could ever have wished for, even if he was annoying at times. They had been through so much together. She kissed him gently on the cheek. If they had to die this time at least they were together.

Cuán placed her hand on Lottie's shoulder. "Albert, Lottie, it's all right. You will be saved if you join in the circle with us. *The Book of Wolves* just says that five Wolf Children must be gathered in order for it to work."

"We must hurry," Günther warned.

"Take my hand, Lottie!" Cuán cried.

The children formed a circle and held hands. Then their eyes were met with a blinding light. Moments later they heard a thunderous roar and the ground beneath them shook violently. The children screamed. The roof from the tower exploded to reveal the night sky. All of the stars were shimmering above them. The children could feel an energy between them. Lightning moved through their fingertips. In the depths of the earth far below them lay the bones of one thousand dead wolves.

Then they heard a welcome sound as Deathhound and his warriors howled in fright.

The children watched five bright, shining stars twirl and fall from the black sky. They landed in the centre of the circle. Lottie and Albert broke the circle to shield their eyes, the starlight was so bright. Blaise, Günther, Cuán, Faolán and Madigan each seized a star and ate it.

"Lottie, look!" Albert was at the window.

The others joined him. As far as the eye could see, there were hundreds of wolves, beautiful peaceful creatures who had been ruled by wicked werewolves for too long. They covered the mountain tops. Strong, powerful animals. Each one a survivor. They came from each province.

There was one wolf that led the pack. A white wolf with piercing blue eyes. They were the eyes of a Wolf Girl who had turned into a wolf forever. She was the Elder Wolf, Thorn.

Tears erupted from Madigan's eyes, when she saw her gentle friend.

"I knew she would come. The Elder Wolves sent our cry for help out to all the wolves in Wolf Land!" Overcome with emotion, she ran to Faolán and hugged him.

"We did it, Faolán!" Madigan cried.

"Yes, Madigan, we did!"

Below they saw Deathhound and his warriors retreating from the tower.

The children bounded down the spiral steps and down the wooden ladder.

Outside, beneath their feet the bones of a thousand dead wolves united. Then they rose up together to form the body of a giant Spirit Wolf. It was so large that it managed to block out the entire moon. The stars appeared like a halo around its head.

Deathhound quailed and cowered before him.

The Spirit Wolf was filled with rage at the way the Wolf Children were treated and it gripped Deathhound in its mouth. It lashed the Wolf Tower with one swish of its tail and set it tumbling to the ground. The Spirit Wolf held the body of Deathhound in its massive bloodthirsty jaws. He looked small in the mouth of the giant wolf. Then the Spirit Wolf plummeted towards the ground, faster than the speed of light, and the bones of a thousand dead wolves sank back into the belly of the earth taking Deathhound with them.

The children hid amongst the trees a safe distance away and watched as his evil band of warriors retreated back into the forest.

Moments later the children witnessed the most spectacular sight. A stampede of wolves bounded through the Portal of Starlight into Ireland. There were hundreds of them. They were beautiful and peaceful creatures, with peaceful eyes and kind hearts.

A tear fell from Blaise's eye and Lottie guessed his thoughts. They had been through so much together. Lottie felt as though she had known Blaise all her life.

"Your mother would be so proud of you, Blaise."

"I wish she was here with me, Lottie, to witness this glorious sight."

Lottie hugged him tightly. "She is here, Blaise. She will always be with you."

Blaise smiled. "Thank you for everything, Lottie. I am so happy that you came into my life."

Lottie, Blaise, Albert, Cuán, Günther, Faólan and Madigan then left Wolf Land.

Cuán watched as the last of the wolves entered the shimmering light. A great responsibility lay on her shoulders. She was the leader of Wolf Land now. It was up to her to finish what her mother started. She thought of Oisín and prayed he would stay safe and decide to escape from Wolf Land, now that he could no longer work as a healer for Deathhound. She needed his help now, to take care of her wolves. She would hope for the best and expect him to come. Bringing her wolf cub with him.

Cuán walked over to Lottie. "Thank you, Lottie, for being so brave and for coming to rescue me." Lottie was a remarkable girl.

Lottie threw herself into Cuán's arms. "I will never forget you, Cuán! I will tell Mother all about you. She will be so happy that we met."

"Tell Nancy that I am sorry I frightened her all those years ago and that she will always have a special place in my heart."

Albert ran to Blaise. He was the big brother that he always dreamed of having. When he grew up he wanted to live in a caravan just like Blaise, and to travel the world.

"Where will you all go now?" Albert feared that he would never see Blaise again.

Blaise hugged him. "I will find a new home with the Wolf Children, Albert. Please don't worry. I will always be near. I will spend the rest of my life wandering through the hills and mountains."

"What about Snowdrop?"

"She can come with me."

"I don't want you to go. I love you. Please stay with us. You can be my big brother!"

Blaise picked Albert up in his arms. His blue eyes were pleading with Blaise to stay and he wished that he could.

"You are a brave little man, Albert Hope. I promise that I will come and visit you sometime."

"My house is in Manchester, near Manchester United Football Club."

"I will find it, never fear, and I will never forget you."

Cuán placed her hand gently on Albert's head. "Blaise, I am so sorry to interrupt but we need to go now. We must gather all the Wolf Children of Ireland together. We need to plan our future! They will be waiting for us at the historic sites around Ireland, Albert. Every time that you visit one, know that the Wolf Children are near."

Faolán held out his hand to Günther. "I am proud to have met the Great Warrior Wolf. I hope that you will join us, Günther. We need a warrior like you on our side."

"Yes, Faolán, my home is with you and the Wolf Children now. Although I will visit my home in Germany from time to time. You would like it there. It is a land full of beautiful green forests."

"I'm sure there are wonderful things ahead for you all, now that you are free of Wolf Land," said Lottie, a little enviously. She and Albert must still live out their own war.

"We hope so," said Faolán with a grin.

A thought struck Lottie. "I wonder how Wolf Land will be, now that Deathhound is dead?"

A shadow fell across Faolán's face. He glanced at Madigan and then at Cuán.

Then Cuán said, "I am sorry to have to tell you, Lottie, but it is written in *The Book of Wolves* that Deathhound will rise once more."

Lottie couldn't believe what she was hearing. Her heart sank.

Cuán placed her arm around her shoulders. "Don't worry, Lottie. When he does we will be ready for him. And today is a day of rejoicing. We must not let the thought of that wretched Deathhound spoil it for us. Come on – let us say goodbye to this terrible place."

Then they all held hands and entered the portal side by side. It glistened like a million stars. It felt cool on their skin. Then it turned warm. It reminded Lottie of being in a warm bath. The whooshing sound of shooting stars whizzed past their ears and they each felt weightless. It was as though they were floating through time and space. They held each other tightly and did not let go as brightly coloured lights flashed before their eyes. Although it could only have taken a second to cross the portal, it felt like a lifetime. When it was all over they fell onto stony ground at the other side of the portal.

They were back in Ireland. They stood and watched as the shimmering portal to Wolf Land closed.

Blaise then said, "I must go to get Snowdrop and some things from the caravan – like my mother's photograph. Though it will break my heart to leave the caravan behind – it is the only home I've ever known and where my mother lived and died."

An inspiration came to Lottie. "Blaise, why don't you take the caravan to Maeve's house and leave it there? She will guard it for you and you can come back and see it when you are able?"

"And I can play in it!" said Albert.

A brilliant smile lit up Blaise's face. "That's a wonderful idea, Lottie! I will do just that!"

"Yes, that's a perfect solution!" said Cuán. "Lottie and Albert, come with me. The others can join us later." Tears sprang to her eyes. "I must go straight home. Home to Ma."

Chapter Fifty-five

Home

The farmhouse emerged like a bruise at the end of the long lane. Creeping ivy trailed up the walls. Cuán couldn't believe her eyes. It was exactly as she remembered it. Although the large front door was in need of a lick of paint. And the windows in the house had been boarded up with wood.

Suddenly a black-and-white sheepdog bounded out of the forest and ran around the yard, chasing its tail. Then it ran towards Cuán and knocked her off her feet.

"Bonnie!" Cuán cried. She burst out laughing as the dog licked her face. "But it can't be!"

"It's Bonnie's pup, Cuán," said Albert. "Bonnie came home safe and sound after you left! Isn't that right, Lottie?"

But something had caught Lottie's eye.

She stared and then hurtled across the farmyard.

"*Mother!*" she cried. She could scarcely believe her eyes!

Her mother Nancy was running towards them, arms open wide.

"My beautiful children! I thought I would never see you again!" she said as she threw her arms around them. Her blonde hair flowed over her shoulders. She wore a beautiful green dress and smelt like buttercups.

Then Nancy looked beyond them and her heart almost stopped beating when she noticed Cuán standing there. She looked exactly as she had twenty years ago. It was as though time had stood still.

"Cuán, is that really you?"

"Nancy! You grew up while I was away!" Cuán screamed in delight as she ran towards her friend. Although she was older now her eyes remained the same.

In great wonderment, Nancy held Cuán's hand and led her to the front of the house, with Bonnie beside them.

Maeve was standing there. She wore a purple dress and had a green shawl around her shoulders, secured at the front by her mourning brooch with the twist of Cuán's black hair inside.

Cuán gasped. She could not believe how old and frail her ma had become since she went away.

"*Cuán, my child, you came home!*" Tears sprang from Maeve's eyes. "I always knew you would!" She reached out her bony hand towards Cuán and touched her gently on the cheek as if she couldn't believe she was real and might disappear at a touch.

Cuán could see her skin was paper-thin, veins like blue ribbons clutching to the narrow bones on the backs of her hands. She hugged her and she felt as frail and delicate as a small bird in her arms.

"But, Cuán, you still look like a young girl – how can that be?" said Maeve, marvelling as she looked at her.

"It's such a long story, Ma," said Cuán. "Let us sit down and I'll tell you all about it. But – forgive me, Ma – I have to leave again soon. I have people that I am responsible for and must take care of. But, as soon as I can, I will come back to spend some time with you. And don't worry – I am never going to disappear from your life again. I promise you."

Tears slid down Maeve's pale cheeks. But she smiled through her tears. "I understand, my dear child. Just to see you again and know that you are alive and well fills me with joy. And don't worry – I have Nancy and her children to keep me company – and Bonnie of course."

Albert and Bonnie were now playing chase and the dog started barking madly.

Suddenly Albert ran back to Nancy.

"Is the war over, Mother?" he asked.

"No, Albert, it's not. But we are going to be staying here in Kilbree until it is."

"Not with Pooey Prudence!" he cried.

"No, Albert. I heard all about your time with the Dunlivins from Maeve. And, before that, the fact you were almost split up before you had hardly left and almost never made it to Ireland at all. When Miss

Bentwhistle told me that, I got such a fright that I left Manchester immediately and came here to make sure you were safe – I have only just arrived. So, don't worry – we will be staying here with Maeve."

Albert turned to Lottie and smiled. He loved his big sister even if she was a bit bossy at times. He knew that everything would be fine as long as they stayed together. He could not wait to get home to England after the war to tell his friend Billy Bright all about it.

But Lottie was staring into the forest. The sound of wolves howling in the distance suddenly brought tears to her eyes. And in that moment, something told her that she would have many more adventures with the Wolf Children and that the battle for Wolf Land had only just begun.